SPACE CAPTAIN

ADELAIDE

A CRIME LORD'S DEBT

SPACE CAPTAIN

ADELAIDE

A CRIME LORD'S DEBT

YVONNE YOURKOWSKI

Prologue

Earth's population had exploded in the last century, causing a drain on natural resources, which in turn started WWIII in 2055. The war had lasted for five hellish years. Earth had been decimated, and billions of people were killed. The majority of countries were forced to band together, forming the Coalition of Nations in order to end the war. Once the Coalition constructed the first space ship and space station, nothing could hold the explorers back. During the next ten years of exploration, another suitable planet was discovered, and Earth sent delegates to colonize it — calling it, unoriginally, Earth2.

During Earth's years of space exploration and discovery, humans had encountered many species bent on the subjugation and slavery of Earth's inhabitants. The alien races loved using Earth for target practice. Growing up, Adelaide Zedler remembered seeing the sky crack open to rain fire and destruction down upon what remained of Earth's cities. Adelaide still woke up with nightmares thirty-one years later. So many lives had been lost. It was why she had joined the military and was now the captain of one of Earth's battleships. But now, in the year 2108, Earth was in the middle of another war that, if not won, could see the end of their civilization.

SPACE CAPTAIN ADELAIDE ZEDLER
BORN IN 2075; 33 YEARS OLD

OCCUPATION: CAPTAIN IN EARTH'S MILITARY

PLANET: EARTH2
- Earth has become very careful about preserving unsustainable resources
- She lives in the capital city, Transmont
- Hollow Peasant is her favorite watering hole
- Earth is part of the Multi-Species Accords

PHYSICAL DESCRIPTION:
Red curly, shoulder-length hair; thin, straight, freckled nose; green eyes; small waist; large chest; 5'5" tall; communications unit attached to wrist (looks kind of like a large square watch); high muscle tone and definition; very pretty.

WEAPONS:
Blaster on each hip, knives in each boot and a smaller blaster on her thigh.

PERSONALITY/EMOTIONS:
Strong-willed, nerves of steel, fierce, feisty, sarcastic.

FAVOURITE FOOD AND DRINK:
Meat pastry from Gaeaf, Toph non-alcoholic beverage from Zartuth, garpel drink from Zartuth

Chapter 1

"Captain, we've received the coordinates."

Captain Adelaide Zedler turned from analyzing the computer data to looking down her thin, straight, freckled nose at the ensign. Trying to rub away the pain pulsing at the back of her head from her severe bun, she demanded, "What are the coordinates?" Adelaide frowned, swiping at the few red curls that were escaping from her hair elastic to land smack dab in front of her eyes. There were so many times when she had been tempted to chop off her hair, but it was only worse short.

"The destination is Earth2," the ensign said.

"Engage," she said, sitting down in her chair and pushing the comm button on the arm of her chair. "Attention, battle stations. We are on a trajectory to Earth2, where our enemy has engaged our allies. Hopefully, this is the last battle, and we'll beat those bastards back. Captain out."

Cheers echoed in agreement throughout the ship, as the alarm sounded the battle warning. Adelaide looked around the bridge at the crew that, over the past years, had weaseled their way into her heart. The battleship was large, with a compliment of two hundred members, and housed one of the largest arsenals in Earth's fleet.

As she stared out into the vastness of space, the ship's massive cannons shifted in the corner of her eye. The ship was built in three square segments. Cannons stuck out on either side of each segment. The bridge sat above the middle segment like a large periscope, acting as the backbone of the ship. Either of the end segments could be jettisoned if damaged beyond repair, but if the middle went, they were all doomed. When no one important was listening, Adelaide would call it the caterpillar.

Adelaide watched as the ship moved to enter a jump gate. Eight years ago, in 2100, Earth had signed the Multi-Species Accords with the hope that the defences they offered would provide Earth's citizens with protection against any non-members. The jump-gate technology Earth had received by signing the Accords was a godsend. They were able to reach locations within their galaxy in hours, compared to earlier estimates that it would take at least a billion years to cross the Milky Way galaxy. It opened up endless possibilities for exploration, and for some, exploitation. Not many jump gates existed. They were built near Accord-member planets, so the gates could be easily defended. Other species could pay the planet an exorbitant fee to use the gate or try entering by force. Only a few were ever able to pass through and cause problems throughout the galaxy. Of course, this rule encouraged innovation, and many scientists were trying to duplicate the technology and even improve upon it, in hopes of making it smaller.

Adelaide had an inkling that the Raykar may have developed this new gate technology, for how else they could travel such distances so quickly? Everyone in the Accords was aware of the travel ban prohibiting the Raykar from using the gates. The reigning government of the Accords constantly sent out bulletins listing the peoples and planets who were on their shit list. Shaking her head, she set aside the concern for the moment, and instead, Adelaide tried to mentally prepare herself for the fight ahead. Earth's three battleships and ten warships would engage their enemy, the Raykar, along with their allies from the Accords. Hopefully, the Raykar would be beaten into submission, and Earth could finally know peace.

Adelaide adjusted her mandatory uniform jacket. It was a dark blue double-breasted jacket with large gold buttons running down the front in two lines. She was grateful for her small waist, because the jacket cinched very tightly, and she could barely breathe as it was. You would think the higher-ups would realize that girls had boobs, and hers were larger than most. With today's medical advances, women were getting breast reductions and lifts in just hours, with no recovery time. Surgery might be in style, but Adelaide had no plans on changing her God-given natural assets.

"Captain, we'll be exiting the gate within minutes."

"Everyone prepare for arrival," Adelaide commanded. Space seemed to zoom past the ship in streams of light as they shot across the galaxy. When they exited the gate, Adelaide sucked in a breath and said, "Contact Admiral Arteaga." As she waited, Adelaide watched the massive amount of debris floating in their path.

It was a requirement of the Accords to provide support during war. The sensors showed that only nine Earth ships were left, fighting alongside five allies. From the reports she had received, there were originally twelve allied ships. This was not good. The biggest problem was the group of twenty-five Raykar ships plowing straight towards them. The enemy ships were shaped like massive sting rays, and their sleek black shapes seemed to glide through space effortlessly, as they blew one of Earth's ships to kingdom come. They were down to eight.

She had a bird's-eye view of the battle. There had been skirmishes throughout their galaxy, but this was the final one. The Raykar were trying to break through the Accords' blockade to reach Earth2. Three other planets surrounded the battlefield like a fighting ring. Two were uninhabited, and the third was primitive. The locals lacked space travel and the desire to advance, much to the surprise of all spacefaring species. Adelaide could understand the simple life, though. It would be a lot quieter and easier than dealing with these issues, but she enjoyed the excitement. She was surprised the Raykar weren't trying to subjugate them, but maybe the planet had nothing they desired.

"I have Admiral Arteaga."

"Sir?" Adelaide responded.

"Captain, the Raykar are advancing through our front line, and we can't hold them off. Cover that hole!" ordered the admiral.

"Yes, sir. You heard him — maneuver us now. Be ready to engage."

She watched as an Earth ship exploded on their left, and the pieces blew apart, a few hitting their hull and sending shudders rippling throughout the ship. Seven Earth ships remained. Crewmen swore as their ship reached its destination, and they witnessed the destruction. The noise was deafening within the ship, which continued to shudder as it was bombarded by the fragments. Some were the size of large boulders, and the flashes from the blasts lit up the space around them.

"Ensign, ensure there are no breaches," Adelaide commanded. "Here they come. Fire!"

The ship jerked as all cannons fired towards the oncoming vessels. Time seemed to slow as ship after ship lit up. With all of the remaining ally ships directing their energy on the incoming enemy, they were finally able to slow the advance.

"Captain, a ship is coming in fast on the starboard."

"Concentrate our firepower. We need to slow them down and take evasive maneuvers."

Adelaide watched as the ship continued on its path, straight for them. "Shields at maximum. Divert power from every system that can afford it. Everyone, brace for impact," she yelled, as the incoming ship collided with theirs between its front and middle segments. The crew was thrown forwards, and alarms sounded throughout the ship. Adelaide gripped the arms of her chair, forcing her body to remain rigid. The lights flickered off and then burst back on causing little sparks in front of Adelaide's eyes. Their ship was skewered, damaging both the front and middle segments. Adelaide gazed in horror as the front of her ship slowly peeled away, dragging the enemy ship with it.

"Status?" she demanded, staring at the jagged edges of the ship.

"Shields are at minimum, but we can still shoot the bastards, Captain."

"Do we have propulsion?"

"Yes."

"Move us a few degrees to port side. There's a gap that the enemy is trying to penetrate. Keep firing." There was no way in hell that Adelaide was going to let the Raykar win.

"Yes, Captain."

The ship teetered before righting itself and inched forwards. Reports were coming in from all over the ship. Adelaide scrolled through them, mentally sorting the priorities. There were hull breaches in the rear segment, but as long as their segment survived, they would be alright.

"Captain, half of segment three has been compromised, but it's holding strong."

Just then, the ship was hit with a barrage of cannon fire, and they tilted to the right. The roar was deafening as her crew yelled and the ship squealed, then popped, while slowly beginning to pull apart.

"Captain, the ship's lost life support and firepower. We're dead in the sky."

"Everyone, to the life pods," Adelaide yelled. The crew began scattering as she stumbled to the control station situated at the front of the bridge. She needed to pilot the ship.

"Move it, Ensign," she ordered a remaining crewman.

"Captain, what about you?" he asked.

"I'm staying. Someone needs to pilot this bucket of bolts until everyone is safe."

"Then I'm staying," he stated, and a few others echoed him.

"No. Everyone, evacuate. I'll be close behind. That's an order." Many crew members argued, but Adelaide held firm, and they eventually ran for the life pods.

Adelaide sat in the pilot's chair and grabbed hold of the stick in order to steer the battleship manually, staring intently ahead. Hopefully, she could at least guide them away from friendly ships, while everyone escaped. If she could take out some Raykar ships on her way, all the better. The lights began to flicker, and smoke swirled under the door and onto the bridge. Adelaide watched the computer and counted the life pods as they ejected. She slammed her ship into an enemy vessel, and her body flew to the ground. *Time to go,* she thought, scrambling to her feet. Adelaide's battleship screeched past the other ship and was now on a direct trajectory towards the enemy line. The ship groaned and seemed to scream in agony, or maybe that was just her, as the bridge exploded just as Adelaide ran through the door. She ducked and dodged the falling debris while stumbling to the pods.

One of the hull breaches had been close by. Broken bodies littered the hallways as she drew closer to the pod room, but there was no time to mourn. Flames shot out of a mechanical panel, and Adelaide threw her body to the ground, but she hadn't been quick enough.

"Crap!" Adelaide ripped off her jacket, glad she could take a breath, and stomped on the smoldering sleeve.

"Captain," a crewmember called out, crawling towards her on the floor.

"Lieutenant! Let's get you out of here." Adelaide gently grabbed the man's muscular arm and heaved up, helping him stand. A large gash ran down his leg, leaving a trail of blood behind them as they hobbled towards the escape pods.

"Watch out!" Adelaide yelled, pushing him forwards as a beam fell. Adelaide dove for cover but didn't move fast enough. Her leg was pinned beneath the beam, and her head crashed against the hull. She groaned, trying to hold in a scream. Blood dripped down her forehead, blurring her vision.

"Captain, are you alright?"

"Get out of here."

"No. Try to pull out your leg when I lift the beam." The lieutenant braced his back against the wall and tried to lift, grunting with the effort. The pressure eased slightly, and Adelaide wiggled her leg.

"Hurry, I'm about to drop it."

Adelaide moved faster and let out a shriek as she yanked her leg free. It was broken, and she might have to crawl, but there was no way she was staying here. Flames were now making their way down the corridor, causing little explosions along their path. She coughed as smoke filled the area, and she tried to glimpse what was ahead.

"Help me up," she said. The world dimmed and her eyes briefly closed as she stood. "Give me a sec," she said gruffly. Agony shot up her leg with every step.

When they reached the pods, Adelaide shoved the protesting man into one and pushed eject. It was her turn next. She dragged her leg to the last waiting pod and stumbled in, closing the door. As Adelaide's escape pod shot into space, the ship reached critical condition and exploded, sending her into a tailspin and making her head smash into the wall. Thankfully, she blacked out.

Chapter 2

"Captain!"

Adelaide felt a cool breeze across her face, breathing air into her depleted body. She gasped and struggled to open her eyes. Pain swamped her body, and Adelaide moaned as her consciousness and awareness flooded back.

Where was she? The pod still cushioned her sore body. As her eyes peeled open, a crewmember's face came into view. Blinking from the bright sun glaring down on her, she could just make out a silhouette that shifted, spreading merciful shade across the pod's hatchway. Her eyes readjusted, focusing on a human form: a thin, gaunt male in his early twenties with short black hair, a prominent overbite and small, thin glasses.

"Where are we? How long has it been, Jacob?" Adelaide croaked.

"I've been wandering for about an hour on this forsaken rock, before I finally found you."

"Are there others?"

"Not that I've come across."

"After you help me out of this coffin, you'll have to set my leg," Adelaide said.

"What!" Jacob grimaced, looking like he was the one in pain.

He hesitated before bending over, grabbing both of her arms and slowly pulling. She sat up, and then with great care, stood on her good leg. Her leg buckled, and she grabbed tighter onto Jacob's arms, almost dragging him over. He grunted in surprise, as his body adjusted to the weight.

"Hang on a moment," Adelaide whispered, as her head began to pound and sweat formed under her shirt. She gave a few huffs before cautiously swinging her injured leg over the dented side of the life pod.

Her first glimpse of the planet was depressing. There was an ocean of light orange sand reflecting the bright sun as far as the eye could see. Her pod had crashed in a cluster of rock formations. The front had caved in like an accordion, luckily her five-foot-five frame was short enough that it hadn't taken her head off. A path of destruction could be seen behind the pod. Tufts of sage brush spotted the landscape, so it at least didn't look completely dead. Adelaide guessed they had crashed on Carraig, one of the uninhabited planets surrounding Earth2. From pictures, she had seen the planet was one big rock, and she was surprised anything could survive on it. *Yeah, of course, she and Jacob would beat the odds*, she thought sarcastically.

"We need to find something to brace my leg. Which direction did you come from?"

Jacob pointed off to the left of their location. She could see what looked like cacti and more rocks.

"Did you see anything we could use?" she asked beginning to pant from the pain.

"No."

Adelaide collapsed on the edge of the pod and inspected it for anything useful. Part of the top panel was ripped halfway off.

"Here, Jacob, use my blaster to laser off this section." She lifted her blaster up with a shaky hand, and Jacob quickly grabbed it, probably afraid she might accidentally shoot him.

Her body temperature was rising and thirst was starting to set in. They needed to find something soon, or they wouldn't survive till rescue. The metal screeched as Jacob slowly removed the loose piece.

"Okay, maybe I can rip up one of my sleeves, so we have something to secure it," Adelaide said. She reached up to her white not-so-crisp-anymore sleeve and yanked as hard as she could. After a few attempts, there was a ripping sound. Digging her finger into the small hole, she yanked one more time, and it came loose. She made quick work of ripping the sleeve into a few long strips and laid them across the pod.

"One piece of metal will have to do," Adelaide said trying to breathe through the pain. "Alright are you ready?" she asked.

"No."

"Tough," she snorted, "I'll hold onto the pod, and you pull hard until you hear the pop."

"Ready." Jacob crouched in front of her and grabbed her ankle. "One, two, three." He gave a massive jerk while Adelaide gripped the edge of the pod in both hands. Adelaide gasped and let out a scream as her leg popped into place. She was sweating profusely, and her body began shutting down, as her eyes tried to close. Forcing her breathing to even out, Adelaide passed the strips to Jacob.

"Okay, place the metal along the side of my leg, and tie these real tight. The medics will be able to fix it, when we're rescued."

"Are you sure?"

"Of course. They can fix anything, nowadays."

"No, I mean about rescue."

"Yes. They'll be looking for survivors. This planet is close to the battle. I think it's Carraig."

"My beacon was destroyed," Jacob admitted quietly.

Damn, she thought. Hers was, too. She had been hoping his was still working. They really needed to produce better life pods with beacons that wouldn't be damaged by the slightest impact. She glanced down at the ruined pod and grimaced — maybe it wasn't just a little impact.

Adelaide looked down at the comm attached to her wrist. It was a tiny computer with a band that wrapped around her wrist and was hardwired into her body. Another piece of tech that was beyond her thinking but that she was immensely grateful for. Since she was a captain, the military had paid for the comm, and it was hers for life. Once attached it was extremely

13

difficult, if not impossible, to remove. But it had proven itself worth the cost of her blood and tears throughout the years. The holodisplay appeared with a touch, and Adelaide tried contacting the fleet.

"Damn it, there's some kind of interference. I can't contact the fleet on my comm. But it's working enough to confirm that we did crash on Carraig."

"Can it pinpoint where we are? Or our surroundings?" Jacob asked leaning in for a closer look. The display flickered, and Adelaide snarled in frustration.

"I don't think so. Maybe there's some type of alloy on the surface interfering with the signal." There was another flicker, and a 3D picture of the planet appeared with a red dot.

"There we are," she said with a sigh. There were a lot of sharp brown peaks and very little green covering the globe.

"Someone saw the life pods escaping. They'll be searching. We just need to survive until then." Jacob nodded in agreement, but a frown marred his face.

"Do you still need to rest?" he asked.

"I need to find water and get out of the sun." Her fair complexion was a natural hazard in the sun, and her skin would begin burning soon.

Jacob stood up, straightened his back and held out his arm.

"Can you reach in and grab the pack of rations," Adelaide asked, pointing to the compartment in her coffin. "Do you have yours?"

"Yes. But they won't last long."

"We can survive a day or so on them," she stated, watching him wrench open the little door guarding the unappetizing package. With the large advancements in Earth's technology since joining the Accords, it was surprising that food rations hadn't improved from tasting like chunky dirt to being at least a little appealing.

"Let's go." Adelaide grasped Jacob's arm, took a deep breath and stood up on a shaky leg.

"Before we leave, let's leave a message for any rescuers or fellow crashers. We'll keep it simple." Adelaide directed Jacob to scrape an arrow into the hard sand, which pointed in the direction of the large red and brown rocks.

"We need some rocks to outline the arrow in case the weather blows it away. I see some this way." She hopped painfully closer to some small rocks in the distance. Jacob hurried forwards.

"I've got it Captain." He bent over and began piling the rocks into his folded-up shirt. Once his design was complete, they started their journey.

Adelaide looked at the 3D image on her wrist comm and sighed as it flickered again and disappeared.

"I don't think this will be much use. Let's head in the direction of those larger rock formations."

Adelaide hopped beside Jacob, using his arm for support. The pain came in waves, crashing through her body. The heat was stifling, and sweat seemed to drip off her body, as they walked across the open desert. The rocks that her capsule had crashed into offered nothing in the way of water or food. So, into the open expanse they went to die under the scorching sun. Eventually, another ridge of rocks came into view, and Adelaide heard Jacob sigh. He didn't seem to be doing any better than she was, and having to support her as well must be a strain. They struggled between the rocks, once in a while reaching a shady spot, where they could take a quick rest. *Why in the hell couldn't they have landed on the one inhabited planet?* Even if the locals were a smidge hostile, it was still better than being stuck here sweating like a pig.

With each painful shuffle, the sand and dirt rose, coating Adelaide's body, itching with every movement. The sun beat down upon them relentlessly, making her want to remove almost every inch of clothing, but then she would burn to a cinder. Along with her lovely red hair, her body was as pale as a ghost — with plenty of freckles to go around. The only way for her to achieve the gorgeous glow that many humans developed naturally was to seek out the tanning fanatics. Over the centuries, the fake-baking method had advanced to a surgical procedure allowing the results to be almost permanent. No one went to the tanning beds, like in the old days: surgery it was. *No way in hell* was Adelaide going for surgery to change her skin tone. If the sun couldn't do it, then she was stuck the way she was born.

Every so often the breeze picked up, teasing them briefly, and then died down just as quickly, leaving the air around them hotter than before, if that was possible. As they trekked over the flat, dry sand, some unknown creatures would scurry across their path, towards the safety of the rocks. None of them appeared threatening, but looks could be deceiving.

"Hey, Captain, why don't we try the cactus for a drink?" Jacob suggested, as they came upon another patch of the spikey-looking plants.

"No!" Adelaide said sharply. Jacob looked at her in surprise.

"It can make you sick, so it's not worth the risk. I need to rest. Let's sit over by that overhang. Maybe you can search around the rock face for water." Jacob nodded but looked disheartened as they stumbled to the left.

Adelaide dropped onto a rock jutting out from the wall of a tall cliff. Her body was starting to shut down. The heat was sucking out what little moisture she had left in her body. Her eyes were beginning to droop by the time Jacob came running back with a Cheshire-cat grin.

"What?"

"I found water."

"Great! Where is it?"

"It's just a trickle, but it's better than nothing."

"Lead the way," she said, but it took a few painful tries before she could stand enough to follow.

"Did you see anything I could use as a crutch?"

"No. It's pretty bare. I'm surprised we haven't seen more animals."

"It's probably too hot. They're the smart ones. I do feel it cooling off, though, so we may spot more now."

*   *   *

Adelaide could hear the drips, before they turned the corner, almost tripping on some brush appearing out of nowhere. *Or maybe she just needed to pay more attention,* she thought with a grimace, struggling to stay up right. Adelaide sighed in relief, as she leaned in and let the cool liquid trickle down the cliff face and drip into her hand. It was slow going, as they took turns sipping the heavenly, metallic-tasting liquid.

"We should stay here in the shade for a while," Adelaide said, feeling the fatigue set in and her eyes begin to close.

"Sure, I'll check around to make sure it's safe," Jacob volunteered.

"Be careful, we're not sure what's around."

"Agreed," Jacob said, as he scooted off over the rocky terrain. Adelaide checked her rocky perch for creepy crawlies, before leaning back with her hand resting lightly on her blaster. The only sound was the wind whistling through the cracks and crevices. Every so often, there would be a growl or a clicking sound, and her eyes would snap open, her heart rate increasing as she searched for the culprit. She didn't know which would be worse, finding the creature or never seeing it at all. Sometimes having an imagination was a terrible thing.

"Captain," Jacob whispered, treading lightly towards her.

"Did you find anything?"

"There was a rather large creature coming from the other side."

"Did it look dangerous?"

"Not sure. It was probably about ten feet long with six thick, stubby legs. Had a round scaly body and a huge head that looked like a hammer. It was using either side of its head to dig in the sand."

"Hopefully, it's an herbivore," Adelaide said, swallowing.

"Do you think we won?" Jacob asked, changing the subject abruptly.

"I don't know. We were winning, before we went down," she answered. But Adelaide knew that could change in an instant. Earth had been winning their last skirmish with the Raykar, until the Raykar had pulled out a new weapon and decimated their fleet at the last minute. Not many of Earth's ships had survived, and hers was one of the few that had limped away, defying capture.

"Because if we didn't win, there probably isn't going to be a search party. Or do you think the Raykar will hunt for survivors?" Jacob looked around nervously.

"We are going to survive until rescue, no matter how long it takes," Adelaide said forcefully, crossing her fingers behind her back. With her being injured and only on laser between them she didn't like the odds if they were discovered by the Raykar. She shuddered remembering a previous battle where she'd watched a Raykar bite someone's arm off. Their teeth looked human but were they ever sharp. "We might as well stay here for the night. Let's eat some of our lovely rations," Adelaide stated, just as their stomachs grumbled in unison. For the next few minutes, the only sound was the of two of them trying to chew and swallow the tough, crunchy bars.

"We need to keep watch. You can take the first rotation. I need to crash," Adelaide said as she finished her rations. "Wake me in a couple of hours. Here, take my blaster, and see if you can find a dead cactus to cut apart for us to burn. We don't want a fire big enough to attract animals, but we may need some heat when the sun sets."

"Sure," Jacob replied, taking the blaster and heading off between the rocks.

Adelaide tried using her comm again but no luck. About half hour later, Jacob returned dragging a small, dried-up-looking cactus. He lasered it into small chunks with the blaster and then stacked a few pieces in front of Adelaide. He focused the laser on the pile, and it eventually began to burn.

"Good job," Adelaide praised. "We'll keep this low, but don't let it go out."

Jacob nodded before wandering a few feet away and staring off into the distance at the setting sun. It was spectacular, with red and orange hues across the sky.

Adelaide shifted on her perch feeling a sharp pain. She reached beneath her butt and pulled out a small sharp rock. Frustrated and in pain, she threw the offensive stone against a nearby boulder. Jacob jerked around as the rock shattered.

"Sorry," she whispered, trying to relax enough for sleep to take hold. Times like these reminded Adelaide why retirement was looking better and better. Eleven years of constant fighting would appease any adrenaline junkie. Her family had been harassing her for ages to work for their cargo business.

*   *   *

Adelaide must have finally dozed off, when a creepy tickling feeling jerked her awake. Staring into the black night, she couldn't hold back the scream that ripped out of her throat. The fire illuminated the largest bug she had ever seen. Its multiple hairy legs were crawling up her leg, waving long pincers in the air. She used her fist to bat it away, grimacing in pain as her hand contacted with it's hard black shell body. As Jacob ran to her, Adelaide yelled for him to shoot it.

"What was that?" Jacob demanded, firing at the nasty thing. Green goo sprayed at the surrounding rocks, and they both grimaced.

"I'm not sure, but it was massive." Jacob shivered, searching their location for any more offending creatures.

"Help me up — you can rest," Adelaide offered.

Struggling to rise, Adelaide longed for a med bot. Nausea rose and she shakily stood beside her perch, waiting for her body either to vomit up her meager meal or let it sink back into her stomach. Eventually, her equilibrium returned and her stomach began to settle.

"Okay. You try and get some sleep," she ordered, hobbling some distance away to a waiting rock. Jacob looked after her with anxiety. It was a few minutes before she heard the scraping as he finally settled down on the ledge. She sighed in exhaustion. They needed to be rescued soon, or she wouldn't last. She glanced down at her swollen leg — *was it twice the size?*

*   *   *

Light was beginning to shine across the desert, bringing with it some much needed warmth. Adelaide could hear whirling in the distance, causing her heart rate to increase.

"Jacob, wake up!" she yelled, pulling out her blaster.

It was either their saviours or their captors. There was rustling behind her, a few curse words and then running steps.

"They're here," Jacob said excitedly.

Adelaide kept her dark thoughts to herself and just nodded. The wind picked up and the dust lifted as the ship neared.

"It's one of ours," Adelaide exclaimed, recognizing the shape of the ship and the noise of the engine. Earth's ships had a distinguishable sound from other engines.

The ship settled a short distance away, and the door slid open. A large white metal med bot emerged, along with two officers. One was a friend, Captain Makar. *Thank goodness*, Adelaide thought with relief. The other man she didn't recognize.

"We are detecting a severe break along with other external injuries. Do you require pain medication?" the med bot asked, floating towards her. The latest model of med bot didn't have legs. Instead, it hovered over the ground and could move at a fast clip if required. All med bots were programed with the medical knowledge and anatomy of all the known species that Earth had encountered.

"Of course. Now would be nice," Adelaide answered, trying not to yell.

The med bot's stomach opened, and its arm reached in, pulling out a pain relief strip and placing it on her arm. Adelaide felt immediate relief and grinned as the pain receded.

"Rescuing you again," Makar said with a smirk, striding over.

"Haha, just get me out of here."

Chapter 3

Adelaide slowly opened her eyes to a blinding light, which bounced off the sterile white walls. She turned her head slightly, gazing at all the tubes protruding from her skin making her feel like a pin cushion. Thank goodness, there was no pain. Her bed was the only object in the sterile room; if she reached out, Adelaide probably could touch both walls. The tubes ran into the ceiling and went god knows where. There was a clatter outside the door, before it slid open, and a nurse walked in carrying a tablet with a holodisplay showing Adelaide's body floating above it. Her crisp white uniform rustled, and her heels clicked on the marble floor, as she strode into the room.

"Captain, you're awake."

"Yes," Adelaide croaked. "Where am I?"

"Back on Earth2, at the military health facility."

"How?" Adelaide asked, blinking her eyes against the glare.

"Captain Makar immediately brought you here after your rescue."

"Did we win?"

"Yes. Thanks to you." Adelaide looked at her in surprise.

"What do you mean?"

"It has been all over the reports. When your ship went down, colliding with a Raykar's, it turned the tide. Everyone is calling you a hero."

Adelaide stared at the nurse in shock, as the woman moved around the table, inspecting the tubes and pushing a few buttons.

"Any pain?"

"No," Adelaide said, following the nurse with her eyes. "When do I get out of here?"

"You should be healed by tomorrow. You may have a slight limp for awhile. Multiple bones in your leg were shattered. We were able to synthesize new bone, but because of the complexity, it will take longer to heal. Your file says not to contact your family?"

"No," Adelaide interrupted. "It's not necessary."

"Alright." The nurse frowned before leaving the room.

*   *   *

Adelaide didn't want to explain about her family disapproving of her career choice. If they knew about her injuries, it would just give them another reason to berate her. She still remembered what had happened a couple of years back, when the health facility on the Earth base had contacted her parents, because she'd been injured. Man, did they give her an earful. They hadn't even come to visit her or ask about her status.

Adelaide sighed and shifted on the table, trying to get comfortable. *How could anyone like laying on these things? Couldn't they at least give you a proper bed?* She'd probably develop back issues because of this table.

Before this last battle, her mother had sent a message pleading with her to help her father with the business. He was having health problems and needed to take it easier, but every time she talked with him directly, no issues were mentioned. She was also a little worried that her brother Dante was hanging around too much; nothing good could ever come from that. He gambled excessively and dealt with the underbelly of society. Maybe it was time to give into her parents' harassment and join the business.

* * *

Arriving on Earth to be debriefed brought back plenty of memories that Adelaide had tried to bury, but they were still sitting on the surface. Before she had shipped out after basic training, Adelaide had gone home to see her parents and Dante. Her hope was that they would wish her luck and give her their approval. *Boy, was she wrong.* Adelaide knew that her parents loved her, but since she had been little, they had been planning out her life around the family business.

It still irked her that Dante was given lenience on his role in the business, but her life was theirs. Her mother had made a delicious meal of all of Adelaide's favourite foods, steak and potatoes along with desert. It was a bribe, and when Adelaide didn't cave in and agree she'd made a mistake, the fighting began. The evening had ended with her stomping out of the house, leaving a crying mother, a growling father and a smirking brother.

After that, Adelaide had only visited every couple of years. Eventually, her parents came around enough that she could talk civilly with them and provide updates on her life. Her mother also decided that, if Adelaide was going to stay in the military, she could find a handsome hero to bring home for them to meet. That new scheme made Adelaide choke the first time she'd heard it, and she had no plans of complying with that suggestion either.

Adelaide stepped off the shuttle at the entrance to Earth's main base and showed her badge. The armed guards checked her credentials before waving her through. The forcefield flickered and disappeared, allowing Adelaide to walk through it quickly. She turned around to watch the entrance close, and the guards' profiles blurred. Someone really needed to develop a transparent forcefield. Since it was a little blurry, anyone could see where the forcefield ended and would, therefore, have a better chance of destroying it. She flagged down a jeep for a ride to General Williams's office, which was about a twenty-minute walk across the base. With the fatigue already setting in, she didn't know if she'd make it.

Adelaide walked into the general's office and stopped at the dragon lady guarding the entrance. Adelaide was here for her debriefing. Everyone within the ranks knew to have a healthy fear of the woman sitting at the desk in front of her. Mrs. Turner's tongue could cut through anyone before they had taken more than a few steps, and her glare sent shivers up Adelaide's spine. There were plenty of rumours circulating about how she had ended up manning this station. Most of them involved her leading crucial attacks in the early days of WWIII until a wound had forced her into early retirement. *Hey, they had something in common,* Adelaide snorted.

"Something funny, Captain?" the dragon demanded, staring in Adelaide's direction.

"No, ma'am. The general is expecting me."

"Just a moment." She picked up her phone and spoke quietly for a moment before nodding Adelaide through to the inner sanctum.

"General," Adelaide said, as she stepped into the room and saluted, standing at attention.

"At ease, Captain," General Williams said with a smile. Adelaide relaxed her stance and waited. "Have a seat," he continued. "There is much to discuss."

She gave a quick nod, before sitting in one of the soft-cushioned leather seats. Glancing around, Adelaide noticed how neat and organized the office was. She wondered if that was the general's doing or the dragon lady's. The last time Adelaide had been to this office was when she had been offered a promotion, which she'd promptly declined. It would have meant a desk job, which was not for her. The military had taught Adelaide many lessons, including that she was an adrenaline junky. The thrill of a battle coursed through her veins, energizing her body, but Adelaide also had a healthy dose of fear that had kept her cautious and alive throughout the years. A desk job wasn't her thing.

One thing Adelaide found disconcerting was that most of her nightmares were still from the alien attacks on Earth when she was younger. Maybe, because she was a soldier now and this was war, her mind could compartmentalize the current horrors into the forgivable category. She shook herself out of her musing, only catching the tail end of the general's question.

"I only know what has been reported in the news. Did I really crash into the lead Raykar ship?" she asked, still not convinced.

"Yes. The Raykar ship you collided with was carrying the vast majority of their arsenal. We were able to use that to our advantage and disable the rest of their ships," the general confirmed. Adelaide tried to keep the grin off her face.

"Do we know how they were able to reach Earth2 so quickly?"

"Not yet. The leaders of the Accords believe the Raykar may have developed some kind of advanced technology. The latest theories are that their ships have been outfitted with a new method of travel. We have some of the debris from their ships, but it may be too damaged to salvage any information."

"What about the surviving Raykar?" she demanded, leaning forwards in the chair.

"They won't talk, not with any amount of persuasion." The general grimaced. Earth didn't agree with the Accords' methods of information extraction, but they were bound by it, especially during a war when other Accord members were involved. Adelaide had not been present for these interrogations but had heard about them. From what she had been told, there were many different methods employed, from electrocution to appendage removal. If these Raykar hadn't talked after that, Adelaide was very worried about what they were hiding, or who.

"I know you were severely injured, and that you're still recovering, but we want you to captain a new ship."

Adelaide wasn't surprised, but she was done with war.

"I'm sorry, General, but I plan to retire," Adelaide said, making the decision on the spot.

"You still have lots of life in you," the general said, clearly trying to reason with her.

"I know," she sighed, "but fighting is no longer in the cards for me."

"What will you do, then?" he asked curiously, staring at her intently.

"I plan to help with the family business."

"You won't be happy with that." The general was probably right, but she wanted to give it a try. Hopefully, exploring new worlds and seeing the sights might be enough to give her the high she craved.

"I plan on giving it my all," she said determinedly.

"Are you sure? We could use someone like you in the field." Adelaide felt warmth fill her bruised body, and she almost second guessed her response, but she held firm.

"I am, sir."

"I need you for one more assignment," the general insisted. Adelaide tried to hold in a groan while pasting a smile on her face.

"What is it?" she asked.

"Head up the team inspecting the Raykar ships. We need to know immediately what technology was used. They are on base at the lab." He gave her a knowing look. "Then, you can leave, if you really want to."

"One last time," Adelaide agreed, standing up. Saluting one more time, Adelaide walked stiffly out of the office with her head held high, striding by the dragon lady.

"Goodbye, Captain. They are waiting for you at the lab," the dragon lady said. Adelaide kept the surprise off her face and just nodded before exiting. *Of course, the general knew she would say yes, and the dragon lady was all-knowing*, Adelaide grumbled as she headed to the science lab only a ten-minute walk, so she pushed through the pain and fatigue. This base was Earth's main military installation, and therefore, the largest. She came to an abrupt halt to allow a line of weary recruits to stumble by. Sweat stains covered their brown uniforms, and Adelaide knew from experience that beneath the sweat, dirt caked their skin. The soldiers carried large backpacks for strength and stamina, which now dragged their shoulders down.

A few nodded her direction, and she held back her grin, when they all grimaced as one. The drill Sergeant was coming up behind them, yelling out commands. It hadn't been one of her favourite activities either. Once they were gone, Adelaide strode past the motorcade where about two dozen trucks and tanks sat waiting for repairs. She eventually made it to the far end of the base and felt like crying in relief. Her leg was throbbing and sharp little pinpricks shot up the length of it. She took a deep breath before pushing through the heavy metal door and leaning on the frame.

The lab was just a hanger that the scientists had confiscated from the ground force a few years back, which had caused an uproar until the general stamped the appropriation with his approval. The hanger could accommodate multiple ships from Earth's fleet at once. Throughout the hanger, people in lab coats ran around like chickens with their heads cut off, yelling out comments and questions. Their main focus seemed to be the large hunks of twisted metal that were piled in the centre. While in space, staring down the barrel of the Raykar fleet, one couldn't really appreciate the beauty of their ships. The pieces seemed to mesmerize Adelaide, as they flashed between black and dark blue, reflecting the large lamps shining down on all the fragments. Their ships patterned alloy reminded

Adelaide of a Raykar's scales which had very similar appearance.

Adelaide stood at the entry trying to absorb all the commotion and debating if she should quickly walk out without being seen. She might love ships but the science behind them? *Not so much.*

"Captain," called a large balding man. He was wearing a lab coat, jeans and a shirt that was a tad too small, showing his stomach, as he hurried in her direction.

"Damn," she said, under her breath.

"We were expecting you. Do you want to see the data we have gathered so far?" he asked breathlessly.

"Yes…?"

"Oh, my name is Dr. Clayton Spook. Follow me, please." He spun around quickly for a big man and practically ran towards the fragments.

Adelaide hobbled around the different types of equipment littering the ground and wondered how they could work in these conditions. The noise level increased significantly the closer they drew to the object of their scrutiny. Sparks flew as some individuals used instruments to cut into the fragments.

"This way," Clayton yelled, waving her past the hunks of metal towards a bank of computers."

"How is it going?" Adelaide asked as they came to a stop.

"Great!" Clayton replied excitedly, leaning down to type on the keyboard for a minute. "I didn't realize the Raykar were so advanced," he said glancing back at the wreckage.

"They weren't supposed to be," she responded with a frown, staring at one of the other screens. "What does that say?"

Clayton glanced back at her and replied, "That the hulls of their ships are made with an unknown alloy."

"From what I remember hearing when the war first started, they weren't very much more advanced than Earth," Adelaide interrupted.

"You are correct, Captain. From the previous wreckage we have on record, the Raykar's ships used to be built from a metal similar to the alloy used for Earth's ships. The properties of this new alloy are vastly different from anything we have seen before. It is a lot stronger and has the ability to repel our blasts." Adelaide frowned as she turned to glare at the fragments.

"Why are we the only scientists?" she asked.

"What do you mean?" he asked, not looking away from the screen.

Adelaide gestured around the room. "Where are the other members of the Accords?" Clayton drew himself up and puffed out his chest.

"They're not necessary. We were given the lead."

"Of course, they are," she said in surprise. "Contact the other scientists. Are there any other fragments around?" she demanded, rubbing her head in an attempt to stop the headache from forming. *How was she going to survive this project without killing Clayton?* She could already feel her annoyance building after talking to him

34

for five minutes. Her temper was not usually this quick to rise.

"There are some fragments at Segundo," he muttered. "But, we'll figure this out before them." Segundo was the capital city of the planet Straim, where the ruling members of the Multi-Species Accords lived.

"We don't have the time for your pride," Adelaide snarled, her face flushing and her body straightening. Clayton backed away a few steps with a look of surprise on his face. *Didn't anyone ever question him?* she thought.

"Discovering their technology is top priority, and we will use all the resources available to us. I want to see a report by 0800 tomorrow morning explaining *all* the findings," she said, stressing the "all" before stomping away from the infuriating man. It pissed her off that the good doctor wasn't trying every avenue to solve the mystery of the Raykar's new technology after so many people had been killed. Many of them had been her friends.

Adelaide pondered the origins of the strange alloy. *Where they hell did the Raykar acquire it?* Someone had to be helping them. Hopefully, the origin of the new technology would be self-evident. Exhaustion was setting in, and her leg was sore. Time to lay down. There was temporary lodging on the base and no point in staying elsewhere. She looked back as she left the hanger, seeing Clayton on the comms, hopefully to his colleagues, before she hobbled stiffly out of the lab. She would have preferred to stomp out making disgruntled noises, but her body wouldn't allow it. Slamming the door was all she could accomplish.

*   *   *

An insistent buzzing dragged Adelaide from her sleep. She groaned in denial while groping for the offending machine.

"Captain, it's 0600," Adelaide's computerized alarm clock announced.

"I know." She slowly peeled her eyelids open a crack. It was too early to be awakened so rudely, even if she'd made the request.

"Captain, I don't sense any movement," the alarm clock stated.

"I'm getting up," she yelled at it.

Before falling asleep last night, Adelaide had taken a pain strip, so her leg wasn't nearly as stiff today. The plan was to partake of the wonderful food in the mess hall. By the time breakfast was over, Dr. Spook should have a report ready for her. Slowly spinning her legs over the edge of the bed, she tentatively put weight on her injured leg. Grinning with relief, Adelaide stood and walked over to her suitcase. Rifling through it, she pulled out a pair of slacks and a dress shirt, quickly pulling them on. Carrying a light jacket, she stepped outside into the crisp air. The sky was clear, giving the sun full access to the land below. It was going to be a scorcher today, and the solar generators would have a chance to fully charge. Since WWIII, the people of Earth had changed their views about "Mother Earth" and decided she was worth saving.

All major centres used solar power almost exclusively. Scientists had made great advancements in perfecting the panels. They were now half the size of earlier ones and collected twice the amount of energy.

"Move it! Move it," Adelaide heard as a squad ran by panting.

Rapid gunfire could be heard in the distance. Someone was always trying to improve their accuracy. When she had lived at the base, the biggest excitement was elicited from the new weapon advancements. Soldiers were allowed to test them. People packed into the shooting range, providing commentary during the trials. Some scientists welcomed suggestions and opinions, while others, not so much.

Adelaide stumbled as a couple of men brushed past her, hurrying out of the mess hall.

"Sorry, excuse me," one of them said.

"No problem," she replied, stepping into the building.

Adelaide walked up to the serving line and grabbed a tray. Her stomach growled as she stared at the selection. Adelaide's cheeks grew warm, and she glanced around to see if anyone had heard before reaching for the ladle. With her plate piled high of eggs and meat, she picked a corner table, sitting down and smiling in anticipation.

* * *

Adelaide's comm beeped, signaling an incoming message. She glanced down at the holodisplay on her wrist. It looked like Clayton had come through with the details. Adelaide pulled up the report and scrolled down. Scientists from the Accords had theories on the strange alloy but nothing concrete. Their fragments were too damaged to ascertain the type of technology being used by the Raykar. Clayton's team had been able to piece together some fragments, though, and the preliminary results showed that the new technology existed. It left a strange residue that hadn't been recorded before. His comments implied that the Raykar had developed a jump gate that was fully integrated into their ship. Adelaide seriously doubted the Raykar were responsible. Their species stole and salvaged all the technology the Raykar used. They lived by one rule: "Why build what can be taken from another?"

If it was a smaller version of a jump gate, the thing would probably have some extreme security. Adelaide decided to visit Clayton to pound the idea of collaborating with the Accords into his head and monitor their progress.

* * *

A week later, Adelaide was back in the general's office giving her final report.

"Are they finished?" General Williams asked her.

"The main portion. I'm sure the scientists could find a reason to continue. They're fascinated with the fragments."

"And you're not?" he asked, with a small grin.

"No," she stated. "I don't find it interesting to stare at objects and analyze them to death. I'd rather use them." The general flipped through her report.

"What are your observations?"

"It's all in there."

"I want you to give me an overview," the general said, leaning back in his chair and steepling his fingers.

Adelaide took a deep breath and said, "Through collaboration with our allies, our scientists have determined that the Raykar have developed a small device that allows them to travel great distances."

"Do you agree?"

Adelaide paused for a moment. "Yes, I believe the device exists, but not that the Raykar developed it."

He looked at her intently and asked, "Why?"

"The Raykar have never advanced their own technology. It's always been discovered through others, usually by force."

"Agreed." He nodded. "Do we have any theories of the mystery race?"

"No, and there weren't any markings or materials that point to a specific race or sector."

"We'll have to keep that investigation going. Our allies had no ideas either?" Adelaide tried not to frown, she didn't want to be stuck with that.

"They are all puzzled as to where the tech could have originated from." The general stared at Adelaide for a few minutes making her shift uncomfortably.

"So, you still want to leave?"

"Yes," she replied simply and waited silently for his response.

"Mrs. Turner," he called. The dragon stepped in carrying a stack of papers. "You will be sorely missed," he continued. The general took the papers from Mrs. Turner and grabbed a pen.

"There are some discharge forms that we'll need your signature on." Adelaide slid to the edge of her seat and leaned over the desk, ready to start a new chapter.

*   *   *

Adelaide walked out of the office a free woman. Now to make the dreaded call.

"Adelaide, is that you?" her mother, Aquila, said peering through her glasses at the comm screen. She was sixty-five years old but didn't look a day over thirty. While Adelaide worried about the ramifications of surgery, Aquila embraced these new surgical techniques. The one exception was that she never altered her red hair, which Adelaide had inherited. At least Aquila still look like herself, just a younger version of it. It was commonplace for women and men to alter their bodies beyond recognition these days. There were plenty of alien technologies that humans could take advantage of. People had also started adding features from other species to themselves in an effort to look more exotic. Thank goodness, her mother had never done that. Adelaide pasted a smile on her face.

"Yes, Mom. I wanted to let you know that I've retired from the military."

"Great, dear! Your father will be pleased. Are you going to the ZOO now?"

"I was thinking of coming home first for a visit," Adelaide sighed.

"You should hurry to the ship. Your father needs you now."

"Fine. I'll see you later, then." Adelaide tried not to let the hurt show on her face as she shut down the communication. It would have been nice to have a little downtime before facing her father. There would be no point in contacting him, as her mother was probably already communicating with him herself. With that thought, her comm beeped to indicate receiving a message from her mother with the ZOO's coordinates. Grabbing her bag and slinging it over her shoulder, she headed out the door to her exciting new life, hopefully.

Chapter 4

Adelaide felt a hard lump of dread in the pit of
her stomach as she limped to the ZOO.

Her dad, Barrett Zedler, had started the
cargo business Zedler, Odin and Owen Shipping,
or the ZOO for short, back when space travel had
first begun. He had a terrible sense of humour,
and his business partners had, for some unknown
reason, agreed with him. Barrett had dragged
Odin and Owen, a couple of his close friends, into
the risky business venture, and they were some
of the first people to explore space. Her dad had
accumulated enough wealth, by storing a few
extra items that couldn't be found on the
manifest every now and then, to buy out his
partners and add two more vessels to his fleet.
Adelaide suspected that his friends didn't like the
way the ZOO was being used and were glad to get
out before something bad happened. They were
more like silent partners anyway, only once in
awhile joining her dad on board for a job. Soon,
the ZOO was widely known in both the

commercial sectors and the criminal underbellies of dozens of planets ranging across the galaxy.

Adelaide rubbed her sore leg. Medical had done all they could for it, which was extensive, but it was going to take time to heal fully. Even with the leaps in medical technology, the body could still only do so much. Working for her dad almost felt like acknowledging that her parents had been right about her career. But, Adelaide reminded herself that it had been eleven years, long enough to prove herself and justify her choice. She had no idea how, but news about her retirement from the military had travelled fast. She'd received multiple career offers but had turned them down because of her family obligation.

As Adelaide approached the ZOO, a crewman zoomed by pushing multiple crates up the plank and into the cargo bay. She entered the ship in search of her father, trying to slow her heart rate as she went. Walking onto the bridge, she spotted her dad joking with Dante.

"Adelaide, you made it." Barrett jumped up and pulled her into a massive hug. Surprised, she slowly wrapped her arms around him. He had never been an overly affectionate man. Over his shoulder, Dante rolled his eyes and grimaced beneath his tiny mustache.

"Great," she muttered.

"What was that?" Barrett asked, pulling away.

"Nothing, Dad," she said, giving him a tight smile.

It was hard to believe that she and Dante were siblings. Sometimes, jealousy reared its ugly head when they were together. Dante had inherited their mother's curls and thin frame, but his six-foot-two stature and black hair was all her father. Of course, he wrecked his gorgeous looks with the caterpillar on his lip. Adelaide almost laughed every time she saw it. Meanwhile, she was stuck with wild curly red hair and freckles. The only way her body stayed in it's great physical shape was the constant training she subjected herself to.

She and Dante used to be close growing up on Earth post-war. The landscape had been horrific, especially in the major cities. It had taken probably ten to fifteen years for the major plant life to begin growing again because of the weapon fallout. The Coalition had had their work cut out for them trying to feed the citizens of Earth. There were areas around the Earth that were only slightly damaged, and vast gardens had been cultivated in these regions. The products were shipped worldwide to ensure the survivors would thrive under the new world order. There were still shortages, and poverty was a way of life for most, but her family had been fortunate. With her dad's steady job, her parents had been able to move the family to the area that used to be Chicago. Everything was at a premium, and the streets were filled with beggars. There were never winners in a war, and WWIII proved that. It had been horrible growing up in the city of demolished buildings with no green in sight. The Coalition had focused more on developing new technology rather than fixing old buildings. Fancy new structures had risen and dwarfed their predecessors, rising to the stars. These new places were built out of advanced materials developed by the military to withstand a war, which hopefully wasn't coming anytime soon.

Back then, Dante would escort her all over town, ensuring her safety. At school, the necessity wasn't as high, because the police patrolled. Adelaide had been a quiet, scrawny kid prone to harassment. Dante had always stepped in and defended her. These days, it felt like Dante would rather leave her than save her. She wasn't sure when things had changed, and she didn't care. There was too much bitterness between them now. And yet, a few times during her career in the military, Adelaide had searched out Dante's whereabouts to confirm that he was alive and not incarcerated.

Adelaide stepped away from her father, looking around the bridge. Her dad really needed to upgrade the ship. There were dents throughout the ZOO from the previous owner that had never been repaired. Over the years, it grew worse from regular wear and tear. As parts broke down, her dad would replace them with other used pieces. So, now, it was just a hodgepodge of metal and machinery. As far as she knew, the business made enough money for upgrades, but weapons were pretty much nonexistent, and the engine had seen better days. The other two cargo ships in his fleet weren't much better off. He kept the crew at a bare minimum so his profits were higher. If there was any trouble, the meagre crews of 25 men would be screwed. On previous visits, Adelaide had suggested changes or improvements, but she had met with resistance and backlash. She didn't know anything, her military wasn't better than him, and on and on.

"What's the plan?" she asked, coming out of her reverie.

"We have some cargo going to Zartuth," Barrett replied.

"Really? What would we be delivering *there*?" Adelaide asked suspiciously.

"Just some equipment," Barrett said evasively, glancing at Dante as he shifted away from her. She noticed the quick exchange, and dread filled her stomach. Adelaide frowned. Zartuth was on the edge of their current solar system and the place to go for anything illegal. Anyone wanting to disappear chose Zartuth as their destination. The planet's government let the local factions handle any conflicts that arose. It had worked well so far. Adelaide had only heard of a few skirmishes turning serious enough that the combatants couldn't be contained and the military had been called in.

"Well, let's see the great Captain fly," Dante said snidely, pointing at the pilot's chair with a glare. "We hear you're some kind of hero."

"We don't need to discuss that part of her life. She's here now, where she belongs," Barrett said, glaring at Dante. Adelaide shook her head. Of course, her dad didn't want to acknowledge her achievements. They had been achieved by going against his plans for her life.

"I bet that sticks in your craw," she couldn't help
saying, before settling into the chair with a
chuckle. There were a few coughs around the
room as the others turned to their consoles. It
felt nice sitting in the driver's seat again. She
grabbed hold of the stick and said, "Hold onto
your pants, gentleman." Her dad sent the
information to the station, and Adelaide slowly
lifted out of the bay. As soon as the ZOO was
clear, it shot towards the closest gate. They
would arrive in approximately two hours at
lightspeed. Because of Barrett's cargo-ship status,
they received a discount to travel the gates. As
members of the Accords, travel was usually free
through the gates, but businesses were required
to pay a small fee. At least it was less than the
fee for non-members.

"How long do we plan to be on Zartuth?"
Adelaide asked.

"Not long. We're just delivering the cargo,
and then we're out of there," Barrett answered.

While flying through the gate, she wasn't
required to pay complete attention, so Adelaide's
gaze wandered around the bridge. Some of the
crew, she recognized, but most weren't familiar.
The crewmen began talking quietly amongst
themselves, every now and again glancing her
way with a frown. There were no other women on
board, and she knew that, just like sailors on the
sea, some believed girls were bad luck to have on
your ship. Her brother probably didn't help, with
his snide comments. It had been better in the
military, where seeing a woman in uniform was

commonplace. Many of Earth's top-ranking generals were women.

*   *   *

The flight was uneventful, and Adelaide was glad to arrive. She resisted feeling for the hole that Dante had surely drilled into the back of her head with his glare.

"So where are we going?" she asked, turning to her dad.

He looked at her in surprise. "You don't need to worry about it."

"No problem, Dad. I want to learn everything. That's why I'm here."

"Alright," Barrett stuttered, "I wasn't expecting you yet. That's why Dante is here. We're going to the surface."

"Really?" Adelaide said. When the ZOO dropped off its cargo, it was usually just at the station. Adelaide had never ventured to Zartuth's surface, as the space station orbiting the planet was large enough to supply anything you could want. A few years back, the military had been conducting drills nearby and needed to replenish their supplies. Only a few of her ship's crew had been brave enough to venture onto the station to find the required parts. The rest had decided a break wasn't necessary.

"No problem," she said nonchalantly. "I'll get us docked, and we can head out." Docking the ZOO at the space station was quick and painless.

"Ready?" Adelaide said, standing up and looking at her dad and Dante expectantly. *Of course, Dante was up to something,* she thought. Walking behind them, Adelaide unconsciously patted her blaster.

"Aren't we missing something?" Adelaide asked, coming to a halt as the men were leaving the ship. Dante looked back at her frowning.

"We have to meet the buyer, er, *customer* first and make arrangements." She frowned at their backs as she followed them out of the ship.

Bright colours assaulted Adelaide's vision as they strode through the market towards the shuttle bay. Vendors displayed their wares under brightly coloured canopies scattered throughout the station. She heard multiple languages being shouted around her — thank goodness for the translator chip that she'd had implanted by the government. There were a barrage of translations bombarding her brain, and Adelaide groaned, not used to the sensory overload. On her military ship, most of the crew spoke English or the common language of the Accords.

It had been part of signing the Multi-Species Accords that an individual operating a business had to either speak the common tongue of the Accords or have a translator chip installed behind their ear, connecting directly to their brain. Of course, Earth's government was all over it. No complaints from her — it was free. Adelaide was terrible with languages and excited for the technology. It was funny, even with the chip, the one speaking still had an accent for any language that wasn't their native one. Adelaide must have received the travelling bug from her father, because she loved to explore and discover new places and species, so language was vital. There were not a lot of things she could say the two of them had in common since she had supposedly abandoned the family — his words.

"You get used to it," said a small, wiry man from behind her. Adelaide spun around in surprise.

"Thanks. You look familiar." She frowned in concentration, studying the older man. He looked to be in his early sixties, with intricate tattoos across his head. Adelaide didn't want to stare while trying to decipher the pictures, but some numbers caught her eye.

"My name's Gil." He stuck out his hand. "The ship's engineer." Recognition dawned on Adelaide's face.

"You were recruited for this farce as well?" she asked, nodding to the disappearing backs of her family members.

"Yep. We better hurry to catch up."

"You know what's going on?"

"Nothing good," he growled quietly.

Adelaide muttered under her breath, hurrying to catch up, but her leg was already feeling fatigued and achy. She needed to get a pain strip when they returned. Adelaide should have known to keep some on her for now until her leg completely healed. A few vendors tried stepping in front of her, but Adelaide said no and pushed through to the waiting shuttle. She could almost guarantee Dante was encouraging them to take off without her.

"Don't worry, your brother won't leave without me," Gil whispered with a grin.

Adelaide smiled, looking surprised. Either Gil could read minds, or her feelings were showing again. It had taken extensive training during the early stages of her career to control her feelings and hide them from the world. Her crew didn't need to see their captain panicking, and the enemy didn't need to know when they had the upper hand. It had been drilled into her time and again by her instructors.

It was a quick ride to the planet's surface, and they landed in a cloud of dust. Emerging from the shuttle felt like entering a sauna. The planet's two suns glared down from the green sky. Adelaide did a double take. *Wait, a green sky?*

"Hurry up!" Dante called. "We don't have all day."

"I'm coming."

There were plenty of scantily clad, for a lack of better term, female and males wandering down the street. With some species, she wasn't sure how to identify their genders, and it was easier to apply the term "female" or "male" instead. Adelaide tried not to gawk as she kept pace with her father. He never glanced around once, but Dante sure let his eyes wander. Some species had extra limbs or different limbs than humans or even a glow around them that Adelaide couldn't explain. On a ship in outer space, Adelaide hadn't had much contact with other species from worlds away from here. As a captain, she'd been able to satisfy her exploration bug, but there weren't very many different species to be seen on Earth's space ships. This was an experience that she would be remembering and planned to duplicate, hopefully many times, in the future.

Their groups' stomping feet kicked up more dust as the wind picked up, blowing it around. Adelaide was jostled as multiple people — beings not human — pushed past her, hurrying through the crowd. There were yellow, green and brown bodies all smushed together looking like a rainbow. She tried not to stare at all of the different species gathered together in one place, many of whom weren't familiar to her.

"Is that a green horse?" Adelaide asked quietly, but gasped as the "woman" turned. Her green skin was a stark contrast to the white hair that flowed down her back and over her shoulders, partially covering her two bare breasts. Her four legs were thin and shapely, ending in tiny hooves. Adelaide could see now that her back was just a quarter the size of a horse, and there wasn't enough room for carrying someone. The proportions were just enough to accommodate her many appendages, making her very pretty. Adelaide wasn't in Kansas anymore. She grinned to herself, remembering growing up and watching that movie with Dante. Of course, *The Wizard of Oz* had been remade multiple times. She had been ecstatic when the original had been found and released. Feeling something at her waist, Adelaide grabbed for her blaster and peered around, but the sensation stopped abruptly as a little black body, with what looked like horns on the front of his head, scurried back the direction he had come. Gil snorted behind her.

"They have to eat, too. Around these parts, you need to keep your weapons and belongings safe. The kids will steal anything not attached to sell for food. If you stick with us, you'll meet many interesting beings. Come on, we have to catch up."

Even though humans had been travelling through space for twenty-five years, they were still small in numbers compared to the other races found across the galaxy, so they weren't seen in large quantities on the different worlds. The human population was slowly growing and expanding, letting its presence known. It was comforting that, after so many wars, humans were still going strong. They were resilient.

Buildings sat side by side along the streets of Zartuth. The bottom halves were made out of a muddy white stone, while the tops were made of red wood. The planet had plenty of rock to spare, and these buildings held up under the onslaught of the wet season. Floods were commonplace, and wood foundations would rot quickly. She wasn't sure what the purpose of having the top halves of the buildings made out of wood could be — why not make it all out of stone? The poor inhabitants of Zartuth went from enduring floods and soaked clothes to the heat waves that they got to bake in during the dry season. But, beggars can't be choosers. If someone needed to be off the grid, this was the place to be. Of course, it seemed unusual that the local inhabitants wouldn't want to leave the moment they were able. Yet, the stats Adelaide had read yesterday to prepare herself had said that the population was rising on Zartuth and that the planet boasted a healthy economy.

Crates were being moved at a steady pace, in and out of the buildings, mostly heading to the shuttle bay and landing docks. Dirt packed all of the streets, and tufts of brush peeked through in places. She was surprised — *wouldn't something more permanent, like paving stones, be better than watching your street wash away all the time because of the flooding?* The planet was wealthy enough to cover the costs, and the stone was readily available. The landscape reminded Adelaide of the Old West, from Earth's history, but with many different and strange plant species like the purple grass and large brown trees that grew in peoples' and businesses' yards. From what she could discern, aliens outweighed the native Zartuths, who were easy to spot with their almost hairless heads and large round eyes. She recognized the Tu'Val, with their large He-Man bodies, and the Gaeaf, which was surprising since most didn't venture far from their frozen planet.

"How far is it?" Adelaide asked.

"Not too far," Dante responded.

"We're going to the pleasure district," Gil piped up. Dante glowered in Gil's direction. Adelaide could hear the laughter behind her. She was really starting to like Gil. He seemed to enjoy irritating her brother, and she was all for that.

Dante stopped in front of a building with the name "Narwhal Tavern" carved into the door. She could already hear the music — it must be deafening inside. Adelaide gazed in wonder at the massive metal door. It was over ten feet tall, and it appeared to accommodate two or three people side by side.

"Adelaide, why don't you stay outside with Dad. Gil can come inside with me."

"I don't need to be babied," she snarled, immediately reacting to his condescending-big-brother tone. It was fine for him to be protective when they were growing up, but not now, after insulting her for so many years. He didn't have the right.

"Fine. Your funeral," Dante said, grinning as he pushed open the door.

The first thing Adelaide noticed was the wonderful drop in temperature. The second thing was her throbbing eardrums. She let her eyes adjust to the lighting before continuing on. Not far into the bar, a rather large Tu'Val from the Raau planet strode up to Adelaide. Her eyes took stock of his seven-foot, muscle-bound body. His green skin seemed to shimmer in the dim light, drawing her gaze to his bulging biceps.

As Adelaide had been admiring the male before her, he was clearly doing the same. But with his appraising look, she felt like he had stripped off her clothes with those purple eyes. His voice startled her, when he suddenly spoke.

"You're new. I have a place where we can't be interrupted." Adelaide laughed.

"I don't think so." She watched a frown cross his handsome face. *Probably not that many girls told him no,* she thought.

"I don't think you heard me," he said insistently, grabbing her arm. Adelaide noticed a few patrons moving away slowly, but none stepped in to help. That's alright, she didn't need it.

"I would let go if I were you." It was his turn to laugh.

"Really, what are you going to do, little girl?"

"I won't tell you again. Release me," Adelaide snarled, feeling a tug.

"Is he bothering you?" Gil asked from behind her.

"I'm good," she answered, as the tree trunk in front of her grinned. She twisted her wrist sharply and pulled free, lurching the Tu'Val's body slightly closer. With a quick jerk, she lifted her knee, making contact between his legs, and brought her elbow down a second later, connecting with his head. His body dropped to the floor, and she heard the gasps in the room and then dead silence. The quiet didn't last, and it wasn't long before she couldn't hear herself think anymore and Gil was chortling beside her. Adelaide's leg almost gave out, and she bit back a groan of pain. *Damn thing, when would it heal?*

"What the hell did you do?" Dante demanded, pushing his way towards Adelaide through the crowd of onlookers.

"He attacked me! Where were you?" she replied, rounding on him.

Dante looked at her in astonishment and then down at the body slowly uncurling on the floor of the tavern.

"Damn it, Adelaide, he's our contact."

"Oh, shit," she whispered.

"Taurian, meet my sister," Dante said as Taurian stood. Adelaide didn't expect the grin that split his face to make him almost irresistible, but it did.

"So, we will be seeing lots of each other," Taurian said, leering at her.

Not bloody likely, she thought but just smiled tightly. Her father approached the group, arriving next to Adelaide just in time to here Taurian's next comment.

"What did you say your name was?" Taurian asked.

"I didn't."

"It's Adelaide," Barrett answered, looking at her with a surprised expression. *Probably never expected me to have the ability to defend myself.*

"Adelaide Zedler? I've heard that name," Taurian muttered, staring at her.

Oh crap, she thought.

"No, you haven't. Let's get this over with," she interjected, hopefully derailing his train of thought.

Dante moved a short distance away with Taurian, leaving Adelaide standing with her father and Gil. Adelaide watched Dante lean forwards, waving his hands, a frown marring his face. Taurian stood impassively until Dante finished his spiel before barking a few words. Dante shut up and took a step back. It wasn't long before Dante stomped back over.

"Let's go. We need to pick up the cargo and meet Taurian back at the warehouse."

"When?" her dad asked.

"A couple of hours."

"That won't be enough time to get back."

"For what?" Adelaide interrupted.

Her dad waved his hand in her direction and continued speaking.

"Taurian damn well knows the consequences," he muttered, practically running for the door. The others hurried after him. No one would answer Adelaide's questions. They would only chuckle and say, "Wait and see." She'd taken on the Raykar — she could handle this, right?

The first thing Adelaide did when they arrived at the ZOO was visit the medical bay. Their med bot checked over her leg and handed her a pain strip, which she slapped onto her arm, sighing in relief and flexing her leg. The ache was already receding, and her limp was not as pronounced. She decided to use the time to familiarize herself with the ZOO. It had been ages since she'd walked these corridors. Most of the crewmen were around, and they cautiously welcomed her. But, the minute her back was turned, there was quiet, rapid conversation and laughter. Her ire was rising, and Adelaide was tempted to march onto the bridge and demand an explanation. These men gossiped more than an old woman, and she seemed to be the butt of their jokes. But instead, she decided to observe the transaction and gather all the ammunition she could. Her dad had to stop letting Dante destroy the company. If they were ever caught smuggling, there'd go the business, because they'd all be in prison.

TAURIAN CASSINI
BORN IN 2068; 40 YEARS OLD

OCCUPATION: SMUGGLER
- *Dealt with Adelaide's Brother Dante*

PLANET: RAAU
- *People called the Tu'Val — a warrior race, love to fight and pillage*
- *covered in jungle, warm and humid*
- *species wore very little clothing*
- *Not part of the Mult-Specie Accords*

PHYSICAL DESCRIPTION:
Seven feet tall, light green skin, sculpted body, vivid purple eyes, blond hair to shoulders, and a hairless body. He has a chiseled jawline and defined cheek bones.

WEAPONS:
A long sword strapped to his back and a laser gun strapped to his hip.

PERSONALITY/EMOTIONS:
Strong, entitled, cocky

Chapter 5

Adelaide was raring to go at the designated time, and she ensured she had a few pain strips stashed in her pocket. If she wasn't careful, they would become an addiction — not something she needed to deal with — but they were necessary for now. Dante was directing the unloading of his precious cargo. A large wooden crate holding god-knows-what was pushed down the plank.

"Okay, let's head out," Dante said.

Her dad stayed back, so it was Adelaide, Gil, Dante and Brandon — a tall, dark-haired crewman from the ZOO. Adelaide ensured that her blaster was charged before they left. No way was she going out there unarmed. She'd heard about some of Dante's previous escapades from her mom and again from some of the crew today.

"How are we getting this down to the planet's surface?" Adelaide demanded, staring at the huge crate standing up to the level of her hips. "It must be at least eight feet wide and long."

One difference between Zartuth and most other planets was that they banned any ship from landing on the planet's surface. The space station was the only approved landing site. But, there was no way they could fit this thing onto the shuttle. Adelaide figured that the individuals in charge didn't want to chance a large landing party having direct access to the planet and taking over. At least, with the station as a checkpoint, they could control the amount and type of visitors who made it down to the surface.

"Don't worry your pretty little head about it. I've got it covered," Dante blustered.

"Bribes," Gil said under his breath. Adelaide whipped her head around and glared at her brother, trying not to snarl. Well, at least he'd called her pretty. It was the first compliment he'd given her in a long time. What was he doing to their dad's business? It was a good thing she was here. She could feel Dante's impatience as they skirted around the umpteenth group of people. His face had a permanent frown, and he gripped his blaster in its holster. Dante was leading them to the opposite end of the station where the shuttle pad was located. He motioned for them to stop and continued towards a closed door. After a couple of knocks, the door opened slightly, and Adelaide could hear a voice. They talked, Dante's hand was scanned where his personal chip was embedded, and he walked back in a matter of minutes.

Personal chips were another lovely invention Earth had received because of the Accords. All employees of any company operating within the Milky Way galaxy were required to get the personal chip implanted into the top of their hand. These chips transmitted a person's name, employment status, resident planet and banking information. The idea was great, in Adelaide's opinion. Paying for items was quick and easy now, and fraud was virtually impossible, because the chip also transmitted a person's DNA signature. A personal chip connected directly to the brain, and a person had to allow the transaction for it to work. Another thing Earth's government had jumped on board with. All military personnel were implanted immediately, as well as all inmates. Inmates would then be tracked and monitored upon release. However, many people on Earth were resistant to the chip. The government could watch and track people — blah, blah, blah. Adelaide remembered a news story where a child was kidnapped on Earth. Before the offender could attempt to leave the planet, the police had traced the girl's chip and rescued her. After the story broke, a wave of sales for implants flooded Earth and the colony.

"We're good to go. Hurry up," Dante said upon his return. They strode up to a small ship and pushed their cargo up the ramp and into the cargo bay. Adelaide glanced around, but no one came to speak with them or inspect their crate.

"Hold on," Dante said, as the door closed and the engines fired up.

A back door, Adelaide thought, bracing herself against the crate. It was cramped quarters even though the cargo area was otherwise empty.

They quickly reached the planet's surface, and Brandon maneuvered the crate out of the ship using their hyperlift. Dante yelled at him a few times, trying to motivate his speed. If it had been her, her response would have been to slow down, not pick up her pace. Of course, Dante couldn't fire her. She wasn't sure how much control he had on the ZOO.

"Enough, Dante," Adelaide barked, glaring in his direction.

Dante opened his mouth but probably thought better of his response, because he turned around and stomped ahead. Brandon gave her a nod before following.

"You'll be good for the ship," Gil commented, walking by. Adelaide tried to keep the grin off her face, but a smile slipped through. *Maybe it wouldn't be so bad,* she thought.

Dante stopped at the door of a large warehouse, glanced around and then cautiously entered. The few working lights hung from the thirty-foot ceiling, casting a paltry light within. Adelaide squinted in the darkness, spotting all the lovely hiding spots between the multiple crates scattered throughout the warehouse. Some were stacked halfway to the ceiling, and all the ones she could read didn't have the proper stamps. They could hear a noise further into the building.

"Taurian, where are you?" Dante yelled. There was silence for a few minutes, and Dante opened his mouth to call out again.

"We're back here," Taurian answered.

"Come on." Dante waved them forward and led the way, moving farther from their escape route. Adelaide and Gil pulled out their blasters, peering around as they followed him. Brandon was a step behind, pushing the crate while trying to balance his blaster. They found Taurian standing under one of the lights, surrounded by men armed with large swords and blasters. The instant Adelaide appeared, Taurian grinned in her direction and stepped forwards.

"Glad you came along, so we could finish our discussion."

"What discussion? From what I recall you were lying on the floor."

"Adelaide," Dante hissed, as the Tu'Val roared with laughter.

"Let's get this over with," Adelaide said.

"You heard Red," Taurian said, winking at Adelaide as he turned to Dante. "Let's see them."

Dante strode over to the crate, using the crowbar to pop the lid. Adelaide leaned forwards, wanting to catch a glimpse of the goods. Taurian reached into the crate, pulling out a large blaster. It was the length of his arm and probably weighed a ton. But, Taurian seemed to have no difficulties holding the weapon and twisting it around, inspecting all of its nooks and crannies. A pleased smile crossed his face as he said, "Transfer the credits."

Dante visibly loosened as his comm beeped. He glanced down at the holodisplay and grinned.

"Let's go, we're finished," he said. Their group was headed to the door when a commotion started behind them.

"Hurry," Dante whispered, urging them quicker. Adelaide stopped in her tracks.

"Shouldn't we see what's going on?"

"Are you nuts? It's probably another gang. Doesn't concern us," Dante said, pushing her forwards. She glanced back and saw someone move between the crates. Adelaide growled and pushed Dante aside just as the door exploded. They dived for cover and returned fire.

"You're surrounded. Hand it over, Dante."

Adelaide glared at her brother. "Who the hell is that?" she demanded. It seemed like her brother had pissed everyone off, and Adelaide wasn't surprised.

"I have no idea," Dante snarled from behind her.

She peeked around the crate and jerked back as they fired her way. She glanced around the room, searching for a way out. Brandon was crouched beside Dante, and about twenty feet to her right, Gil was crouched behind a stack of crates with his blaster at the ready. Before she could yell out a warning, two human men stepped around the corner. This wasn't the place that Adelaide wanted to see more humans. She grimaced and took aim, but Gil stood and moved in a flurry, taking both men down in a second. Adelaide couldn't stop her mouth from dropping open.

"Did you see that?" Adelaide asked Dante.

"He can take care of himself."

Pieces of wood exploded, and Adelaide ducked as they sailed above her head.

"This is crazy. Where's Taurian?" she demanded.

"Probably snuck out the back. The bastard."

"We need to get out of here."

They all fired again, and she heard a scream.

"You guys cover me. I'll try to distract them," Adelaide ordered. Dante and Brandon began firing, and she scooted around the crates, moving silently towards her targets. Adelaide smirked as she heard Brandon's whispered "man, is she amazing." Of course, her leg began screaming at the abuse, but she grimaced and continued on. Both unknown assailants and Dante were yelling back and forth, creating some distractions to cover her advancement. More shots were exchanged, and Adelaide reached their hiding spot. She peered around waiting for the right moment. When the coast was clear, she attacked. The first man went down like a ton of bricks, and the next wasn't far behind.

"We're good," she yelled, stepping out. Luckily none of their people were harmed.

"Hurry, before more show up," Dante said, running for the door.

They burst out of the gaping hole into the cooling air.

"Don't we need to let someone know?" she asked, limping beside Dante.

"Who in the hell would we tell? The corrupt government or another gang?"

"I don't know. What about the bodies?"

"They'll disappear by morning," he said, swivelling his head back and forth, as they headed for their shuttle.

*   *   *

The suns were just beginning to set as they neared the shuttles. It was a ghost town. Where the hell was everyone? A buzz was drawing near, and Adelaide glanced behind them. Dante flinched and picked up his speed. A swarm of black objects were nearly upon them.

"What are those?" Adelaide screamed. They were humongous flying *somethings*.

All four of them dove into the shuttle just as a group of the creatures splattered against the glass. Adelaide took a cautious step closer and whispered, "What are they?"

Gil snorted and said, "The wildlife. Comes out at night."

That made things clearer, Adelaide thought sarcastically. A few seemed to shake it off, and they flew away. The others slowly slid down the shuttle as the engine engaged. Their beady red eyes stared right through her, giving Adelaide the heebie-jeebies. The creature reminded her of a mosquito, but it was the size of a small bird.

"Do they suck on people?" she asked in horror, staring at the very long nose.

"Yep," Brandon said, grinning at her.

A shudder ran up her spine as an image flashed through her mind of the bug latched onto her neck. She was definitely going to have nightmares about those things.

* * *

Adelaide stomped into the ZOO. "Where is the Captain?" she demanded of the first crewman she saw.

"On the bridge." He pointed the way, staring at her wild hair. She was sure some blood also spotted her body from the exploding crates.

Her dad was sitting in his chair, joking and laughing with three of the bridge crew. She hadn't been noticed yet, as one man was in the middle of telling a crude story about a woman he'd met on Zartuth. Of course, knowing she was there probably wouldn't make a difference.

"Dad, we need to talk," she interrupted.

Barrett turned his head and glared in her direction. "When I have time."

Great, she thought. *He's being a man.* Her dad and brother didn't help with all of the sexist stereotyping from the crew. *Why, then, did her dad want her on board so badly?* Adelaide wondered.

"It's important."

"Fine." He slowly stood up and gestured for her to follow.

They stepped into the room off the bridge, the door sliding shut behind them. The instant they were alone in his office, he yelled, "I am the Captain of this hunk of junk. Show me some respect."

"Then don't be an idiot," Adelaide growled, prowling in front of him. "I just came back from a situation where my dumbass brother caused a shootout."

"Don't swear about your brother. He's been here helping with the business while you've been out gallivanting."

"Gallivanting?" Adelaide clenched her teeth, breathing out her nose. "What he's doing isn't helping. It'll get you arrested, and then what would happen to Mom?"

"It's only once in a while."

"Arrrgh." She threw her hands up and turned away, trying to calm down. "Dad, you can't take these chances," she said quietly.

"It's my business, and I can therefore do what I want. You've been here a whole day and already believe your word is law?" Barrett paced in front of Adelaide, a frown on his face.

"I'm trying to help, Dad. I can't watch Dante wreck what you've built."

"I'm not an idiot! I know perfectly well what Dante is up to. Why do you care so much? You never did before," he demanded, glaring in her direction. "You want to take over my business, don't you? Dante warned me that this would happen."

Adelaide tried to stay calm and not let the hurt colour her words. "I've always cared, Dad. I knew you could handle it, I just want to learn the business, and family is important. Dante is wrong about me. I don't want to take this away from you. I love you."

71

She watched her father stare in her direction, before collapsing in the chair.

"You need to stop encouraging Dante in this. It will destroy you. Why doesn't he captain one of your other ships? He's a great pilot."

He sighed. "It's not for him. He needs to be free to leave for business."

"That's what he calls it nowadays," she said snidely, shaking her head.

"Don't take that attitude with me," he said, scowling. "I know you and your brother aren't getting along, but if you want to learn, that had better change," he threatened.

"You need to tell that to Dante as well. I'm warning you — I'm not going to put up with his shit. I have no desire to go to jail for him."

"I'll take it under advisement."

Adelaide nodded, silently fuming as she stepped back onto the bridge. The three crewmembers were staring in her direction, watching her hurry off the bridge. She straightened her shoulders and strode in the direction of engineering. She would hunt down Gil, and maybe, he could provide her with some answers about what Dante had been up to.

"Did you tattle to Dad?" Dante demanded, stepping in front of her.

"Get out of my way."

"Where are you going?"

"None of your business," Adelaide snapped. "And you should be thinking about Mom and Dad," she continued.

"I am. This is making them more money," he stated.

"Yeah, before you get them arrested. How could you tell Dad I would take advantage of him? I'm nothing like you." Adelaide clenched her fists trying to hold back a swing. Dante snorted derisively, stepping back and waving her through with a bow.

"What happened to you?" she whispered, walking away.

Chapter 6

"Hurry up, Adelaide, we need to reach the market before it closes," Aquila urged, trying to grab the running six-year-old's hand. Adelaide giggled and skipped up to her mother with a smile.

"Can we get a candy?"

"If you're good and you hurry up. Your father is coming home, and I want to make his favourite supper."

"Daddy's coming!" Adelaide squealed in delight. She did a little dance in the street and a woman passing by smiled at her antics. Who wouldn't love a little girl with red curly hair down her back, freckles across her pert nose and a twirly dress?

"Come on, Mommy, hurry up," she called, hopping ahead.

Aquila laughed, trying to catch up while navigating the floating box in front of her. They were almost to the market when a screeching noise filled the air. Adelaide yelled and covered her ears, crouching down.

"Mommy, what is that?"

Aquila rushed over to Adelaide, touching her shoulder and looking for the cause. Soon, others were pointing upwards and screaming in terror, and Adelaide's mother was dragging her towards a nearby building. The noise drew closer, and Adelaide tried to keep up with her mother's running stride, but she made the mistake of glancing up. It looked to her like millions of ships covered the sky, and large red balls were hurtling towards them. Her body seized up in panic, and she came to an abrupt halt, jerking on the connection to her mother. The pretty sparkling balls were almost upon them, memorizing Adelaide. They reminded her of her ball at home — the one her brother, Dante, would bounce to her. She remembered the laughter as she ran after the ball with Dante chasing her.

"Adelaide, we need to move now!" her mother screamed, grabbing her daughter up into her arms and running.

They made it to the building as the first ball slammed into the ground and destroyed their floating box. Adelaide screamed, and tears ran down her face. That wasn't at all like her ball at home! It was terrifying to see the other people running in every direction, trying to dodge the multiple balls as they exploded. Before her mother had a chance to pull Adelaide's face into her body, she saw a woman get thrown through the air, landing beside the door. To this day, when she closed her eyes Adelaide could still see the bloody stump where the woman's leg should have been.

Adelaide screamed and sat up, gasping for breath. *What the hell?* She hadn't dreamed like that for awhile. The day of the first bombing had changed Earth, some said, for the better. *How?* she had always demanded. For years, they had suffered through the aliens' bombardments and thousands of their already depleted population had been taken into slavery. The Coalition liked to send out propaganda that, without these terrible situations, the Accords would never have stepped in and invited Earth into their fold. Adelaide thought it was a bunch of crock. The Accords took in new members all the time. To join, you just had to agree to their terms and meet their membership requirements.

Glancing at the clock, Adelaide decided there was no point in going back to sleep. There was no way an hour would make a difference. She grabbed a change of clothes and stepped into the tiny bathroom for a quick shower. *Maybe that would help give her a new outlook for the day, but probably not,* she thought and grimaced. Dante had to leave the ship sometime, didn't he? It would be so much easier integrating with the crew if he wasn't around.

*   *   *

Adelaide was feeling better as she stepped onto the bridge. She needed to stay positive and make the best of it, or she would never last.

"Hi, Dad. What's the plan for today?" she asked. Barrett swivelled towards her with a smile.

"We're going home," he answered.

"What?" She looked at him in surprise. "Don't you have another job?"

"We have a few days. Your mother wants us home for a visit, and the boys can have some shore leave. Last night, we changed course for home."

"Is Dante still here?"

"Of course. We're all going." He turned back to the front, dismissing her without another word. Adelaide stood rooted to the spot for a moment before spinning around. Getting familiar with the ship would keep her busy for the short trip home.

*   *   *

Adelaide felt the small jolt as the ZOO docked at the terminal on Earth. They were close to her parents' home in Chicago. A shuttle landed in front of the crowd, and Adelaide, Barrett and Dante all stepped inside, squishing in towards the empty seats in the back. The doors slid closed, and there was a small shudder before they began to rise slightly, hovering about ten feet off the ground.

They zoomed towards Chicago at a fast clip, and Adelaide stared out the window, watching the scenery fly by. It was amazing to see the transformations that Earth had experienced. Before WWIII, Adelaide's family had lived a few miles outside of Manhattan. She'd enjoyed running free through the trees and fields. Then, the war had devastated all plant life, and they'd lived in the barren wastelands, staring at the dead, shrivelled trunks sticking out of the ground. The animals were also few and far between, many of them mutated from the chemicals such that they could no longer be used as a food source. It was still all right living there, but once the aliens had attacked, her parents had packed up their family and moved them to Chicago. It had surprised Adelaide, because the aliens had really only bombed the large cities. *Why would they move to a potential attack zone? What was wrong with living just outside of Manhattan?* she had wondered at the time.

Chicago came into view, and she spotted the tall, slim white pillars powering the city's forcefield. They matched the other buildings that had been erected over the years. It was a city of white. Everything shone in the sun, and to Adelaide, it looked like a lovely beacon for their enemies to attack. *Nothing like the threat of annihilation as a motivator.* After the first attacks, which had lasted three days, the Coalition had sequestered the top scientists of Earth until a prototype forcefield was developed. She remembered seeing the military set up these huge, hulking metal casings to enclose the precious technology that was promised to save them all. There were six pillars that surrounded the city, protecting it in a dome. All major cities were given forcefields of their own. *Guess it was good her parents had moved to Chicago, because Manhattan hadn't received any,* she thought ruefully. Outside the range of these forcefields, the people were on their own. Earth couldn't afford to protect everyone everywhere. There were still families that lived on the frontier, refusing to leave.

In the early stages of the forcefield technology, the whole grid would need to be turned off for anyone to enter or leave its field of protection, not that many wanted to leave the cities. That meant a curfew was instated, which only allowed people to exit or enter the cities at specific times. People waited in long lines until the city officials deemed it time to lower the shield, rushing everything and everyone through before an attack could happen.

As the years passed, Earth eventually joined the Accords. Humans had gained better technology as a result, and the forcefields were enhanced greatly. Over the next fifteen years, in spite of the bombings, green began to sprout across the Earth. A few uncontaminated animals had been discovered and were bred in installations to keep any mutations from occurring. Eventually, to continue the breeding program, the government began selling the animals to qualified families that met the heavy conditions placed on the animals' habitats. Ocean life, however, had been devastated by the fallout, and Earth's scientists had not yet been able to determine which species had survived. Adelaide's heart ached whenever she saw the oceans and there were no creatures frolicking through the waves. Adelaide was glad to see a few trees and patches of grass dotting the landscape.

The shuttle slowed as it neared the gate, and a guard waved them past, raising part of the forcefield. A doorway opened, and the shuttle zipped through. They had to travel to the far side of Chicago to reach home, so Adelaide watched the passengers with interest. It had been a few years since she had travelled outside of the military base on Earth. The civilians had changed to match the times. The beings moving throughout the city were still predominately humans, but she saw other species mingling in the crowds. It was midday, so the city was bustling as bodies rushed about their business.

*   *   *

Half an hour later, the three of them stood in front of the family home. The door opened, and Aquila stepped out with a huge smile on her face. Running down the sidewalk, she enfolded Adelaide in a hug.

"I'm so glad you're here," she said, before hugging Dante, too.

They followed Adelaide's mother up the walk and into the house. Adelaide had been worried that the night would end in a big fight like their last family supper. She was pleasantly surprised when everyone got along and Dante seemed like his old self, laughing and teasing. But, the fuzzy feelings didn't last long. The very next day, Adelaide and Dante were back to arguing about his activities aboard the ZOO. Their dad finally had to send them to separate corners of the ship.

*   *   *

To Adelaide's surprise, Dante stayed on the ZOO for four months after her arrival. She figured he thought leaving would give her a foothold. One morning, she awoke to find out that Dante had taken off in his ship, probably to go con someone. With him gone, Adelaide was finally able to relax and enjoy getting to know her dad and the business. With each job, Adelaide became more invested in and excited about the prospect of staying on the ZOO. She was able to feed her need to travel, and even though the crew was human, she met many different species on the multiple planets they visited.

Six months after Dante had left, he made a sudden reappearance while they were docked at Gaeaf, demanding a meeting with their dad. Barrett and Dante headed to the office just off the bridge, with Adelaide following closely behind them. She wasn't letting Dante take advantage of their dad again. She stepped into the room just before the door slid shut.

"What are you doing here?" Dante demanded with a frown on his face.

"I'm part of this family and this business. I have a right to be here," she stated, parking her butt into a chair, crossing her arms and daring Dante to say anything.

"Leave it alone, Dante," Barrett said. "What do you have?"

"There is a shipment that I need to acquire and deliver to Raau."

"You mean steal something and sell it to the highest bidder," Adelaide said.

Barrett turned his glare to Adelaide before asking, "When?"

"Now. The shipment is on the planet Brauk, just a hop skip and jump from Raau."

"Why don't you take your ship and retrieve it?" Adelaide demanded.

"Enough!" Barrett yelled. "This is still my ship, and I will make the decisions." He turned to Dante. "I have another job that will take us by there. We can probably stop at Brauk. Why do you need my ship?"

"The ZOO is a cargo vessel," Dante said, thinking that explained it all.

"How much trouble will this cause me?" Barrett asked.
Dante looked hurt as he stared at Barrett.

"None," he replied. "I wouldn't do anything to cause you harm." Barrett snorted as he glanced at Adelaide.

"What is involved with this mission?" he pressed.

"We need to land on the planet, take a few guys, and retrieve the items," Dante replied.
Barrett sighed as he paced in front of Dante.

"Fine. But, you're paying me the going rate."

"What! I'm your son — how can you charge me that?" Dante protested and gave Adelaide a dirty look, probably thinking it was her fault.

"I've been thinking about these jobs, and as Adelaide has pointed out, it's costing me a fortune. Even if you pay me a cut, it's not enough to cover my expenses."

Adelaide gaped at her father. Was he throwing her to the wolves? It might be worth it if it actually stopped Dante, but she shouldn't be made out to be the bad guy.

"Did she now?" Dante snarled. "Fine, I'll pay you." He stormed out of the room. Barrett gave Adelaide a shrug and followed. Putting her head on the table, Adelaide moaned. This wasn't going to end well, for anyone.

*   *   *

Dante's visits lessened over the course of the year. He made a couple of reappearances, but they were minor compared to the excursion to Brauk. They had ended up running from the officials on the planet, and a couple of her dad's crewmembers were injured. They hadn't signed up for anything dangerous. The job was supposed to be pretty mundane, just delivering goods. That was the first sign that her dad was finally clueing into the damage Dante could do to the business. Of course, Adelaide was still getting calls from her mother, demanding why she wasn't willing to help her brother. No matter what Adelaide said, or how she tried to explain it, Aquila still thought everything was her fault. Adelaide always tried to keep the hurt from surfacing during those calls, but it was near to impossible. Adelaide wondered how her mother managed not see how it was affecting her.

Eventually, Dante stopped coming altogether, but he did take the time to phone their mother and complain about his treatment by Adelaide. It was soon after this that Barret finally listened to Aquila and retired. Adelaide ran most of the business now, but her dad still helped out with running the three ships. Coming aboard two years ago, she hadn't known what to expect, but she was surprised how much she enjoyed it. The job ticked off all the boxes and more.

Chapter 7

Adelaide bowed her head, and a few tears fell to the cold tile floor. Dante stood silently beside her as they stared through the glass at their parents' bodies being cremated. Because of the wars and the damage done to Earth, it was decided that burying bodies no longer worked. The dead were now incinerated quickly and quietly at medical centres. It was very impersonal, in Adelaide's opinion, but they didn't have any other options. Burying someone was now a punishable crime. She was surprised Dante had shown up. Over the past year, she could count on one hand how many times he had contacted their parents. Dante had blamed Dad for siding with Adelaide about the business. But, she was sure Mom had still communicated with him constantly, because Adelaide had still been hearing a lot about Dante's troubles from her mom.

Adelaide had been running a shipment when the police contacted her about the accident. Her parents had been eating downtown when a vehicle had lost control and crashed through the restaurant, killing four people, both of them included. Adelaide had sent a message to her brother, but she'd never received a response. Her heart had almost stopped when he'd stepped through the door today.

"Are you sticking around?" she asked, turning to look at Dante.

"No, I have to get back."

"What about all their things?"

"Do what you want with them. I don't want anything." Dante nodded curtly in her direction before leaving the room.

Adelaide swiped her hand across her red eyes and sniffled, following him out. Time to find a transport. The doors to the medical centre slid open, revealing a swirling black sky and big, fat rain drops landing on the road. Adelaide grimaced, pulling her jacket tighter around herself. This was one thing she didn't miss about being planet side, even if it was a necessity.

Finally able to flag down a transport, she quickly slid into the backseat, giving the driver her parents' address. The surroundings changed drastically the farther they travelled from the city centre. The city had repaired its downtown core but left the edges to deteriorate. She was surprised her parents had willingly lived where technology didn't rule. The driver scanned Adelaide's hand for payment, before she stepped out and stared at the tiny house. The rain had receded, and only a few drops landed on her head. She swiped at the frizzy curls blocking her view and muttered to herself.

Time to quit stalling, as she couldn't afford to leave the ZOO for long. The crew were already harassing her with questions, and it had only been two days. *Can't they think for themselves?* Her parents had coded the door to open for both Dante and herself, so entering was easy. The place was just as she remembered it. The stark white walls shined in the nearly empty living room. Her parents had installed these new foldaway couches, which slid into the walls, compacting themselves away to provide more space. Her butt hurt just thinking about them. Adelaide swore her dad only agreed, because the hardness encouraged shorter visits.

The screen, which was usually playing, hung silently on the far wall. The news used to play constantly, even if no one was in the room. She remembered her mother cleaning in the other rooms and the screen blaring. No one dared touch her beloved shows, or they'd get a dressing down. Adelaide worked through the day, organizing their belongings and piling boxes upon boxes in the empty living room. She couldn't believe how much crap her parents had. Night was falling, and she was too exhausted to make up the guest bed, so her parents' bed it was.

* * *

Three days later, Adelaide closed the door of her parents' home for the last time, holding one small box in her hands. This place wasn't home. She liked her house on Earth2. Her parents had moved to this particular house after she'd already left home. There were no fond memories here, just fighting and heartache. A realtor would look after the sale, and the funds would be split between her and Dante. After accounting for all their bills, the amount left over wouldn't be large. *You would think, since burials no longer happened, the costs would have decreased,* she thought. *Not the case, as it turned out.* The realtor was also arranging for most of her parents' belongings to be donated. Adelaide had found a few mementos to keep, depicting a happier time in their family.

During the ride back to the ZOO, Adelaide's mind was running a mile a minute. Thank goodness, her dad had given the business to her. It was one less thing to worry about. She didn't think Dante knew about that little tidbit yet. Her parents hadn't wanted a confrontation. It was now going to be up to her to explain the situation, when Dante eventually tried to claim the ZOO, which she could almost guarantee he would do.

After she arrived at the shipyard, Adelaide hurried to the ship's door, and it slid open. She was extremely grateful for the silence, as she headed to her quarters. The crew was on leave till tomorrow, when they had a cargo run. Maybe by then she'd have a plan. It was going to be a challenge to manage all three ships while also being a captain. Not that she couldn't. The question was, *did she want to?* Exhaustion eventually took over, so she stripped down, climbed into bed and fell asleep.

*   *   *

Adelaide groaned as her internal clock woke her at six in the morning. There was time to have a shower and eat before everyone arrived. They would fly to Earth2 to load the cargo, which would give her a chance to stop in at home. Before her parents' death, the ZOO had been in space for over a month with no real rest. Adelaide wanted to ensure her place was still standing and grab a few essentials.

She stepped into the shower, pushing the button to release the shower gel. It coated her hair and body and immediately began its job of eating away the dirt and grime. In minutes, Adelaide was able to wipe away the dried gel, and her skin underneath it was clean. It was too bad they hadn't developed a nice-smelling body cleaner. Maybe they thought that, since gel showers were utilized mostly in space, people didn't care if you had a flowery scent afterwards.

Rifling through the drawers, she grabbed black pants and a top, pulling them on before heading for food.

"How are you doing?" Gil asked, walking into the galley.

Adelaide wiped her eyes and grimaced.

"Alright. Just tired."

"I'm sorry about your parents."

"Thanks," she sighed. "Not sure what I'm going to do now."

"You'll figure it out."

She nodded, shoved the eggs into her mouth and chewed.

"What would you do?" she asked quietly, after swallowing the mouthful. Gil looked at her and rubbed his bald head.

"Depends if you like it here."

"I do." She paused, and Gil waited silently. "But, I'm not sure if running their company is what I want. Flying and commanding a ship is what I enjoy."

"You've answered your own question, then," Gil said, grinning and turning to his plate. Adelaide stared at him in surprise before a small smile played across her lips. Things would work out, whichever direction she chose.

*   *   *

A week later and with another job done, Adelaide was tired and looking forward to a couple of days off to recharge. She walked away from the ZOO, heading into the throng of workers pushing crates and pallets towards Transmont, which was the capital city of Earth2. The port was built on the outskirts of the expanding city, and it was quicker to use foot power than to wait for a transport. She was glad that Earth2's council allowed ships to dock planet side instead of just relying on the space station. She hated having to wait for a shuttle, when flying directly here made more sense. The sun's warmth worked its way through Adelaide's clothes, and she smiled. Out in space, she didn't miss much about being planet side, but the sun was a given. Adelaide could soak up the heat all day and not move. She reached the cobblestone path and stopped to remove her jacket. The council was trying to go *au natural*, so there were no paved paths on Earth2. Stones were either taken from the local quarries or purchased from Zartuth.

Transmont's short square buildings came into view, bringing with them a multitude of voices. Each building was coloured brightly, glittering in the sunlight. Sometimes, it was difficult to stare directly at the buildings, if the sun was too bright. It had been determined by the council that tall buildings would scar the beautiful landscape — Earth2 was going to be better than Earth. Restrictions were imposed on all companies. Adelaide didn't think it would last long. Humans weren't the best at respecting environmental issues and concerns. Just looking at their history was depressing. Hurrying through Transmont to the opposite side of the city, she turned a corner, and her house came into view. Someone was sitting on the stoop, and she paused, before slowly advancing. Dante's features came into focus, causing Adelaide to grimace. *Why's he here?*

"Dante," she greeted him neutrally.

"Adelaide, what did you do?" he demanded.

"I don't have any idea what you're talking about." She scanned her hand, and the door slid open. Dante followed her in. *Wonderful.*

"You know — Dad's company."

"What about it?" She hung up her coat and untied her boots. "I'm tired, Dante. What do you want?" she sighed, as he trailed behind her.

"Fine. When did you con Dad into giving you the company?" Dante demanded. Adelaide whipped around, furious.

"Conned? What the hell are you talking about?"

"You've been around for, what, a couple of years, and you get the company? I was around the whole time you were gone," Dante insisted.

"First, I've been working my ass off for him for the last three years, ever since you took off. Second, you only ever risked getting him arrested." Adelaide and Dante were now almost toe-to-toe in her living room. She clenched her fists, trying not to deck him.

"At least I was around," he yelled.

"Oh, give me a break. You were helping yourself. Taking advantage of your parents isn't something to be proud of. If you care so much about the business, you can run one of the ships," Adelaide contended.

"I don't need your charity. Stick your offer up your ass, and leave me the hell alone." Dante stomped out of her house and down the front steps.

Damn it, Adelaide thought. *That went so well.* It was no surprise her parents had put it off. She trudged to her bedroom, shedding her clothes on the way to the shower. The warm water cascaded down her body, and she smiled in pleasure, finally able to relax. Having a gel sprayed on your body, which then dried, was not how she thought the cleaning process should be. Twenty minutes later, she stepped out with a towel wrapped around her body and padded to the closet. Rummaging through the hanging clothes, she finally settled on her customary tight black jeans and t-shirt. It was nice not to be in the confines of her uniform. She missed what it represented but not the suffocating material itself. The next step was to assuage her hunger, and then she would decide her plan of attack.

"Steak and roast potatoes," Adelaide commanded the food replicator, waiting a few seconds until the wonderful smell filled the kitchen. Since the invention of food replicators, the trend in most homes was to forgo a kitchen, as rarely anyone cooked anymore. But, Adelaide enjoyed cooking once in a while, so she'd had her builder add in a small, compact kitchen. She didn't have a choice on the style, which was completely white and almost blinded her every time. But, at least she had one. *Beggars couldn't be choosers.* Carrying her plate to the living room, she turned on her television. A message flashed across the screen that some unknown culprit had harvested from one of the forbidden forests. Only a few areas were sanctioned by the planetary council for harvesting, and they were heavily monitored. It would have been difficult for someone to get in there, drop the trees and escape. With the harsh penalties, there were easier places to acquire wood. Adelaide frowned as her brother's image popped into her mind. She hadn't been surprised he'd refused her offer. He wanted the profit without doing the work. She snorted, realizing he was just like half the people she met.

During the last week, Adelaide had thought long and hard about her dilemma. Her decision was to sell the other two ships. If she was able to book steady jobs, then only the ZOO would be needed. With just one ship to manage, Adelaide could actually enjoy doing her job. She probably wouldn't get top dollar for them because of their condition, but it would be enough money to upgrade the ZOO and outfit it with some cannons.

Her next shipment wasn't scheduled for a week, so hopefully, that would be enough time. The crewmembers of the other two ships had already been informed of her decision, and they weren't terribly upset. The crew probably would have stayed on, with a little bit of grumbling, but it would be easy enough for them to find other work. She hadn't bonded with any of them, and they didn't seem keen on taking orders from a girl, which was the complete opposite of the military. *Didn't matter your gender or species, you followed rank and showed respect.* It was something that was missing in civilian life.

Adelaide was still debating about the fate of the ZOO and its crew. Depending on the cost, there was a new ship's brain available that could run most of the ship. The artificial intelligence would be a dream. It could monitor and control all of the ship's systems at once. She could link it to her comm and her translator chip, so that she would be able to communicate with the ZOO from anywhere. Adelaide sighed as she carried her plate to the automatic sanitizer. She loved this invention almost as much as she loved traditional showers. It was a big step up from the dishwashers of the past. The machine blasted the dishes with an intense ultraviolet light, and in seconds, they were clean.

She needed to spread the word about the sale of her two ships. Perhaps going to her favourite watering hole would be a splendid idea.

She'd have a few drinks, listen to the gossip and maybe take in some entertainment. It was hit or miss what the Hollow Peasant offered to its customers, but maybe she would be lucky enough to catch something good.

*   *   *

Thank goodness, Adelaide thought. *One night to spare.* She grinned, watching her two previous ships lift off for the last time. A weight seemed to have lifted from her shoulders, and the numbers that had been transferred into her account definitely helped. The ZOO needed to be updated into the 22nd century. She'd have plenty of time during the next trip, as they would be going steady for the next month. The upgrades could be accomplished when they returned.

*   *   *

The last pieces to her ship's brain were now installed, and Adelaide wanted to jump up and down. She felt giddy, and tingles ran up her spine. The upgrades were spectacular, and she couldn't wait to take it out for a spin.

"Looking good, Captain," Gil said, walking up beside her. Adelaide grinned.

"Sure is. You ready?" she asked.

"No problem. Looking forward to it," Gil assured her.

Because of the upgrades, she had decided that the ZOO could operate with just Gil and herself. The other twenty-five members were redundant.

"Do we have anything right now?" Gil asked.

"Yep. We're delivering some parts to Raau and then taking food to Gaeaf."

"So, we'll be gone awhile."

"Looks like it. Do you need anything before we head out?" Adelaide inquired.

"No, everything is on board."

"Okay. I'll see you in two hours for takeoff."

Adelaide had a few things left to grab from her place before they left. The trip would give her the chance to tweak the new computer to ensure the ship's brain was running properly. Because Raau wasn't part of the Accords, no jump gate existed near the planet. The closest one would still mean a month's travel, which was why the profit would bring in such a tidy sum to add to her bank account. Raau's climate produced some of the best food, which was in high demand. Adelaide was surprised they hadn't appealed to the Accords for an exception to the rules, so they could build a jump gate closer to Raau.

One drawback to reducing the number of ships she owned was having to turn down jobs while out on longer hauls. She'd already had a request this morning. *It was good to be wanted,* she thought with a grin. Throwing some items into her bag, she grabbed a bite to eat. Maybe while they were on Raau, they'd take a couple of days of R and R. The planet was largely covered with jungle. If it wasn't for the He-Man attitudes of the males, Adelaide could spend some enjoyable time exploring. Her father had mostly assigned the shorter routes to her, so this was going to be her first time on Raau. She'd met plenty of men from the planet, so she knew their attitudes. They didn't seem to modify their behaviour when they left their planet in the slightest.

Adelaide stepped into the ZOO, and the first thing she noticed was how new and shiny it looked. The second was the silence. It was going to be strange having only one crewmember aboard for the long journey. She made her way onto the bridge and sat in the captain's chair.

"Computer?"

"Yes, Captain," replied the computer over the ship's comm system.

She grinned at the prompt reply and commanded, "Systems check." There were a few minutes of silence.

"Everything is within acceptable parameters."

"Great! Gil, are we ready for takeoff?" she called into the comm.

"Yes, Captain," he answered, and some engine noises could be heard over the comm. Adelaide could picture Gil drooling over all the new equipment. The upgrades had drained most of the credits from the sales — *but who cares? It was worthwhile.* Engine efficiency had increased by 50%, and their defenses were up 100% since weapons of any kind had previously been absent. Gil said he'd spent most of the night familiarizing himself with the new equipment. There'd be plenty of time to sleep on the journey.

Adelaide scanned her chip and commanded, "Computer, take us up." The engines purred as the ZOO slowly lifted from the planet's surface. Once they cleared the atmosphere, the ship shot forwards with just a hint of vibration. *So much better,* she thought. "Set our travel coordinates to the nearest gate."

"Arrival is estimated at four Earth hours," the computer replied.

Adelaide stood up and walked to the ship's main computer terminal, staring at the screen. She could see their trip plotted as dots. Bending down, she opened the panel and peered in at all the wires and gears. She tinkered around with the upgrades on the bridge for awhile, inspecting all the shiny new parts.

Chapter 8

It had been a long haul to Raau and back, and Adelaide was excited to wined down. She did get her chance to explore Raau, and it had been beautiful. Adelaide had basked in the heat as she trekked through the sites, trying to ignore the looks she received from the locals. Gil had left her to her own devices, staying mostly on the ship. He'd said that, at his age, traipsing around wasn't a good idea. Adelaide had snorted at that, as Gil was fitter than most people who were younger than him. She figured he'd wanted to stay at the city and visit the taverns.

Speaking of bars, Adelaide pushed open the tavern door in front of her, and the smell of body odour and alcohol reached her nose. She didn't flinch but instead breathed in deeply and smiled. The Hollow Peasant was her retreat on Earth2. It was a local watering hole at the edge of Transmont, so it was unusual to spot any other species than humans inside. Side stepping a patron who was passed out on the dirt-encrusted floor, she made her way to the small bar by the stage. The offerings were slim, but they imported the best alcohol from the planet Gaeaf. It wasn't for the faint of heart, but during her military years, she had developed a fondness for it.

"Hey, Rocky. How's it going?"

"Great, you're usual?" the bartender replied.

"Yes."

"How come I haven't see you for awhile?" Rocky asked, slowly pouring the red drink into a short glass.

"I was on a long haul. I'm heading back out on a job tomorrow." Adelaide scanned her chip then turned and stared around the room. She really didn't want to sit at the bar today. Rubbing the back of her hand where her chip resided, Adelaide made a beeline for a table in the back. With all this tech attached to her brain, Adelaide sometimes thought about the possible consequences. *Oh well,* she thought. She loved progress and technology. Pushing back the heavy metal chair at the table, Adelaide sat down, her butt already feeling sore in expectation.

The furniture was a mishmash of metal and wood. Since the council didn't want to spoil the landscape here like we had on our first home, there weren't any industries on Earth2 yet. So, that left everyone to scrounge for items from Earth or buy from other planets, but they had to pass all the restrictions placed on imported items. Taking a sip of her drink, Adelaide tapped her foot to the woman singing and gyrating at the opposite end of the bar. She wasn't too bad. There had been worse here. Adelaide remembered one band that had been booed off the stage. Of course, they were from a different planet, she couldn't remember where, and what they considered good music was as a constant scream. Her ears had hurt for days after that. Since then, the Hollow Peasant seemed to keep the entertainment closer to human preferences.

The noise receded as the woman bowed and left the stage, weaving her way around the tables and touching as many male patrons as possible. Adelaide snorted — she wouldn't be surprised if Rocky had hired an exotic dancer to entertain after the woman's sets were done. *Not sure where they would go,* she wondered idly. The bar only had a couple of bathrooms at the back and what she'd always assumed was an office. Over the hum of conversation, Adelaide heard the door slam open, and a large shadow filled the doorway. She looked back down at her drink.

"Hey, Adelaide. Where's your good-for-nothing brother?" a voice she dreaded called out, as its owner pushed his way through the crowd. She looked up with a grimace.

"Taurian, what do you want?"

The Tu'Val grinned at her as he pushed a patron off his seat and sidled up to her table, dragging the chair behind him. The poor man on the floor didn't complain. He just scrambled up and ran out the door. *Who would argue with a seven-foot, muscle-bound male carrying a very large sword?* Apparently, only she was dumb enough to do that.

"I know this is Dante's favourite place," Taurian persisted.

"It used to be. What's it to me? Do you see him here?" Adelaide asked, leaning back in her chair and gulping down her drink while trying not to grimace.

"You're his sister."

"Again, so what?" Adelaide demanded. Taurian looked at her quizzically for a moment before something seemed to dawn on his gorgeous, chiselled face, and she felt her stomach drop.

"Well, if he's not here, I have the next best thing."

Adelaide figured it was getting a little cramped and hot in the bar, and a quick glance around revealed that all the patrons were trying to ignore them. *Time to leave.* She stood up, and Taurian followed suit, his hand snaking out to grab her wrist. She looked down at their connection and glared up at his towering bulk.

"Where are you going?" Taurian asked. "I think, since your brother isn't here, you might as well take his place."

"Not bloody likely. Take your hand off me," she demanded.

Taurian laughed and asked, "And what are you going to do?" He glanced up and down her slight frame in derision. He seemed to have forgotten their last encounter in a bar. *Time to remind him.* Adelaide tried walking around the table, but he kept a firm grip on her wrist.

"If you value your privates, I would let go now," she said quietly. A few people around them scrambled out of the way, heading towards the bar. She was sure they didn't want to miss watching her get her assed kicked. She grunted to herself — *not likely*.

When Taurian just smirked, Adelaide decided she'd had enough. She stepped into his personal space, and with a fast jab to his man junk, she twisted her other arm out of his grip. As he was bending over, she grabbed his massive forearm with both hands, jutted out her hip and threw him over her shoulder to crash onto the table. Before he could move, Adelaide had her blaster levelled at his head.

"When a female says no, she means it," she snarled. You could hear a pin drop as Taurian gazed up at Adelaide with what she was sure was admiration. That was not something she wanted from him.

"Put the table on my tab," Adelaide called out to Rocky, as she stomped to the door and exited the establishment. Once she was clear, speed became the priority. *No way was Taurian going to catch her.*

*   *   *

Adelaide gazed lovingly at her cargo ship, sitting in its bay at the docks, with her family's logo larger than life on the side — large green letters spelled out "The ZOO" above an image of two planets with a brown crate between them. The usual fear and trepidation that came with seeing it was no longer present, and her smile widened. It usually reminded her of the condemnation she'd received from her parents about joining the military and "leaving them in the cold " — their words. She could still recall accepting her diploma and then marching down to the recruiting office. Her mother had trailed behind her, trying to convince Adelaide of the error of her ways.

"What could a skinny redhead do against a bunch of men?" Aquila had said. Adelaide was still a skinny redhead, but over the years of intense training, her body had filled out with muscle, and her hair colour had only intensified. In all her travels, her hair still earned comments, especially from the different species who wanted to touch it and inquire if it was natural. Personally, all she received from it was grief when she tried to tame the curls and frizz. Now that she'd had the chance to reconcile with her parents before their death, the name no longer brought out that fear.

Adelaide sidestepped an oncoming cart, filled with parts, being pushed by a Zartuth male. They were one of the few species that closely resembled humans. The biggest difference was their wider brows, accentuated by their almost hairless heads. Adelaide sometimes had difficulty looking directly at them. A Zartuth's large round eyes, which were the size of golf balls, were a little bit freaky. The male waved his four-fingered hand in thanks before hurrying on. Four other ships were in the loading bay, in various stages of docking and collecting their cargo.

"Watch where you're going!" a man yelled, followed by a loud groan and a crash. She turned to watch as a loader tried to stop on a dime — *not possible,* she thought — and the slow motion of the machine as it tipped over, its heavy load dropping to shatter on the ground. The individual responsible for the catastrophe shivered and quaked, staring in horror at the surrounding chaos. Station personnel poured from the tower, yelling orders and pushing people out of their way. *Hopefully, the cargo wasn't expensive,* Adelaide thought, making her way closer to her ship. She was jostled a few times and glared at the offending parties. She didn't have time for this. The noise had reached an almost deafening level, and she was tempted to cover her ears. Earth2 wasn't usually such a busy station.

At this point, different species seldom stopped on Earth2, because the planetary council still hadn't developed many exports, and no one promoted Earth2 as a destination planet. Occasionally, a few beings would immigrate to Earth2, though. The air quality and native plants were extraordinary, and other species were beginning to take notice. She was alright with that, because Earth2 was now her home. Nothing tied her to Earth anymore, and she'd rather hang up her hat here.

"Have you heard?" a man whispered, from off to Adelaide's right.

"War?" the other male asked.

"I was talking with my brother-in-law, who works for the government…" another man responded, his voice trailing off.

Adelaide whipped around, trying to find the men, but was dragged along with the crowd. *Damn it,* she snarled to herself. Being a captain through years of war as Earth expanded into the galaxy hadn't been a walk in the park. Another war wouldn't be good for Earth. The planet hadn't recovered yet.

Walking up the ramp to the ZOO, Adelaide ran her hand along the ship's side and entered the cargo bay, which dampened some of the shouting. A low hum could be heard coming from the engine room, and it vibrated through the ship. She loved the sound and feel of a ship, especially her ship. With the upgrades, she'd had a new engine installed that could reach lightspeed in 2.2 seconds. It ran on carbidihyde, making it very efficient for long hauls, because the system used the carbon dioxide and waste from the ship, converting them to energy. The cargo bay was stacked floor-to-ceiling with crates carrying their next shipment. It gave her a sense of satisfaction that the ZOO was keeping afloat after her father's death.

"Hey, boss," Gil greeted her.

"Hey, Gil. Are we ready?"

"Sure thing. You're good-for-nothing brother showed up here, though."

"What the hell!" she cursed under her breath. "What did he want?"

"He came with an offer, but he completely forgot about it when he saw the upgrades."

Adelaide swore again as she walked to the bridge and asked, "How did he see them?"

"He decided a tour was in order, and he went wandering around the ship while he was trying to sell his idea."

"And?"

"He started mouthing off, and I got sick of it, so I threw him off," Gil admitted. Adelaide roared with laughter.

"I wish I could have seen his face." She wiped the tears from her face.

"You can. The ship recorded it," Gil snorted, slapping his hand on his knee.

"I think a viewing might be in order. Thanks," Adelaide said with a grin.

"No problem. Anything for you, girly," he said, before hobbling down the walkway.

Adelaide gazed fondly at his back. *Was he getting slower?* she wondered briefly. She might have to check out the video to see how the little man was able to evict her six-foot-two brother. Of course, not many who met Gil were willing to mess with him. Over the years, she had watched the fat melt off Gil, leaving behind a skinny, toned, toughened and grizzled old man. Working in the engine room gave him plenty of opportunities to develop the muscles covering his body. But, his age was working against him, and even with modern medical advances, his sixty-plus-years body was catching up to him.

Adelaide grumbled about her brother while heading to the bridge. Lights lit up following her progression, and she stopped, taking a deep breath. Looking at all of her hard work and sweat always calmed her. There was no way someone who had been on the ZOO previously would miss the changes. Monitors were now scattered throughout the corridor, so at any time, Adelaide could pull up information or control the ship. Adelaide had even had all the inner panels changed out to a new thinner, harder material. It was a light grey, and when the lights shone, the panels sparkled without a scratch on them, and she was hoping to keep them that way. Fighting on board shouldn't be a common occurrence any longer. With Dante around, there'd been multiple times when the ZOO had been boarded. The old panels had been well used and showed their age.

She continued down the corridor, stepped onto the bridge and sat down in the captain's chair, pulling up their schedule. The spare parts in the cargo hold were crucial to the generators on the planet Gaeaf. They had only one season, maybe two: winter and mild winter. Adelaide had read the history of the planet, and surprise, surprise, when they began travelling in space and discovered the existence of other worlds, many of Gaeaf's citizens had left. And it was for greener pastures, which they'd never seen before. Gaeaf had since become a big tourist attraction, and it reminded Adelaide of the Swiss Alps on Earth. People had two choices of where to live: one side of the planet consisted of multiple mountain ranges, while the other was predominantly flat. Most people preferred living in the few larger cities to be near a working, mostly reliable generator. During the colder months, the planet's temperature dropped down between minus forty and minus fifty. Most buildings were connected by above-ground tunnels. But, you would still find many of the natives walking outside. They would say they did it "to enjoy the fresh air," but they were nuts in her opinion. She could now run the job blind folded. This was already her second run this year.

Adelaide began her pre-flight check by asking, "Computer, are we ready for lift off? Did the system checks show anything?"

"Nothing, Captain. Everything is functioning at optimal levels," a female voice spoke over the comm system. When Adelaide had had the computer installed, a choice of voices was available. She couldn't pick a man's voice, because there was no way that his voice would be waking her up in the middle of the night. *Way too creepy.* So, she'd settled for a girl's voice, but it couldn't be too squeaky or whiney either. Adelaide still hadn't decided on a name, but she wanted to choose something more personable, because calling it "Computer" all the time wasn't appealing. It would make her feel less alone, if she could pretend someone else was aboard the ZOO. Adelaide was glad Gil had stayed on; he knew this ship inside and out. His company was good, too, and when he put up with shit like dealing with her brother, she was immensely grateful for him.

"Have you sent our manifest to the station?" she asked the computer.

"Yes, Captain. They want your scan."

Adelaide swiped the back of her hand above the scanner situated in the arm of her chair. Her computer chirped, and the station acknowledged their departure. They were still not advanced enough for computers to pilot a ship without a warm body, which sucked, because Adelaide had to be woken in order to pass through the jump gates. The panel in front of Adelaide lit up, and a multitude of lights flashed across it. In her early years in the military, she'd had to push all those buttons. So, if necessary, she knew what to do, but it was nice to just sit back and watch. The ship slowly ascended. The journey would take approximately 7 Earth hours using the jump gates, compared to the 15 hours the trip would have taken before their invention. Trips to Gaeaf usually worked best if Adelaide left Earth2 by late afternoon. Because of the time difference between the two planets and their orbital rotations, she'd arrive by early morning, which helped with the jet lag.

"Gil are you hungry?" she yelled through the comms.

"When am I not?" he replied, chuckling through the comm. "Meet you there."

Adelaide beat Gil to the galley and punched her food into the replicator, another perk to the upgrades. Adelaide sighed with relief. She liked cooking, but the ship wasn't equipped with the proper equipment. Her food appeared on the tray, and she carried it to one of the tables just as Gil walked in.

"That looks and smells good — so glad you're not cooking."

"Hey! You've never tried my food," Adelaide protested. He laughed and grabbed his plate.

"Rather starve," he mumbled, sitting in front of her. She smiled down into her plate and continued eating. She didn't know much about Gil's story, but he had fought in WWIII. He refused to talk about Earth or his past. Her father had sometimes spoken about Gil's wife; the rumor was that she had left Gil for his best friend right after the war. *What a bitch*, Adelaide thought. Gil was a little gruff and loud, but he worked hard and watched your back. She remembered a few times Gil had helped out during some of their smuggling drops. Some had ended in blaster fire, but at least no one was ever seriously hurt.

"So, this trip should be uneventful?" Gil asked, glancing her way.

"Yep. No planned stops. I was thinking of staying a few days on Gaeaf."

"Sure. I've nothing else to do."

"What do you think of the name 'Advanced Logic Intelligent Command Environment' — ALICE, for short?" Adelaide asked. Gil stared at her blankly. "For the computer," she clarified.

"Oh." Understanding dawned on his face. "Sounds fine to me," Gil said, taking his plate to the automatic sanitizer. "I'll see you in the morning."

Adelaide nodded at Gil and finished drinking her toph. It was similar to coffee on Earth, but so much stronger, and the flavor was like a burst of nuts in your mouth. One of the perks from travelling to Zartuth. She'd have to remember to input the computer's new name when she had time.

Instead of heading to the gym, Adelaide strode to her room. *It was probably time for a wash day,* she thought, glancing around the small room. Hers were the largest sleeping quarters on the ship, with cubbies for her clothes, a desk and bed. Adelaide stepped over the clothes strewn on the floor to her monitor by the supposedly double bed. *Yeah right, it could fit two children,* she sniffed to herself. She called up the video of her brother.

It started with Dante entering the cargo bay and scanning the area before yelling her name. Of course, the computer had already alerted Gil of the entry, and he stepped into the cargo bay minutes later with a frown on his face. The screen zoomed in on Dante, as he wandered her ship, talking animatedly about a great opportunity, but that changed quickly. Soon, he was yelling, pointing at different parts and demanding answers. Gil followed behind him, glaring at Dante's back. Adelaide swore steam was rising above Gil's head. Eventually, Dante realized no answers were forthcoming, and he spun around to confront Gil.

Adelaide smiled when her brother discovered how close Gil was standing to him and stumbled back, mumbling something she couldn't catch. Gil stepped closer and leaned in to whisper, causing Dante's face to blanche. *What did he say*? she wondered, replaying the scene and straining to hear. *Nothing.* Gil turned around and jabbed his finger in the direction of the cargo bay, demanding that Dante leave. He seemed to contemplate ignoring the command, but the moment Gil shifted his body closer, Dante scooted past him and yelled, "I'll talk to my sister later."

"You do that," Gil snarled at Dante, following him out. He stood at the entrance, watching Dante scurry to the station. Adelaide laughed until her sides hurt. *Bet that stung his ass,* she thought.

With the freak accident last year taking both of their parents, Adelaide had been left as head of the family. As if she could allow Dante to control anything. They wouldn't have lasted out the year with him in charge. Both of them would have been incarcerated. Gil felt more like family to her, and he was someone she welcomed. She still remembered Dante's response, when she'd suggested that he captain one of the ships. Dante's answer had been to tell Adelaide to stick her offer where the sun don't shine and leave him the hell alone. Fine with her. They hadn't spoken since.

Chapter 9

A loud beeping startled Adelaide out of her sound slumber. She thrashed in her blankets for a minute, trying to escape.

"ALICE, what the hell is going on?"

"There is a proximity alert fifty kilometres off the starboard quarter. Decelerating. It's a Raau assault carrier. The commanding officer is listed as Taurian Cassini."

"Shit!" Adelaide swore, scrambling out of bed and running to the bridge.

"Gil, get up here," she yelled into the comm. "How far are we from Gaeaf?"

"Three hours."

"Damn it." Adelaide glared at the screen as Gil skidded onto the bridge.

"What's the problem?" he said, trying not to stare at her in her skimpy tank top and shorts.

"Taurian," she replied; it was all she had to say. Gil cursed and watched the ship grow larger.

"What does he want?" Gil asked.

"I don't know. The last time we met, it didn't end well."

"Yeah, I know. You threatened to cut off his privates," Gil said smirking.

"He had it coming."

"But, there, he was alone," he reminded her. Adelaide grimaced as she recalled the exchange from yesterday.

"We're being hailed," ALICE announced.

"Let's hear it."

"Hello, Adelaide." Taurian's smirking face appeared on the screen in front of her. "You couldn't stay away. And you're dressed appropriately," he remarked. Adelaide had to admit she was tempted by the come-on — he looked like a god, with his sculpted green body, blond hair reaching his shoulders and vivid purple eyes. She held herself rigid, resisting the urge to cover her chest, and glared at the screen. It was difficult to be taken seriously in her current attire, but you would think she'd fit right into Raau culture. It seemed that the Tu'Val thought clothing was optional, and the less the better.

"We'll pull up beside you and come aboard," Taurian declared.

"Like hell you will!"

"How else are we collecting our goods?" Taurian demanded, leaning closer to his monitor. She could now see the question in his eyes, probably mirroring her own expression.

"What goods? I have no idea what you're talking about," she responded. Adelaide could see Gil fidgeting out of the corner of her eye and motioned him back. He knew what to do.

"Didn't you bring me my treasure?" Taurian demanded. He was starting to grow angry, and his eyes seemed to shoot daggers her way.

"No! I told you I was done. Can't you take a hint? Were you talking to Dante?" she said, gripping the arms of her chair. Dante was going to die a slow, painful death when she located him.

"You're really telling me you know nothing? If you don't let me board, we'll have to convince you another way."

Adelaide saw his ship cannons move to target her ship, and she cursed. "I don't have anything, and if you think I'm scared, think again. You don't stand a chance. I'll blow you out of the sky," she roared and slammed the buttons on the console in front of her. She watched as surprise danced across Taurian's face.

"When did you outfit the ship?" he asked cautiously.

"After dealing with all you assholes out here. A girl has to protect herself. Now get the hell out of my way, or I'll make you."

"You don't have the guts," Taurian taunted.

"Try me. Remember, I've flown through plenty of battles and come out ahead," she reminded him. His head turned as he conferred with his crewmen.

"You'd better hope I don't find your brother. No one cheats me," he threatened. "And I'll be seeing you again." Taurian winked at her before the screen went blank and his ship moved away. Adelaide collapsed into her chair.

"ALICE, track the ship's progress and inform me if they change direction. Gil, where are you?"

"Coming back. You scare him off?"

"Enough for now. Did my idiot brother say anything about his scheme?" Adelaide asked.

"Nothing. He didn't actually get to the job. He mumbled something on his way out, but I didn't catch it."

"Anything about his destination?"

"Nope."

"We have to find him," Adelaide sighed. She may not be able to tolerate Dante, but she didn't want him dead, and she knew Taurian was serious.

"What about the shipment?" Gil asked.

"We'll finish it, but then we have to track him down. What would possess him to cheat Taurian? Only an idiot would, and Dante values his life too much. Everyone knows that a Tu'Val lives to fight and pillage. The sneakier the bastards are, the better, in their opinion."

"Maybe he's into something," Gil said.

"Yeah, a large pile of shit. ALICE, I'm going back to my cabin. Let me know if anything else changes," Adelaide said, stomping out of the room. *What the hell was Dante thinking?* She couldn't stay on Gaeaf now. The first thing to do would be to track down some of her brother's associates. She still had their contact information.

For the next couple of hours, Adelaide tossed and turned in bed before finally giving up. She pulled up the computer data on her wrist comm and scrolled through it, looking for Taurian's movements. He seemed to be leaving them alone. The sensors had lost his trail about an hour ago with his ship travelling in the opposite direction. She sighed in relief. Adelaide was a little suspicious that Taurian had given in so quickly. Maybe he didn't want to tangle with her until more ships arrived. She knew the firepower contained in her ship could win against him, but it would be tricky. During the war, Adelaide had learned a few interesting moves from a grisly old captain she'd met during training. He'd decided that she needed the benefit of his wisdom and had taken her under his wing. Her old warship was more maneuverable, but this beauty could hold her own now.

They arrived at the station on Gaeaf a few hours later. Docking and unloading time averaged two hours. This time she wasn't searching for parts. Lucky, since she had to find her dumbass brother.

"You ready to dock?" Gil's voice came over the comms.

"Yeah, I'm sending our documents to the station now." Adelaide punched a few buttons and then scanned her chip. Minutes later, an acknowledgement came through.

"Captain Zedler."

"Hi. You ready to unload my cargo?"

"We need some time. Our loader crashed into the door. We're trying to open it."

"When did this happen?" Adelaide demanded. *They didn't have time for this shit.*

"Eight this morning." Adelaide checked the planet's time — nine o'clock. "We should be done in maybe another half an hour."

"Okay, let me know when you're ready. I need to leave quickly."

"Sure."

Might as well try Dante's associates, she thought, pulling up their last known whereabouts and sending out some queries. *That took a whole whopping ten minutes.* Adelaide stood up and stretched as her stomach growled. Her decision made, she smiled, hurrying to grab breakfast.

* * *

"Captain, we're ready to dock." Adelaide sat up from her slouch.

"Thanks, ALICE, let's get on with it."

"Sorry, command not recognized."

"Dock at the station," Adelaide commanded.

The ship slowly inched towards the bay doors. They lurched to a stop, and she heard the click as the ship connected and sealed to the station. Adelaide hurried to release the cargo doors.

"Gil, be ready to leave as soon as we're empty," she called over the comm.

"No problem. I don't have to leave the ship"

"Can you oversee the unloading, then? I want to grab something from the station."

"Yeah, I'll be right up."

On every trip to the planet, Adelaide stocked up on her favourite delicacy that was only available on Gaeaf. The replicator could only provide a limited number of items, but this wasn't one of them. There were chefs who had tried to reproduce the recipe, but no luck. It was a guarded family secret. Her mouth started watering just thinking about it.

Adelaide watched the station employees tromp into the cargo bay and begin unloading the crates. She waved to Gil and headed down the ramp. The station was one big market, selling mostly wares from the planet, but there were a few off-worlders who had gained precious selling space there. A large part of Gaeaf's exports consisted of clothing made from the local animals. Every part was used, from the fur to the skin to even the innards. Many tourists didn't own warm enough apparel to survive the climate. Of course, there were also plenty of food vendors and parts dealers. She zeroed in on the heavenly smell and made a beeline for the stall, weaving around the other patrons. Compared to Earth2's station, Gaeaf was three times bigger and had a constant influx of travellers.

It was a godsend having the language interpretation technology of the translator chip. Thank goodness, the government had covered the expense, or it would have cost her an arm and a leg. Her program needed updating, because it overloaded whenever there was too much input. So, walking through the market was sometimes a challenge, especially since Adelaide was horrible at languages and couldn't distinguish many on her own. She didn't understand the science behind it, only that when someone spoke a different language, her brain articulated her response.

Two males from Gaeaf plodded slowly in front of Adelaide, and she almost snarled at them but stopped when she heard their topic of discussion.

KRANTH
BORN IN 2058; 50 YEARS OLD

OCCUPATION: RUNS A STALL ON GAEAF SPACE STATION
- *Sells Adelaide's favourite meat pastry*

PLANET: GAEAF
- *Half mountain ranges, half flat*
- *Only two seasons: winter and mild winter*
- *Big tourist attraction*
- *15 hours from Earth2 travelling by warp or 7 hours by jump gates*
- *His people are warriors*
- *Part of the Multi-Species Accords*

PHYSICAL DESCRIPTION:
Stalky; 5'5 feet; covered in body hair; skin colour is almost white; has horns (males' thick as arm and green; females' thinner and blue); their front teeth are pointy and sharp with 2 small tusks; bushy eye brows; brown eyes; white hair down to shoulders

WEAPONS:
Double-bladed axe

PERSONALITY:
Loyal, humorous, enjoys drinking and fighting, strong constitution

"U laq fbukkocawr rleh rlay Zartuth sba soxurib tban waq lyugl fbullana," he said, scratching part of his hairy arm that was peeking through his coveralls.

"U swaog ragr iir rev bu a rbowoddus wirxol."

"U rov Graeden lqibj owin. Lrok jkar gruq nug." The male said, his eyes partly covered by his bushy brows stared off in the distance.

Adelaide peered over their horns, trying to figure who Graeden could potentially be. His name didn't sound familiar, so she wasn't sure if it was a shopkeeper. Over the last couple of years, Adelaide had met most of the sellers, and very rarely did they change. If they did, she would hear about it on her next trip through. If there were warships amassing, she wanted to know. The males veered off before she could question them. Pursuing them at the moment wasn't going to work because of her time constraints. She hurried on to her chosen stall, ignoring the beseeches from the other sellers.

"Ikkog buaryax," Kranth said in Gaeaf.

"Hi, Kranth. I'm here for my regular allotment." Adelaide smiled.

"Just a minute while I package it up for you." Kranth bent over picking up a container, his animal hide pants pulled tight over his thick legs. Here at the station his people didn't need their traditional thick jackets with the hoods covered with fur. Their race used all parts of the animals native to on the planet since their bodies evolved to survive in this environment. One of Kranth's sleeve slipped down and he muttered trying to roll it high enough not to interfere. Adelaide resisted reaching to stroke his shirt, she could see the softness from here and new the time and energy to make was tremendous. They still did everything by hand, refusing much of the available technology.

She watched as Kranth scooped up the pastries filled with succulent meat and deposited them in a container. The smell was filled with numerous herbs and spices mixed into a wonderfully tasty treat. Adelaide had asked Kranth once what the secret was to tenderizing the meat so it melted in one's mouth, but he had just laughed and said he'd never tell.

"So, how's business?"

"Great. Busy as hell," he replied.

"Have you guys had any issues with pirates?"

"There's been a few. It seems the occurrences have increased. Not sure what they're thinking. We lost one of our shipments of generators," Kranth said with a frown tugging on his long black beard.

"I hope you were able to replace them."

"At a high cost. We're lucky it's the warmer season, with no generator going for two weeks." He shook his head.

"Where?" Adelaide inquired.

"In one of the mountain villages. But, they're hardy and survived waiting a couple of weeks for a new one. Here you go." He handed over her precious package. "Are you staying awhile?"

"No, I have some family business to deal with."

"Hope it's nothing serious."

"Not sure, but anything involving my brother is dicey. Thanks, Kranth. I'll see you on my next shipment."

Kranth grinned farewell at Adelaide showing his sharp pointed front teeth. She still sometimes had difficulties not to flinch when seeing them. They reminded her of Earth's fairy tale vampires, but with more teeth.

Adelaide did a quick browse on the way back but nothing caught her eye. A common thread that she heard repeated during her wander through the marketplace was the growing chance of war. Most species enjoyed the peace that was earned through the signing of the Accords and the skirmishes afterwards. The other species outside of the Accords still accessed the stations occasionally, but they were few and far between. Far too many fights broke out between the two groups.

One species no one ever heard from were the Cradesions, who hailed from Sipelgas, but they were feared by all. It seemed that sightings of them were becoming more frequent, and Adelaide was hoping it didn't mean that they had plans for expansion again. Before Earth was a blip on anyone's radar, the Cradesions were considered the scourge of the galaxy. Their main goal had been to colonize planets and reproduce as many offspring as possible. From what she'd heard, their species was only four and a half feet tall, with four arms and two legs. A hard, dark-blue shell covered their bodies, and their three eyes stared unblinkingly at a person without eyelids. It was surprising they were so feared, since because of their size, she wasn't sure how they would fight hand-to-hand. Their species must have some spectacular weaponry, and she didn't want to experience it firsthand. They had disappeared when they had all but been wiped out during the war. No one knew where the Cradesions had settled to lick their wounds, but they must have found a secluded spot in the galaxy.

The ship was three-quarters unloaded when she returned, so Adelaide put away her treasure and headed to the bridge. Might as well get ready for takeoff.

"ALICE, have we been refuelled?"

"Yes."

"Great. Let's start pre-launch."

She checked her messages, hoping for information about Dante's whereabouts, but no luck. First stop would be Zartuth. Dante loved a bar called Narwhal Tavern. Maybe he'd been sighted by the patrons. She was almost hoping there would be resistance, then Adelaide could bang some heads to loosen their tongues a bit. From her experience, the saying was true: there was honour among thieves. Even with other species. Hopefully, being related would encourage the flow of information. Space was endless, and someone could disappear easily. Not like when Earth had been the only place out there. She'd just finished going through the ships records and logs, when Gil walked in.

"They're done unloading," he informed her.

"Good. Let's get out of here."

"Have you got a destination in mind?"

"We'll try Narwhal Tavern on Zartuth first."

"That's as good a place as any to begin," Gil replied. Zartuth was two hours from Gaeaf, and as long as Taurian hadn't changed directions, they wouldn't run into him. "Do we have any shipments to pick up?"

"There's some, but we've got time," Adelaide answered. She muttered under her breath about family and began pushing buttons. She needed a distraction, or the whole trip would be filled with dark, brooding and destructive thoughts about her brother. The ZOO wasn't a search-and-rescue company, and it definitely wasn't at Dante's disposal. Flying always soothed Adelaide, and her tense muscles slowly loosened. *Maybe it wasn't his fault*, she thought and then snorted. *Not likely*.

Adelaide hoped they wouldn't run into any trouble on Zartuth, but that was always a possibility. Which races happened to be involved determined the outcome. The Tu'Val, and some Gaeaf, thought it was all in fun, while the humans and others would whine and complain till the cows came home. In her opinion, if someone planned to live on Zartuth or conduct business there, they shouldn't be surprised. During the trip, Adelaide received a few responses, and supposedly no one had seen Dante. He was in the wind. She growled in frustration and hoped he was at the Narwhal, so she could knock some sense into him.

Docking was quick, and Gil and Adelaide rode the shuttle to the planet's surface. She saw a few Zartuths looking her way, and her fingers itched to grab her blaster. Narwhal Tavern was dead centre in the town and one of the popular joints for conducting business. Everyone knew to keep their weapons primed and their comments to themselves. She groaned while pushing open the large, heavy door to the establishment. It was made out of a metal mined on the planet and was almost indestructible. To accommodate the many species who frequented the establishment, the door was well over eight feet tall and ten feet wide, towering over her 5'5" frame. Thankfully, she could easily fit through, or there would have to be some serious dieting happening.

They stepped into a large room filled with metal tables of all shapes and sizes. For the type of customers frequenting the joint, it was kept surprisingly clean — not eat-off-the-floor clean, but she didn't get a dirty feeling from being here. A few customers looked their way, but they were mostly ignored. In the dim light, Adelaide gave a cursory glance around the room before striding to the bar. None of her brother's cohorts were in sight — *damn*. The regular bartender eyed them as they drew closer, and he slid some drinks to a large Tu'Val.

"Hello, Pander," she crooned, leaning against the bar.

"Hey, Adelaide," he answered warily.

"Have you seen my brother?"

"Why?" he asked, wiping the bar with a cloth.

"Family business."

"Maybe."

"Are you going to make me beg for my own brother?"

Pander looked uneasily between her and Gil before saying, "Fine." He blew out a breath and leaned forwards to whisper, "I saw him talking to the trader over at the far table." He nodded in the direction of a large human, sitting solitarily and holding a drink. The other patrons seemed to give him a wide berth.

"Who is he?" Adelaide demanded.

"Not sure. He showed up a few months ago and started throwing his weight around."

"What about Taurian's guys. Have they come looking for him?"

"Not that I've seen."

At least that was one good thing, Adelaide thought, as she frowned in the lone man's direction and nodded at Gil. He would have her back.

"Hello. Can I have a seat?" she asked, sideling up to the loner. The man staring at her gave her the willies. Multiple tattoos covered his head and arms. Small, squinty eyes seemed to assess them, before the man grunted. Since it didn't seem like a negative, Adelaide pulled out a chair and collapsed into it. "I hear you may have been talking to Dante?"

"What's it to you?" he growled in a low, gravelly voice.

"He's my brother."

"Sorry to hear that."

"Why?" She sat up straighter.

"He's a dead man." Now she was getting mad. Only she was allowed to threaten her brother.

"Are you threatening him?" she demanded.

"It's not just me. What are you going to do about it?" he asked, setting his drink down.

"I wouldn't push it. He may be an ass, but he's my brother."

The man pushed away from the table and stood up, way up.

"You think you can do something about it, little girl?" he snapped, giving her a once-over. She slowly stood, hearing shuffling noises in the background as other people moved away. She spotted Gil's hand move slowly to hover over his blaster.

Adelaide had always been underestimated throughout her career. The day she turned seventeen, defence had become her number-one priority. One black belt in Wado kai karate and two other top rankings in hand-to-hand combat later, and Adelaide was justified in her confidence. There were very few individuals, particularly men, who could disarm her. Even with other species thrown into the mix, she could handle herself, and this guy was just human. Hopefully, he didn't have any cyber enhancements, or it could get dicey then. One of the few men who had bested her was Taurian, and they were even in their wins. It still stuck in her craw. She placed her hands on the table, leaned forwards and glared.

"I'm thinking you're going to leave him alone and tell me where you think he is,"

Adelaide said threateningly. His demeanor changed in a blink of the eye. His shoulders drew back, and his chest puffed out.

"I don't like taking orders, especially from a little girl who's out of her league." Adelaide glanced at the blaster on his hip and hoped he wouldn't pull it. Usually, they were stupid enough to grab her first, which was exactly what he did. The man's hand shot out and grabbed her arm, pulling her towards him and knocking over the chairs in her path with Adelaide's ankle, making her grimace.

"Let me go, you ass," she growled. His only response was the laughter that erupted from his chest. Adelaide stepped closer to his body, and at the same time, struck at his throat with her fingers and elbowed his head on its way down. She twisted her arm out of his grip, grabbed his head with both hands and pulled sharply towards her rising knee. She watched as the man's body crashed to the floor. The silence didn't last long before everyone ignored her drama and continued with their drinking and carousing. Kicking him in the head for good measure, she asked quietly, "So, what were you saying?"

* * *

Ten minutes later, Adelaide stomped out of the bar with Gil behind her. Once they were clear of the building, Adelaide slipped into a back alley and leaned against the wall, breathing heavily.

"Crap."

Gil nodded his head, and said, "But, you handled yourself like a pro."

"Yeah." She paused a moment. "I can't believe Dante is involved in that shit." She felt like screaming. It crossed the line that her family had drawn about acceptable cargo. The drugs that Dante was transporting and brokering were used on the victims of human trafficking. The drug caused the individuals to become slow and pliant. Their captors could then move them around freely with no fighting. When the ZOO had gone on its maiden voyage, her dad and his partners had agreed to never transport that drug or anything that helped human trafficking. If her dad had discovered what Dante was doing, Adelaide was sure the shit would have hit the fan. Adelaide shook her head in disgusted exasperation.

"Good thing that idiot had a name and location for us. Let's head back to the ship and continue the search tomorrow."

"Sounds good," Gil said, as they started back to the ZOO.

The streets were quickly deserted as people headed inside before dark. One of the downsides of living on Zartuth was the local wildlife. You didn't want to be out wandering after dark, because you would likely come across the native sucker bugs. Of course, the drunks thought it was a hoot to challenge each other based on how long they could stay outside before one of the bugs attached itself to them. It wasn't a pretty sight to watch one of those things being pulled off its victim. Adelaide remembered the long, deadly-

looking noses that each sucker bug had, which
would leave behind a huge hickey and could even
cause blood loss. She and Gil increased their
speed, not wanting to risk encountering the bugs,
and reached the shuttle just as the planet's two
suns disappeared.

"So, what's the plan?" Gil asked, as the
shuttle took off.

"Tomorrow, I'll find this 'Brokers R Us'
place that guy in the bar mentioned and confirm
a few things before we take off," Adelaide replied.

He nodded in agreement and watched as
the first large insect hit the window, causing a
vibration to run through the shuttle. Adelaide
grimaced, staring into the darkness, searching for
those beady red eyes. They were soon too high in
the atmosphere for the bloodsuckers to reach
them, and she sighed in relief. Adelaide
shuddered, remembering her first time on
Zartuth with Dante. Those bugs had given her
nightmares that the crew had never let her live
down. It was an initiation to all newbies to let
unsuspecting suckers, pun intended, walk outside
after dark with no warning. No one that she knew
of had ever been killed by them, just injured
slightly. Adelaide caught Gil grinning at her out
of the corner of her eye, and she was sure as shit
that he was remembering her initiation that night.
Adelaide turned and glared in his direction, and
he chuckled before peering out the window.

She spent some time on the station asking
questions and listening. She really needed to get
her translator fixed. A headache was developing
fast. First thing upon reaching the ZOO, Adelaide

would grab herself a pain-relief strip. Thank goodness for alien medicine. A cure for most of the diseases or illnesses on Earth could be found on another planet. Adelaide couldn't totally discount human innovation, but most cures were derived from others. Of course, there were still some diseases that were stubborn, which no amount of engineering could cure.

As she moved throughout the space station, she heard the same rumours here about a war starting between the Cradesions and various other species that she had heard on the station at Gaeaf. *Maybe she should be searching for Graeden.* Adelaide really didn't want to fight in another war, but she was sure the military would recall everyone once it started. There were also some whispers about a new faction in town, the one that Dante could be involved with, and they sounded nasty. The temptation to forget his ass was so great that she vibrated. But for now, she'd move forwards with the plan to save him.

Chapter 10

Adelaide finished checking the ship over and planned to leave the planet soon, hopefully with Dante in tow.

"Captain, there's a call coming in," ALICE announced.

"Who is it?" She frowned at the console.

"Pander."

"Put him through," Adelaide answered. "Pander, what do you want?" she continued, after Pander's face appeared on the comm screen.

There was some stuttering before he answered, "Some Tu'Val are here looking for Dante." Adelaide let out some expletives.

"Are they with Taurian?" she demanded. It wasn't necessary to explain who he was.

"Not sure. Haven't seen them before."

"Okay," she said, trying to think — her brain was hurting. "What have you told them?"

"Nothing yet. So far, they've kept it pretty civilized for the Tu'Val."

She snorted in surprise and asked, "Nothing broken yet?"

"No. But, I'm going to have to tell them something."

"Fine, fine. But, try to mislead them."

"What do you mean?" Pander asked.

"You know, send them everywhere but where Dante is."

"I don't know where he is," he said, sounding confused.

"Forget it," she growled in frustration. "Just give them some useless information," Adelaide said, before abruptly disconnecting the call. It wasn't a coincidence that the Tu'Val were here. *How did Taurian figure it out so quickly?* she wondered. It could have been an educated guess, but he and Dante didn't usually meet on Zartuth. The only time they'd met here had been when she first started working for her dad. It had been an explosive meeting. Of course, it was common knowledge that Dante met people on Zartuth to do other business. She began swearing. "ALICE, check for any foreign objects on the hull," she commanded.

"It will take a minute." Adelaide impatiently drummed her fingers on the console, a frown on her face. "Captain, there is a tracking device on the hull."

"Crap. Why didn't you notice it? Our scans should have caught it."

"It seems like the tracker is composed of an unknown substance that doesn't show up on a regular scan," ALICE replied.

"Well, it had better show up from now on. Can you tell how it's attached?"

"No."

"Contact the station, and tell them we have a foreign object on our hull and we need it removed. I have to visit the planet again. See if it can be disabled, so we can study it."

"Yes, Captain."

Adelaide strode out of the bridge and headed to the one place she knew she'd find Gil.

"Gil, you in here?" she called, as she walked around the engine room.

"Back here."

"That bastard Taurian tracked us," Adelaide snarled, as she watched him work.

"Are you heading back out?"

"Yes. I want you to ensure the station gets that tracker removed, and that we're ready to leave when I get back."

"No problem. You sure you're going to be alright?" Gil asked kindly.

"Yes. I'm taking extra firepower." Adelaide patted the two blasters sitting in the holsters resting against each of her hips. She also had a knife shoved down each boot and a small blaster strapped to her thigh. She was dressed in tight black pants, for easy movement.

People gave Adelaide a wide berth as she stepped into the shuttle, which suited her fine. The less blockage the better. Her destination was the docks. Dante was last spotted at Brokers R US, trying to find a way off the planet. Adelaide had no idea where he planned to hide, and she didn't really give a rat's ass. She sidestepped the loaders and hurried towards a building a few feet away. The heat was already on the rise as she shaded her eyes from the two suns above her. Of course, her black clothing probably didn't help the situation. Zartuth had intense heat during the day and scary bugs at night, just a regular tourist place. *Damn it,* she cursed mentally, as she caught sight of some Tu'Val coming down a side alley. They seemed to be heading in the same direction she was. A bell tinkled as she swung open the door to the business and slammed it behind her.

"Ikkog ragq bax U is wide it?" a Gaeaf male asked, from behind a counter that wasn't quite able to hide his impressive girth. You didn't see too many obese Gaeaf unless they were away from their planet for extended periods. Food from other species could really play havoc with their bodies. Adelaide wasn't sure if the atmosphere on their planet had something to do with it as well. Adelaide turned around and flipped the lock before answering.

"Give me Dante," she demanded. The Gaeaf looked at her with suspicion and shook his head in rejection. He then prowled towards her curling his lip into a snarl with his jaw jutting out pushing his two tusks higher towards his eyes. She tried to not stare at the broken tip of one tusk. Their tusks were supposed to be indestructible, what could have happened? There was no way she was leaving without Dante, no matter what this Gaeaf thought.

"There are a couple of Tu'Val coming this way. I don't think you want him here," she said with a sneer, stepping further into the room. "Dante, get your ass out here now! If I have to search for you, I might let Taurian have you," she yelled, looking around the small shop. There was a table, a couple of chairs and a door in the back, presumably leading to an office.

"Keep it down. I'm trying to hide," Dante said, slinking quietly into the room.

"Does this place have a back door?" Adelaide demanded, as she prayed for a yes.

"Through there." Adelaide grabbed Dante's arm and dragged him towards their escape.

"I'm not going with you!" he said, digging in his heels.

"Do you want to live? Then, yes, you are. Keep going." They reached the door just as the front of the shop blew apart. Two Tu'Val ran inside and were confronted by an angry Gaeaf.

"Ragq ogr kkog owa eit fbuis?" he snarled baring his deadly teeth, pulling out a large double-bladed axe and swinging it at them. The Tu'Val roared in challenge, and the fighting started in earnest. A stray blast hit the top of the doorframe as they exited, and Adelaide shoved Dante forwards, spinning around to fire.

"Run to the shuttle!" she yelled at him. Thank goodness, the ship wasn't far, and they sprinted into the shuttle as the doors slid shut. They could see the two Tu'Val coming around the corner, as they lifted up and flew away. Adelaide spun around to her brother and pushed him against the wall, whispering, "What the hell are you doing?" Dante glared mutinously at her, and she groaned in frustration. There would be time to interrogate him on the ship. Right now, she had to concentrate on surviving before she could kick him to kingdom come.

"When we reach the station, you run like your ass is on fire. Got it?"

"Yeah. I want to live. You don't have to threaten me," he whined, which didn't fit his six-foot-two frame and usual swagger. Adelaide turned back to the doors and counted in her head to remain calm. She sent Gil a warning that the ship better be primed and ready, and the minute the shuttle doors swished open, they took off. She assumed the Tu'Val on the planet weren't the only two on their ship, so there might be a welcoming committee.

"Do you have a blaster?" Adelaide asked as they ran, dodging between people and stalls. A few yells were shouted in their wake when Dante knocked over a stand, but it didn't even phase him. In response, Dante patted his right side, and Adelaide nodded.

Their destination was in sight when one of the Tu'Val cronies shouted, "Stop!"

Adelaide put on a burst of speed, and she could feel her lungs burning. A few shots landed close by, and she retaliated. A scream followed, and she smirked in triumph before continuing onwards.

"Hurry up, you two," Gil yelled as they ran up the ramp to the ZOO. He slammed the button as soon as they boarded the ship, since the goons were right on their tail.

"Go! Go!" Adelaide yelled, and they began lift off. "Did you locate their ship?" she asked Gil, as they ran to the bridge.

"Yes. It's at the other side of the station."

"That may give us a few seconds, if they wait for their comrades. You, sit," she commanded Dante, pointing at the chair in front of the controls. Adelaide collapsed, with Gil standing beside her. It was hard to admit it, but her brother was a better flyer than she was. He could help with their escape, since he was the cause.

Dante didn't do his usual complaining but stayed silent, watching the monitor and gripping the control stick tighter. The ZOO cleared the station, and Dante accelerated, trying to increase their safety distance.

"ALICE, where's the Tu'Val ship?" Adelaide demanded.

"They are about to clear the station."

Before she could respond, a shot fired across their bow.

"Damn it!" Adelaide swore. "Dante, hurry up and get us to a safe distance to hit lightspeed."

"I'm trying. Keep them off me for a few seconds."

"How?" Adelaide asked. "They're too close to the station. You're the flying whiz." Dante grumbled under his breath and adjusted their course. She kept track of the ship waiting for the right moment. "Now!" she screamed, and the ship fired.

"Captain, we damaged their propulsions."

"Fire again! Dante!"

"Got it." He pushed the button, and the ship bolted. Her last view of the Tu'Val ship showed it floundering by the station.

"Good thing for your new firepower," Gil said, glaring at Dante.

"Yeah. So, talk," Adelaide said, turning to Dante.

"I tried, and you didn't want anything to do with it."

"You blew a gasket and had to be kicked off my ship." She grinned as the video flashed through her mind. "And I didn't hear from you again. Why are you helping transport that drug?"

"I didn't know what it was for," he denied.

"Bullshit. Everyone knows what the common use of that drug is. You know that's the one line Dad wouldn't cross — the slavery of any race. What the hell is wrong with you?"

"Fine. It was good money. I didn't realize what kind of man he was until later."

"He's involved with peddling flesh, among other things. What did you expect?" she yelled.

"Hey, it's not my fault you cut me off from the family business. I had no choice," Dante yelled right back.

Adelaide closed her eyes, clenching her arm rests to resist shooting him. *Maybe just injuring him would be alright,* she thought grimacing.

"First, it was my company that Dad gave to me." She held up her hand when Dante tried to protest. "You wanted no part of the legal side, so you made a choice. You made another dumb choice, when you agreed to deal with Axis and that drug. So, don't give me the B.S. woe-is-me act. Step up and be a man for once."

"What do you want from me?" he snarled.

"What do I want? I'm trying to save you. If you don't want my help, I can drop you off at the nearest planet, and you can fend for yourself," she snapped turning towards Gil. "What about the tracker?"

"It's in the engine room safely locked up."

"Has it been disabled?" Dante was looking back and forth between her and Gil with a confused look on his face.

"What tracker," he finally asked. Adelaide swung back in Dante's direction.

"None of your business." She stood up, storming off the bridge. Adelaide stomped to the galley for a drink. She needed one after the day she'd had. It would sure make her life easier if Dante insisted being dropped off.

* * *

A half-filled glass sat in front of Adelaide while she tapped her fingers on the table. *How long would he take?*

"Adelaide?" Dante stepped into the galley. She turned around, waiting for him to continue. She wasn't giving an inch. He swallowed. She watched as his Adam's apple move up and down. A bead of sweat trailed down the side of his cheek. Adelaide was almost enjoying his discomfort. "I need your help," he continued hesitantly. He crossed his arms and waited for her response.

"Have a seat, and tell me what you're into." She gestured to the chair in front of her and grabbed her drink. Dante plopped into the chair, crossing his arms with a glare. Adelaide stayed silent, waiting him out. He sighed and slouched his shoulders.

"I was doing jobs for Axis, occasionally, nothing big. He'd want an item found." Adelaide raised her eyebrow at the word "found," not trusting him for a moment. "There were never any real complications. I would visit his casinos every so often, and Axis allowed me to run a tab."

"Are you an idiot?" Adelaide interrupted. "He wanted you indebted to him." Dante frowned.

"I knew it would turn around."

"Really? How did it go for you?" Dante paused, looking around the room, probably trying to decide if it was worth talking to her.

"Axis didn't want to wait any longer," Dante eventually continued. "He demanded that I transport a package to a freighter captain. I was on my way to the drop, when the package ripped open, and I saw the contents. I couldn't deliver it, so I destroyed the drug and then took off."

"Why the hell would you even agree to deliver it?" she snarled, leaning forwards. "And didn't you just tell me that you knew and were doing it for the money?" Dante growled at her running his hand through his hair.

"I had no choice. He wasn't waiting for my luck to turn, so I agreed. I had suspicions of what it was, but until I confirmed it, it wasn't an issue." Adelaide felt sick. That drug was despicable — so many people's lives were destroyed because of it. She couldn't believe a member of her family was involved.

"You really didn't know what was in the package before you agreed?" Adelaide looked at him suspiciously.

"No," Dante replied.

"Axis would have wanted to rub it in your face. There's no way he didn't tell you."

"Well, he didn't," Dante almost yelled, glaring at her. "Maybe, he wanted me to deliver one package, and then he'd spring it on me." Adelaide grudgingly agreed that could be a possibility.

"Fine, what happened next?"

"I contacted Axis and said we were attacked by pirates and the package was taken."

"He believed you?"

"I don't think so, but he said the cost would be added to my bill, and he'd contact me about another job later."

She snorted and replied, "Of course, he didn't believe you. How would the pirates find that small package in your large ship unless you gave it to them? I'm sure you didn't have it sitting in your cargo bay."

"So, what now?" Dante demanded, ignoring her comment.

"Why is Taurian looking for you? Are you stealing from him as well?" she asked, pouring herself another drink.

"No, I'm not an idiot." Adelaide just looked at him skeptically. "I found an item for him and had to hide it, because I didn't want Axis finding it. Taurian is paying me good money for it."

Adelaide sighed, taking a big gulp from her cup, and tried not to grimace as the liquid burned a path down to her stomach.

"We need to avoid Axis, while we retrieve Taurian's goods. Where did you stash it?" she asked.

"That should be easy. He won't be looking." Dante stood before answering, "On Earth2." He said and left the room.

Easy, Adelaide silently scoffed. Dante was jinxing them by saying that. Adelaide frowned. She stood and made her way toward the bridge to alter their course.

"ALICE, change direction towards Earth2. Keep watch for any Tu'Val ships, and let me know immediately if they come within range," she commanded the computer, before she heading to her cabin. *Dante could fend for himself for the moment.*

*   *   *

Earth2 came up on the display, and Adelaide summoned Dante to the bridge.

"Okay, where it is it?" she demanded.

He stared at her for a moment before sighing, "It's on the western hemisphere."

"Where?"

"I'll tell you when we get there."

"How in the hell am I supposed to get there without coordinates?" Adelaide demanded.

"Do you still have the shuttle?" Dante asked, without answering her question.

"Yeah, why?"

"We need to take it to the surface. I'll meet you in the bay," Dante said and was gone.

"Where on the western hemisphere?" she yelled after him. He responded with a set of coordinates, and she punched them in, grumbling about idiots. "Gil," Adelaide said, using the comm.

"Yeah, boss?"

"Stay with the ship. Dante and I are taking the shuttle to the surface."

"No problem. Good luck."

"He might need it. ALICE, is there any sign of the Tu'Val ship?"

"No."

"Keep monitoring, and contact me if it shows up."

Adelaide stopped at her weapons locker and loaded up, before heading to the shuttle bay to meet Dante.

"Let's get this show on the road." She said, climbing into the shuttle. "What are we going to run into?" she asked.

"Shouldn't be much. We're going out to the middle of nowhere."

"What's out there?"

"I've got a safe house," Dante revealed.

"Does anyone else know it's there?" Adelaide asked. *Specifically, Taurian*, she thought.

"No. I haven't told anyone about this location," Dante replied. Adelaide glanced over at her brother, before taking control of the shuttle for the landing.

They stepped out into the hot sun shining through the multitude of trees. The trees were massive. Most were at least ten feet across, and their branches almost touched the ground with bright red leaves. The trees covered the vast majority of the planet. So far, the humans hadn't harvested many. But going by human history, it wouldn't take long before they destroyed the beauty here, like they had on Earth.

"Where to now?" she asked Dante.

"We have to hike about thirty minutes."

"Why? How big is this thing? Can we carry it out?"

"You'll see. I got it there myself."

"Why are you being so secretive?" she demanded, following him between the trees.

"You won't believe me without seeing it," he replied. Dante pushed through the foliage, startling out some small creatures. The similarities between the animals on Earth2 and the extinct ones from Earth were amazing. Of course, on Earth2, the animals weren't domesticated. There were no sentient natives when the planet was discovered. Over the years, evidence had been unearthed that intelligent beings had lived here once. Earth's scientists weren't sure what had happened to them. Enough time had passed to erase most of the traces that remained of their existence. Adelaide pushed aside the branches.

"If you were just here, why isn't there any evidence?" she asked, as she looked down at the trail of broken and flattened grass and plants that they were leaving behind them.

"I go a different way every time to avoid that. The tracks eventually grow over."

"That's smart," she said grudgingly. It was a blessing the trees were large enough to block part of the sun. She could already feel trickles of sweat running down her back. Hopefully, they'd arrive soon. She hadn't planned or dressed for a long hike in the heat. "How are you able to keep your place secret from the council? They monitor the forests heavily," she asked.

"Not this place," Dante answered. "It's far enough away that I'm not observed. Not sure how long that will last."

"Why hasn't anyone else found this place yet?"

"Probably, because they're not looking. I also have security set up around the perimeter," Dante bragged. Just then, a rundown cabin came into view. "Come on, it's in the cabin," he explained. Dante lifted his arm punching some commands into his comm unit. There was a little flash of light, and he continued on.

"You wouldn't happen to keep any drinks here?" Adelaide asked hopefully.

"There's a well around back for pumping water."

"Really?"

"I didn't want a bunch of electricity here, but I had to worry about upkeep if someone had to stay here. So, yeah, there's a well. I'll meet you there."

Dante jogged off to the front of the cabin, and Adelaide veered towards the promise of water. He had found a beautiful spot. Trees surrounded the cabin with mountains peaking out over top of them. She wondered how the heck he'd found this. Adelaide reached the well. Pumping quickly, she splashed the clear water that escaped onto her face and hands and then drank deeply. Adelaide was enjoying the view, when Dante stomped towards her.

"We don't have time for sightseeing. Let's go," he urged.

She held her tongue, barely, and just asked, "Where is it?" He wasn't carrying or pulling anything. Dante pulled a small box out of his pocket. "That's what this is about?" she said in surprise.

"Yep. It's one of a kind."

"Well, let's see it," she demanded. He slowly removed the top, and Adelaide peered in at the shiny gem nestled inside the box. The gem was the deepest purple that she'd ever seen, flawless and about the size of her fist. "Where did you find this?" she asked reverently.

"I can't reveal my source," he said smugly. Dante covered it with the lid and placed the box in his pocket.

The branches whipped past Adelaide's face as they ran back to the ZOO, and she already sported a few red marks across her cheek. They were within a few metres of the shuttle, when she heard a crackle through her wrist comm.

"What, Gil? I can't hear you."

"Taurian... your... and almost..." came Gil's voice over the comm.

"What was that?" Dante yelled.

"I think we've been discovered. We've got to hurry," she urged. Adelaide drew her blaster, and they tried to cautiously hurry the rest of the distance. However, the instant they stepped into the clearing, a grinning Taurian and his men surrounded them.

"What do you want?" she demanded.

"My property. Hand it over, Dante."

Dante wrenched the box from his pocket and stepped forwards. Taurian's men levelled their weapons on him and growled. Dante glanced fearfully around him and froze.

"I was going to find you, Taurian, I swear. But, Axis started some trouble."

"That scum," Taurian snarled. "What are you doing dealing with him?" Adelaide glanced at Taurian in surprise, watching and waiting for her brother to do something stupid. "Not my problem," Taurian continued. "I've got to make an example out of you now." Adelaide watched in horror as Taurian raised his blaster, and she swore Dante was a goner. Her gut wrenched, as Dante fell to the ground clenching his side.

"You bastard!" she screamed, running to her brother's prone figure.

"He's fine. I made sure it wasn't fatal because of you," Taurian reassured her condescendingly. She glared at Taurian before turning back to Dante. "I can't let people get away with cheating me," he continued. To her ears, it almost sounded like he was begging for understanding, but that couldn't be. She hadn't heard the men stepping up behind her until Taurian said, "Take them."

Her arms were seized roughly, and she was yanked up. A grinning Tu'Val grabbed her weapons and slowly ran his hands down her body, searching for more.

"Don't touch me!" Adelaide said through clenched teeth and made a well-aimed kick to his groin. He fell like a ton of bricks, and the surrounding men broke out in laughter. Taurian stomped over and kicked the man in the stomach.

"Remember what I told you," he snarled.

"Pud Vesyeom," the man said meekly, quickly rising but keeping his head down.

Well that was new, Adelaide thought. Not normal behavior at all. He should have bounced up and tried to punch back. Which, of course, would cause a fight to ensue. Fighting was the primary source of joy in a Tu'Val's life, and it could have been the distraction she needed to escape.

"Let's get out of here," Taurian said, leading the way to the awaiting ship.

"What about my ship?" Adelaide demanded.

"Don't worry, I've left it only slightly damaged. Just enough so they can't pursue us."

She swore a blue streak, as her captors pushed her into the ship. Dante groaned behind her, and she glanced back worriedly, before threatening, "Gil and Dante had better both be alright, or I won't rest until your dead," she threatened, straining against the Tu'Val's hold on her.

"Oh, I can't wait. If you want to fight, we can continue this in my quarters," Taurian said grinning.

Adelaide snorted, and replied, "Not in a million years."

"We'll see. Take them to the cells," he said, before striding off.

Chapter 11

The guards had taken all of Adelaide's weapons, but because her comm was attached to her wrist, they'd simply warned her that no frequency could break through the shields and left. But little did the jerks know, Gil could communicate through her translator chip as well.

"How are you?" she asked Dante, watching him move gingerly towards the cot.

"How do you think? I've been shot!" he snarled.

"Hey, don't get mad at me. You're the dumbass who crossed him. You're lucky he didn't kill you," Adelaide exclaimed.

"What did Taurian mean when he said I'm alive because of you?" Dante asked sullenly, ignoring her warning.

"I have no idea," she said, staring out the bars at the guards walking back and forth.

"Are you two hooking up?" he demanded.

"Are you nuts?" she asked, shaking her head in the negative. "Just drop it."

"So, what are we going to do?" Dante asked.

"We wait until Gil contacts me. We can't do anything while we're on this ship anyways."

"How the hell is he going to do that?" Dante broke in, almost yelling now.

"Shut up! You want the guards to hear?" she shushed, looking down the hallway. Dante looked at her mutinously before laying down and turning to face the wall. *Thank god, he finally shut up,* Adelaide thought with a sigh. After a moment, though, she decided to signal the guards herself.

"Guards! Guards!" she yelled.

"Rjey fa pai remy?" asked a large Tu'Val, as he approached the cell.

"We need bandages for my brother."

"We'll see," he said and strode away.

Adelaide grimaced in disgust as she paced the small enclosure. Even in such a large warship, the cells sure were cramped. A single insipid blue light in the top corner threw its meager gleam across the metallic walls, into which previous occupants had tried to scratch messages. Some of the marks were recognizable words, others quite alien. A rancid mixture of body odour and industrial cleaning compounds made her scrunch up her nose, and she coughed a little. Adelaide could just make out Dante's body through the gloomy prison, curled up on the cot about five feet away from her.

"Man. Did something die in here?" Adelaide wondered aloud.

"What are you talking about?" Dante asked, opening his eyes and rolling over.

"Can't you smell that?"

"No," he said, giving her a strange look.

"Never mind," she said. *What the heck was taking Gil so long?* she wondered. He'd better be alright, or no matter how gorgeous Taurian was, she'd hunt him down. Eventually, Adelaide tired of her pacing and gingerly sat on the other cot. She was certain bugs would begin crawling out of the thin, worn brown padding and attack her. There was no way she could lay down and sleep.

*　　*　　*

They had been travelling for what seemed like hours, when suddenly, there was a crackling noise in her mind, a burst of pain and then a faint voice.

"Adelaide?" Gil asked gruffly.

"Thank goodness, Gil. Are you alright?" she asked, trying to communicate silently, but it was extremely difficult not to also voice her words aloud. Using her chip to communicate with the ship was painful and Adelaide could feel a headache beginning at the back of her skull. But, she wasn't going to complain if it could save their lives.

"Yeah, I'm fine," Gil assured her. "They surrounded us and shot up our engines. I have them working well enough to follow you now."

"You can track me, right?"

"Of course."

"Make sure that, if you require parts, you stop for further repairs. We want to be in top shape for our escape," Adelaide instructed him.

"I'll see what planets we pass."

"Fine. We'll try to keep radio silence. I can't communicate like this very well. And we're not sure if Taurian's warship can detect this type of communication," she said.

In response, her mind went suddenly blank, and Adelaide wished for the ability to call Gil back. She didn't like the silence here. Adelaide decided that informing her brother about Gil was out of the question. Knowing him, he'd blurt it out in front of the guards. As if on cue, Dante started moaning and shifting on the bed. *Crap!* Adelaide thought, racing to his side.

A clatter sounded as she hurried over and touched his shoulder. She searched for the noise and saw that she had kicked a metal bowl — *ew*. It wasn't difficult to guess the bowl's purpose. When she turned back to Dante, sweat was forming on his forehead, and his face was flushed. She gently moved his hand away from the wound on his side and grimaced. Even if Taurian hadn't shot any vital organs, Dante could still die from blood loss. He needed medical attention. At least a blaster wasn't as devastating as Earth's old bullet-style guns. From what she had learned in school, a bullet could have bounced around inside him, inflicting permanent damage.

A noise at the bars made Adelaide look up, as a guard threw some gauze and wraps into the cell.

"He needs stitches. I want to see Taurian," she demanded.

"He's busy. When the captain has time, he'll come."

"What about water?" she asked. He threw a container her way and left.

Adelaide muttered under her breath, as she opened the bottle and sniffed. *Smelled alright.* She stuck her finger in and then sucked on it. *Tasted like stale water. Good enough.* Dante flinched as the water touched his burning side. She almost expected to see steam rise up from the wound. Blood was seeping out of the hole that now punctured in his body. Some of the skin around the wound was cauterized, and the black skin around the wound certainly didn't have an appealing smell. Next came the gauze, and she tried to wrap his body as gently as possible. This time, Dante uttered a scream as she pressed down.

His eyes popped open, and he yelled, "What the hell are you doing?"

"Trying to save your life, again. You don't want to lose any more blood. Hold as still as possible, while I finish this," she suggested soothingly. Dante grimaced and clenched his jaw while she completed his bandages.

"Thanks, sis," Dante said softly. She looked at him in surprise.

"What did you say?" she asked incredulously.

"Thanks for trying to help," Dante repeated. "And sorry for getting you into this."

"Your welcome," she said suspiciously, standing up and walking back to the other side of the cell. It had been so long since they'd been civil to each other that Adelaide figured Dante must believe he was dying.

* * *

Adelaide must have dozed off, because before she knew it, a guard was shaking her awake.

"Vaqu am. Yju Vesyeom remyd pai," he said.

"About time," she muttered, groaning as her muscles protested. She glanced once at the sleeping form of her brother before following the guards down the hallway. Adelaide frowned as they passed the bridge. *Where were they going?* she wondered. *No way was she going to ask, though.*

The guards halted in front of a door, and one of them called out. The door slid open, and Taurian stood barely covered in the doorway. *Let's clarify, he was barely covered in her opinion but dressed normally for a Tu'Val.* He ushered her inside and waved off his men.

"Come in, Red."

"That's not my name."

"But it suits you," he said laughing. "Fiery and strong."

He was complimenting her. *What was going on?* she thought warily.

"Why are we here?" she demanded, stepping further away. He grinned, looking pleased about something. "You shot Dante to prove something. Why didn't you just leave us?" she asked. *Was it getting warm in here?* she wondered silently, as she stared at Taurian, waiting for a reply. Taurian looked her up and down, a slight smirk beginning to form on his annoyingly handsome face.

160

"I'm sure you know why you're here," he purred.

"Because Dante screwed you over, obviously." The smirk widened.

"Come now, Red. Do you...?"

"My *name* is Adelaide!" she barked.

"See, that's the warrior's fierceness that I admire so much," he said, nodding in approval. His mental undressing of her slim-but-curvy figure continued without pause. A cold sensation of foreboding started to spread through Adelaide's chest. Yes, maybe she was starting to figure out why she was there. She'd never known him to be this... *creepy* before, but it made a certain kind of sense.

"We are to be married," announced Taurian, with all the gravity of a man heralding his deity. Everything became hideously clear, and Adelaide felt faint.

Trying to keep calm and stay partially sane, she asked, "What are you talking about?"

"Don't deny you want me. I've seen you watching me."

"That doesn't matter. I might have contemplated hooking up but sure as hell not marriage. I'm not the marrying type," Adelaide informed him.

"Hooking up? What is this 'hooking up'?" Taurian asked, frowning in her direction.

"You know, big guy, doing the horizontal tango, making whoopee..." When he kept giving her a blank look, she said, "Sex. Do you know what that is?"

"Of course," he said, understanding dawning on his face. "I will gladly have sex with you. You're a warrior, I'm a warrior. You beat one of my ships..."

"But it wasn't you," she said desperately.

"Doesn't matter. It confirmed you were worthy," he said moving closer. She scuttled farther back but was impeded by a storage unit.

"Worthy! *Worthy?* I have to be worthy to marry one of you?" she demanded.

"Not one of us, me," he said, thumping his chest. "And I have to ensure that my bride can survive our planet and culture."

"I'm not marrying you," Adelaide protested.

"You will change your mind once we reach our destination. There'll be plenty of time to convince you."

"Where are we going?" she demanded. "To Raau?"

"You'll see."

"What the hell was with the tracker?" Adelaide demanded her hands resting on her hips glaring at Taurian. He smirked at her and tried rubbing her arm but she jerked away.

"I wasn't sure if you would find it. Where is it?" he asked.

"Somewhere safe so I can dissect it."

"Maybe I should search your ship. I don't want you duplicating our technology."

"You stay away, or I'll shoot your ass," she snarled. Adelaide tried to step around his large body — *dumb mistake*. His hand snaked out, wrapping around her arm and yanking her against his hard, unyielding form. Before she could utter demands of release, his mouth descended on hers. *Oh, man, she hadn't been kissed like this in a long time,* she thought. Her traitorous body was setting off fireworks. Adelaide finally wrenched her mouth away and punched him. His only response was an I-told-you-so smirk.

"I'll have the guards take you to your quarters," Taurian announced.

"I want to stay with my brother."

"You can see him when we arrive," he stated, opening his door and motioning some guards forward. She tried ignoring them, but they led her next door and pushed her in.

"Enjoy," they said, and the door closed with a resounding thud. *Crap, was she in trouble.* How in the hell was she going to get out of this? Adelaide moaned as she collapsed on the bed. They had to escape. Wherever the final destination was, more than likely, they would be separated. Gil really needed to initiate contact, because her translator chip couldn't.

She paced back and forth for awhile in the room, then decided to snoop. She opened all the drawers and cubbies, but there was nothing. Of course, she couldn't be that lucky. Finally, because of sheer exhaustion, she fell into a deep slumber on the beautiful, comfortable, bug-free bed.

* * *

The quick stop of the ship startled Adelaide awake. She sat up, rubbing the sleep from her eyes, her mind already running a mile a minute. If they could somehow escape while leaving the ship, Gil could pick them up. As the guards led her towards the door, they met another set who were pushing Dante towards her. He stumbled and looked at Adelaide with red bleary eyes and a white face. She could see the tremors that moved through his body. Dante held his hand against his side. She could partially see the bandages, and they were soaked in blood. Hopefully, he could still aid in their escape. They stepped out into a very hectic space station filled with hundreds of Tu'Val. She looked over at Dante, trying to get his attention, but no luck.

"Where's Taurian?" she asked. The men grinned and laughed.

"You missing him already? He will like that," one of them responded. Dante sent her a glare, but she ignored him.

"No, just wondering where your fearless leader is."

"He's completing docking procedures, but he will meet us on the planet."

Good, maybe they'd have a chance, she thought, trying not to grin.

The shuttle ride was short and the doors opened to bright sunshine. Luckily, the shuttle only contained them and their guards — *no problem*. This time, Dante was watching, and she nodded before spinning to her first victim. She had him incapacitated, before the others could react, and attacked the second guard. He was more prepared but didn't last much longer. Dante knocked out one guard, but the remaining man levelled his blaster in their direction, a grin on his face. *Idiot,* she thought, *the guard was enjoying this.*

"What is your plan now?" Dante asked with a grimace, his hand pressed to his side, trying to hold back the dripping blood. They needed to get out of there before Dante's body was drained.

"To disappear," Adelaide said, whipping out one of the guards' blasters from behind her back and shooting the remaining guard in the leg. As he collapsed, she ran forwards and kicked him in the head. "Let's go, Dante." He gave her a weak grin and picked up a blaster.

"Ready."

They ran for a grove of trees approximately 100 feet away from the buildings. About halfway to their destination, a siren sounded from behind them.

"Hurry, Dante!" Adelaide urged, glancing back and watching as he struggled to keep pace. He fell to his knees gasping for breath. If possible, his face had turned whiter, and his grip loosened on the blaster. He looked like a zombie. Adelaide spun and grabbed his arm, pulling him along, watching as their captors gained on them.

"Adelaide," a voice whispered.

"Thank god, Gil. Where are you?"

"Keep running, I'm by the trees."

"Move it Dante, Gil is up ahead," she encouraged him.

"How do you know?" he asked, looking at her in surprise.

"Don't worry, just hurry, and I'll catch up."

"You sure?" Dante asked, stopping to observe Adelaide, as she hunkered down behind a large boulder.

"Go now!" she demanded, waving him away, her attention already on the people coming after them. Adelaide heard Dante scamper away and breathed a sigh of relief. This was just like the good old days. She may be sick and tired of war, but there was no denying the excitement and adrenaline pumping through her right now. The prickly underbrush was hardly noticeable, as she sighted on the incoming threat. The idea was just to slow them down. She didn't want to kill any of them. An unwelcome thought popped into her head — *one of them could be Taurian. Damn it, why did that give her a little thrill?* It was no big deal that a gorgeous barbarian wanted to marry her and was fighting to keep her. She couldn't fathom what was so special about her that he'd go to these lengths. Adelaide shook her head and fired at a boulder close to the approaching Tu'Val, causing an explosion of rocks to rain down. She grinned as their expletives reached her ears.

"Adelaide, I have him, now get your ass back here," she heard Gil say through her comm. She fired one more warning shot and sprinted towards safety. Then, a shower of sparks fell over her, and she heard a shout.

"Adelaide, stop! You're surrounded," yelled Taurian. She took a few tentative steps forwards. "I'll let Dante and Gil escape unharmed," he offered. *Damn it*, she thought. "Not sure how your Gil found you, but nevertheless, they can leave," he continued.

Adelaide slowly dropped her arm, and Taurian's men rushed forwards.

"This will be the perfect match, Red," Taurian declared, as he strode up and tenderly stroked her cheek.

*   *   *

Adelaide was led to a waiting shuttle. Thank goodness for air conditioning, because her clothes were sticking to her like a second glove, and she swore they would have to cut her out of them. Looking over at Taurian, she figured he would find that a very enjoyable task. There had to be some way to still escape, or at least fix it afterwards. *Did the Tu'Val ever divorce?* There was never a reason for her to research that topic before.

Staring out the window, Adelaide watched tree after tree fly by. She couldn't deny it was a beautiful planet, so much green and life everywhere. There was a constant buzzing pain in her head as Gil tried to reach her, but answering him wouldn't be a good idea at the moment. Her concentration was shot, and she'd have to speak out loud.

They arrived at an impressive home.

"Where are we?" Adelaide asked, gazing around in awe. The house was massive, with a sprawling yard full of trees and plants.

"My home, our home now," Taurian said proudly, walking down the marble path to the front doors.

"Your smuggling must be very profitable."

Taurian laughed as he answered, "That's just for fun. I'm the commander of the Raau fleet." Adelaide felt her cheeks warm, and her mouth dropped open. *Holy crap!* she thought. Her soon-to-be hubby was a big uppity up. "You will be introduced to the staff later," Taurian continued. "Now, the guards will take you to your room."

*   *   *

Adelaide's room reminded her of pictures of houses of the rich and famous. She was almost afraid to touch anything for fear of breaking it. *Maybe that would be a good thing,* she thought. It would show her displeasure at being kidnapped. Her whole house, which was nothing to sneeze at, could fit inside this room. A huge bed sat in the middle of the room, with a canopy hanging above it. One corner housed a large dark wood desk and chair with a door to one side that appeared to lead onto a balcony. The other side of the room was covered in drawers and closets with another door. Adelaide heard the lock click, as she wandered the room, looking for an escape. Swinging open the balcony door, she peered below. The drop would probably kill her — *too bad.* The other door led to a bathroom with no window. Collapsing on the bed, Adelaide stared at the ceiling and contemplated her dilemma. She couldn't have picked better scenery to be trapped in, and their people weren't so bad. It was just the whole *forced marriage* thing.

"Adelaide, are you alright? Answer me," her brother practically yelled in her mind. She clutched her head and moaned.

"I'm here, and I'm fine. I couldn't talk before. They took me to Taurian's to prepare for the wedding."

"What?"

She sighed.

"Yeah, he's decided we're the perfect match."

"We have to break you out."

"No. You can't fight the whole planet. Do you know who Taurian is?"

"No, why should I care?" Dante asked.

"He's the commander of their fleet."

"Crap."

"Just keep contacting me. I'll try to figure something out."

"When's the happy day?" Dante joked after recovering from his shock.

"Haven't been told. Hopefully, I'll know soon."

"Okay, I'll contact you in the morning."

Someone knocked, and Adelaide answered, "Come in."

"Hello," said a female Tu'Val, likely a servant. "I've brought you some appropriate clothing from the commander. He thought you would be more comfortable in these garments."

"Did he?" Adelaide said sarcastically.

"Of course," she gushed, not understanding the tone. "He's very thoughtful, the best." The woman laid the clothes down and began hanging them in the closet. They were colourful, and skimpy in Adelaide's opinion, but ideal for this climate. There were various strapless tops and matching skirts. Of course, pants or shorts hadn't made the cut.

"I will be back in two hours to escort you to the dining hall," the woman said and left. Before the door closed, Adelaide caught a glimpse of her guards standing at attention on either side of the entrance. She contemplated whether attending the dinner was worthwhile, but in the end, she couldn't deny her stomach. It would also give her the opportunity to snoop around and get some answers. Maybe there'd be a chance to breakout. She could hope.

Chapter 12

The dining hall boasted a vaulted ceiling, with
multiple murals painted all the way to the top,
many depicting naked males and females. When
Adelaide had first looked up, her cheeks had
warmed and turned red, and she'd quickly looked
away. Taurian had chuckled, making her clench
her teeth and glare in his direction. Their table
sat at the front of the room, with them facing the
fifteen other tables scattered throughout. She
watched as the guests wandered into the hall, all
of them acknowledging Taurian first before
sitting. The other females wore skimpy silk
dresses and had plenty of jewellery adorning
their bodies. The males wore their usual tight-
fitting pants and no shirt, with their swords
strapped to their backs. She was finding it
difficult not to stare with all the eye candy
surrounding her.

Taurian growled low under his breath,
reminding her that, of course, the best was
sitting right beside her. *Was he jealous?* she
wondered, glancing at him from under her lashes.
Streams of servers stepped into the room

carrying trays loaded with delicious-smelling food. She didn't recognize most of the items but was willing to try them. She need to keep up her strength for what was to come. *Yeah right*, she snorted. *She just loved to eat.* Taurian looked at her questioningly, but Adelaide just shook her head, reaching for one of the dishes.

Supper was a long, drawn-out affair with multiple courses and no answers. Adelaide had satisfied her hunger — *man was she full* — but nothing else. She shifted uncomfortably in her chair under all the scrutiny from the guests and staff. It had been tempting to wear her own clothing, but she had felt disgustingly sweaty, and while she was in the bath, her clothes had disappeared. The new clothes were the right size, and she didn't want to ask how Taurian knew. But, man, did she feel naked. As she moved again, pulling down her skirt, Taurian looked over with a smile that warmed her insides and promised heaven.

"I want some answers," Adelaide whispered, leaning over.

"We'll adjourn to the sitting room and discuss the details of the wedding."

Not likely, she thought, staring out into the crowd.

* * *

Adelaide wandered the sitting room, gazing in admiration at the different weapons hanging on the walls, wishing there was time to experiment. She eventually sat on the couch and waited for

Taurian to begin. Adelaide was just beginning to relax, and she jerked awake when Taurian finally spoke.

"Our wedding will be in two days," Taurian said, watching her.

"That quick?" she asked fidgeting. That wasn't much time to devise a plan and execute it.

"Why wait?" he asked. Taurian began discussing the arrangements, and Adelaide just agreed to everything. She didn't plan on attending and didn't care what was involved.

"I need to sleep," she said finally, standing up.

"I'll walk you," Taurian said, stepping up to her, as she shook her head. "I don't want you getting lost," he insisted smirking.

Taurian placed his hand on her bare back and guided her through the house. Heat slowly radiated from his fingers and made its way throughout her body. When she tried moving away, Taurian followed. Adelaide heard his chuckle and resisted the urge to spin around and tell him what for.

"I look forward to our wedding night," Taurian said.

Adelaide mumbled as she stared at the guards, trying to be inconspicuous. Taurian tipped her chin upwards and leaned in for a long, slow kiss before pulling away.

"Night, Red," he whispered, then walked away. She gawked at him for a moment, before glaring at the smirking guards and slamming the door behind her. The lock clicked into place, and she swore at the door.

Sleep beckoned but fleeing was top priority. She could nap afterwards. Adelaide searched through her new clothes for something more appropriate to run away in. It was a godsend that their culture had something similar to undergarments. There would be no commando for her. Especially with these dresses or sarongs. She pulled on a top similar to one of her sports bras and a skirt that reached her ankles. The split up one side made it better for movement, so hopefully, it wouldn't impede her escape. Her captors hadn't left her any footwear, which was going to really suck. So, instead, she grabbed the darkest skirt from the closet, ripped it into strips and wrapped her feet, leaving her toes free. The remaining strips, she stuffed into her waistband for later, and then she flipped through the rest of the clothes for anything that could hold liquid. Eventually, she spotted a blanket that could be useful and ripped off a piece of the shiny, plastic-looking fabric. She pulled the corners together, filled the pouch up with water from the bathroom and waited. When no water leaked out, she grinned in triumph and tied the top, attaching the pouch to her waistband.

The next step was finding a weapon. The only things remotely useable were some lovely, intricately carved golden candelabras. Taking out the candles, she twirled the two rods and grinned. They would work. The plan would be to get away and wait till Gil contacted her in the morning. It would be almost impossible to break through the door, so over the balcony it was. Adelaide grabbed the bedding and began twisting and knotting the blankets. Hopefully, they would get her close enough to the ground to jump without breaking anything. She kept glancing to the locked door, expecting a visitor to disrupt her plans. Once her rope was finished, she slowly opened the balcony doors and peered into the darkness. Voices echoed in the evening but were far away enough not to hinder her descent into the unknown. Adelaide tied the rope to the balcony and threw it over the railing, praying it held.

The drop looked about fifteen feet, which was doable. She slipped the makeshift weapons into her skirt and began lowering herself, dropping to the ground in a crouch and jarring her knees. Grimacing, Adelaide glanced around, ensuring no one was there before she slunk to the back of the house and froze. She'd need to sprint across the open yard to reach the wall surrounding the property. Looking around again, Adelaide saw nothing, so now was the time. With her body low to the ground, she moved quickly across the grass, towards her freedom.

"Rjutu etu pau haomh?" Adelaide heard, just before she reached her destination.

"Damn it!" she said, standing up and pulling out her candelabras. "I'm leaving."

"I don't think the commander would like that," answered the closest Tu'Val. "You're surrounded. Give up." Adelaide twirled her batons.

"Are you sure?" she asked, peering into the darkness for more bodies.

"Pud." Five males stepped closer to her. "We've notified Taurian, and he will be here shortly." So, she needed to be quick, if escape was going to be possible, and get away before Taurian arrived.

"Come and get me boys," she goaded, grinning like a maniac. Adelaide didn't recognize any of the men from the landing party. Good, they wouldn't expect her skills. They were grinning as well, *but not for long,* she thought fiercely. Adelaide began twirling her rods, and she tracked their movements as two Tu'Val slowly stalked forwards. They didn't pull out their weapons, probably in case they damaged her — *not likely*. At least it evened out the odds. The fight began in earnest. She cleared her mind and let her body move in one continuous, fluid motion. Before she knew it, five guards lay prone on the ground. Adelaide dropped her rods, grabbed a sword and scrambled awkwardly over the wall. She probably only had minutes before Taurian reached her location.

Adelaide searched in the darkness for any movement, as she ran hunched over towards the trees towering over the rooftops. She reached the first house and spun around the corner, bending over and breathing heavily. There wasn't time to rest. She hobbled quietly to the next street, trying to avoid the few lights that littered the area. The light was a double-edged sword; she could be seen more easily, but her flight was quicker as any pitfalls were illuminated. Yelling could be heard in the distance, and Adelaide tried picking up speed, as her feet protested their treatment against the rough ground. You would think, in this day and age, this city would have the nice, smooth marble streets or pavement that was common on most planets — other than the cobblestone on Earth2, which was worse.

Sweat dripped down her face, and as she reached the forest, the noise of shuttles could be heard right behind her. Adelaide could just make out a multitude of gigantic tree shapes beckoning her to safety. *Crap,* she needed a place to hide, time had run out. With her legs burning, Adelaide frantically searched for a hiding place. She ran further into the trees, then doubled back and scaled a large tree, using her toes to grip the trunk and the hanging vines to pull herself up. The rough bark ripped off some of the skin from her toes, and she grimaced, hoping a trail of blood wasn't following her now. She passed the first couple of thick branches about ten feet off the ground and continued upwards. Exhaustion was about to claim her by the time a suitable branch appeared, and she crawled onto it, trying to control her breathing. Her captors had reached the treeline by this time, and Adelaide prayed they wouldn't spot her.

The men thrashed through the underbrush below her, scanning for tracks, and she could hear swearing as they shone their lights into the black night. The immediate area was illuminated as well as, shining halfway up to her hiding spot. Adelaide tried shrinking closer to the trunk, and as far to the side as possible, without falling off the branch. Controlling her breathing was hard, as Taurian came into view. Even with her skin being rubbed raw by the trunk, she hugged it tighter.

"Is there any sign?" Taurian demanded.

"Ma dot. Jut ytevld zuef gityjut omya yju gatudy."

"Keep going, she can't have gone far."

Adelaide could hear the excitement in his voice, as he faded from sight. Before continuing forwards, they looked up into the trees, but thank god, not high enough. Soon, she could hear their stomping moving farther into the brush, and Adelaide exhaled a groan. Her legs had long scratches running down them, and the fabric on her feet was shredded, but the wrappings had given her some protection, because there were only a few cuts marring the bottoms of her feet. It could have been a lot worse. She unbandaged them and rewrapped her feet with her saved pieces. The used ones were tied to the branch to ensure none dropped to the ground.

Adelaide slowly inched herself up against the trunk and reached for the hanging vines above, pulling them towards her. She sliced off some strips with the sword and sank back onto the branch. Once Adelaide was as comfortable as possible, leaning back against the trunk, she took the vines and wrapped them around her body and the tree. There was no way she wanted to splatter while dozing. As the noises of the search group dissipated, the forest life began to move. A few twitters and chirps came from above and to her right. She was hoping they were herbivores.

Below her, a creature growled, as branches snapped and something scurried away.

Adelaide couldn't stay hiding there for long. Moving farther away from the city was necessary before daylight. But, her body needed rest for a few hours, then she would continue. Adelaide untied her pouch and drank one gulp of water, grateful it had held. From the little she could see, this forest reminded her of the rainforests back on Earth. Only one remained after WWIII and the bombings from the different aliens. Earth's Coalition of Nations had finally realized the importance of the rainforest to the planet, and they'd put in measures to save and protect the last one. Of course, it was too late for many of the creatures and plants that had called the forest home.

* * *

Adelaide ran for her life as a swarm of creatures flew behind her, their noses stretched out in front of them. She could see the shuttle ahead, but the distance between them only grew instead of shortening.

"Wait she called out." But it was to late, as the swarm attacked. They began sucking her blood and she dropped to the ground with a scream.

* * *

Adelaide jerked awake from the nightmare, as a distant howl sounded, and a shiver ran up her spine. *Man, did she hate Zartuth.* The forest was still coated in darkness, but her vision had improved past her hand. A light mist was falling, as she slowly unwound the slippery vines and stood up, contemplating the ground. Longer vines would be required for her descent. Inching her way down the branch, she reached a cluster of vines and pulled. Along with a few longer vines, a lovely little creature came tumbling out, and Adelaide almost dropped her sword as her hand covered the scream that wanted to escape. The furry thing screeched at her as it scurried along the branch out of sight. It had bared its sharp, pointy teeth at her, which she'd been able to see even in the dark. The white teeth had seemed to glow. With her heart beating a mile a minute, she finished with the vines and crawled back to the trunk. After tying her makeshift rope to the branch, she slowly inched down the trunk, holding the vine in a death grip. *So far so good.* She jerked the vine, watching the knot at the top to ensure it wasn't going to unravel. Her descent took a lot longer than her original climb, but Adelaide didn't want any broken limbs.

Reaching the forest floor, she sighed with relief and released the vine, opening and closing her sore hands as she peered around her. It was only a matter of time before the Tu'Val came back to her point of entry, and she'd be caught. *Time to get a move on.* By this time, Adelaide's hair had curled and frizzed up, moving around her face in a red cloud. She growled in frustration, grabbing one of her ties and pulling her hair back.

Adelaide then took up the stolen sword and swiftly moved deeper into the trees, trying to watch where she placed her feet as well as for creatures. Things were slowly coming to life, and she'd catch the occasional movement out of the corner of her eye. For awhile, she was able to follow in her captors' tracks, until they veered back towards the city, and she continued on her own. As much as possible, she pushed the dense foliage out of her way as opposed to chopping things. No point in making a neon sign for them to follow her. Soon, the sun was peeking through the tree canopy, and engines could be heard from above, but the clouds covered the position of the aircraft. *Crap, they had the ships out.*

Yet, she couldn't help but stop and gaze around in wonder. This forest may have been similar to one of Earth's rainforest, but the tree trunks and branches were a dark purple with green leaves, and many of the vines hanging throughout the forest were a bright, vibrant red. The mist sparkled, as it slowly dissipated from the emerging sun. A tangled growth of dense green vines, shrubs and small trees grew along the ground, making her trek difficult to navigate without leaving an easy-to-spot trail. Adelaide swatted at the bugs beginning to swarm and continued on her course, before dropping behind a tree to allow a large creature to pass by, hoping it would pay no attention to her. The thing swatted the smaller, six-foot trees with its two arms like they were nothing, and a few snapped to the ground. Its leathery skin was good protection against this environment. Adelaide massaged her aching feet, while she waited a few minutes for the creature to pass, before venturing out and staring at the two-toed hoofprints it had left behind. She placed her foot alongside a large print and was relieved she hadn't been spotted. The print was twice as long and as wide as her own.

Even with her thin layers of clothing, sweat trickled down her back as she dodged the foliage. *At least the mist had tapered off, leaving only the humid air,* she thought sarcastically, trying to breathe while constantly swiping at the underbrush with her arms. Brightly coloured flowers littered the forest floor, along with green foliage and roots. One particularly large orange flower caught her eye. Its height reached to her neck, with leaves growing along the stalk that were about a foot in diameter. Thin purple veins ran through the leaves. She leaned in closer to see the six-petal beauty, when suddenly, the centre opened and a thorn shot out, penetrating into her neck.

Adelaide screamed in pain, jumping back and swinging her sword. Vines that had originally lain dormant whipped out, wrapping around her leg and yanking her to the ground. As her head bounced over the roots, Adelaide hacked at the vines, eventually freeing herself. A piercing squeal sounded and another thorn speared the tree behind her. Hopping to her feet, she swung her sword, chopping the flower off at the stem, and watched it fall. Her neck had already started to swell, and she felt lightheaded. *Damn it,* she thought, grimacing as she pulled the thorn out,

along with bits of her skin. It was barbed all the
way down its three-inch length. *No wonder it hurt
like a bitch. Where the hell was Gil, and why
hadn't they contacted her yet?* she wondered
desperately. Adelaide swayed and took a wobbly
step, before collapsing to the forest floor. She
had the foresight to brace herself with her hands,
so at least it wasn't her face that broke the fall.
What in the hell was in that thorn? she thought,
dragging herself through the underbrush to a
relatively safe-looking tree. If anyone or anything
came upon her at the moment, she was screwed.

"Adelaide?" She felt tears pool in her eyes
as the voice sounded in her head.

"Thank god, Gil. Where are you?"

"Trying to hide above the planet. There are
a lot of ships cruising around right now."

"I'm tramping through the forest at the
moment."

"Great! You escaped," Dante's voice came
through.

"Yes. But not with much. And now I've been
shot with some kind of thorn, and I can't really
move."

"Just a moment," Gil said.

"Not going anywhere," she grumbled.

"Okay, is the plant orange?"

"Yeah, with six petals. It's almost my
height."

"You should be alright. It shoots out
paralyzing thorns, so it can capture and eat its
prey."

"Great. How long will I be stuck like this?"

"It doesn't say."

Adelaide swore as she gazed around, looking for any trouble. The forest all looked the same to her.

"Can you tell me which direction to head? Somewhere the ship can land."

"I can lead you, but I'm not sure how quick we'll be. We're dodging a few ships. They know we're out here somewhere."

"I don't know why the hell Taurian is trying so hard. I'm not that special," she grumbled. "Do what you can," Adelaide said, as her legs began to tingle. Thank goodness, it felt like the paralytic was wearing off.

Adelaide pulled out her water pouch and took a few gulps, swishing it in her mouth before swallowing. The two suns rotated around Raau in opposite directions. They passed each other at midday, in their highest zeniths. She estimated there were a few hours till then. Something thrashed in the bush behind her, and Adelaide attached the sword to her belt before half dragging herself and half crawling around the tree as quietly as possible.

"Where the hell is she?" a male Tu'Val growled, stomping to a stop in the clearing. She held her breath, trying not to fidget.

"Why would he go to this much trouble for a female?" the other asked.

"Don't know, and don't go asking him that, either."

"Why?"

"I heard Shamon questioned him and was sent to the infirmary." They both chortled while searching the area.

"Check this out," one male said, and they both leaned down, staring at the chopped off flower.

Crap! Adelaide swore silently, as she peered around the tree. Standing up may be an easier task now, but not fighting.

"This looks cut. She's been through here and may be down for the count as well."

"What was that?" the other asked, as a rustling came from their right. Both males whipped their swords out and slowly moved farther away from her position. A roar sounded, then an animal leapt forwards, knocking both of them down. With one swipe of its massive claw, the creature ripped out the throat of one male and then circled the other, who had managed to rise into a crouch. Its sleek black body was five feet tall and just as long, with muscles rippling under its skin as it stalked its prey on four legs. They circled one another, looking for any moment of weakness. The creature's tail, which was covered in spikes, swiped at the man, who barely jumped back in time. He growled a challenge, raising his sword and swiping it in a large arc. The thing opened its mouth, answering with a roar, and leaped at him.

Adelaide covered her ears, watching its powerful back legs bunch before jumping. To her astonishment, a large pair of wings opened, and the creature took to the air. They had blended in so well with the body that she hadn't noticed the wings before. As they battled, Adelaide searched for her escape route. If she didn't move now, the opportunity could be lost. Placing her hand on the trunk, she slowly stood, keeping an eye on the creature. Her body was beginning to respond to commands, as she hobbled quickly in the opposite direction. Good thing she didn't have to try to go around them. A hoarse scream and then silence made her freeze in her tracks. A thread of fear wove its way through her tired, sore body. After what seemed like hours of listening to the chomping, she continued on, offering up a prayer to anyone listening.

The longer she trudged, the more her body became hers again. Adelaide frowned, as her stomach growled, and looked around. There were trees as far as the eye could see. The suns were just passing one another in the sky, and the heat was stifling. A gurgling sound caught her attention, and she cautiously followed the noise.

"Thank goodness!" Adelaide said smiling, staring at the stream running along under the bushes. She eagerly knelt and splashed her face and neck, before drinking deeply from her cupped hands. Now, she just needed to find some food.

"How are you?" Gil asked. Adelaide jumped, fumbling with her pouch and just catching it before losing her water. She was still having difficulty getting used to someone appearing into her head. It was different with the translator chip, which felt like her own brain talking to her. *This was just weird.*

"Doing alright. How much farther?"

"If you keep going at this pace, you should reach the edge of the forest in a couple of hours." She sighed, not sure if it was good or bad news.

"Have you had any problems?" she asked.

"No. We've been orbiting the sun, staying out of their sensor range. Traffic has slowed down, so maybe they've given up?"

"One can only hope. But I don't think so. I just watched two males get mauled and eaten by some huge creature. So, they're still out here," Adelaide said. "Okay, I'll meet up with you guys there," she replied, once Gil had directed her to the best place to land the shuttle.

After resting and filling her water pouch, Adelaide marched onwards through the trees. The air began to cool, encouraging more creatures to venture out, giving her disturbing images. She didn't want to be in this forest any longer than necessary. Finally, the treeline came into view, and she crouched behind a large bush. Peering into the clearing, she saw no Tu'Val ships or soldiers that were noticeable. *So far so good*, she thought.

"We're going to wait a few more hours," Gil spoke in her head.

"Fine," Adelaide sighed. "I'll find a hiding spot. Contact me as soon as you can. Make sure there's food for me," she joked, staring into the stillness, thinking this was just a little too easy.

"What, you don't want to eat any bugs?" Gil laughed.

"If I had to, but I'm glad you guys are here." Laughter echoed in her head, making her smile. *Time to climb again,* she thought, analyzing her options. The trees had significantly reduced in size as she'd neared the clearing. One looked promising a few steps in, and she quickly scaled the tree now that she was a pro. If you could get over the creepy crawlies, the place might be nice. Hopefully, the boys could reach her soon, as the hunger pains were getting stronger and bugs were not appealing in the least.

Chapter 13

"Okay, are you ready to run?" Gil asked.

"I am sooo ready to leave this planet. Hurry!" Adelaide urged.

"We're coming in now."

Adelaide scrambled down the tree and scurried into the clearing, skidding to a halt at the edge. The wind picked up, yanking her hair loose, and she viciously swiped it away from her eyes trying to glance around. The instant the ZOO landed, Adelaide bolted for the opening. Gil appeared and waved frantically for her to hustle.

"Hurry, I think we've been discovered." Apparently, their luck had run out. She continued sprinting all the way to the bridge, with a grinning Gil right behind her.

"What's our status?" she demanded.

Dante turned around from the controls and said, "Glad to have you back, sis."

"Glad to be back. Now get us out of here."

"There are a couple of Tu'Val ships heading our way."

"They shouldn't be a problem," she said, waving her hand dismissively.

"They might not be, but they also have some warships converging just outside our exit point."

"Damn it, why aren't they giving up? We may have to try engaging lightspeed from within the atmosphere."

Gil and Dante looked at her as if she were nuts.

"You've got to be kidding," Dante stuttered.

"Do you have a better idea?" she asked.

"We can out run them?"

"Not sure we could get through their blockade. Once we're far enough from the ships, punch it," she instructed him. Dante stared at Adelaide, before squaring his shoulders and facing the monitor.

"I'll be in the engine room," Gil stated hurrying out.

Adelaide watched as Dante swerved and maneuvered around the ships as they headed out.

"Okay, get ready," she said leaning forwards. Once they passed their pursuers, Adelaide shouted, "Now!"

A shudder ran through Dante, as he leaned slightly forwards and pushed the button. The ship lurched and shot forwards. An explosion sounded behind them, rocking the ship faintly. *Hopefully, those ships were alright,* she thought clenching the chair arms. They were soon far away from the planet, and Adelaide sighed in relief.

"How is your wound?" Adelaide asked, stepping up beside Dante. He lifted his shirt slightly, showing the pink skin.

"Doing alright. The med bot fixed me up."

"I'm going to shower, change and get some food. We'll talk after," Adelaide warned Dante. "Fine."

* * *

The shower felt heavenly, even if it was just the dirt-eating gel. After eating, she'd stop at the medical bay for a pain strip to help with her aching muscles. With her favourite tank top and shorts on, she headed to the galley. Gil and Dante were waiting, with a tray sitting in front of them.

"We have your favourite food," Dante said with a grin.

"Thanks guys!" Adelaide said, sitting down and pulling off the lid. She couldn't contain her screech, when the large bugs scurried to the edge of the plate. Gil and Dante broke out laughing, until tears streamed down their faces.

"What the hell! Where did these come from?" she demanded.

Dante stopped laughing enough to answer, "Your replicator is surprisingly good. We figured you missed eating on the planet…"

"Get out, before I shove these down your throats," Adelaide threatened, pushing the tray away and trying to keep from grinning. Gil grabbed the tray and carried it to the compactor and then left the room with Dante. Both men grinned back at her and bumped fists before turning the corner. It was nice to see them getting along for once. When she was alone,

Adelaide chuckled and ordered some more substantial food. *Man, was she glad to be back.*

Adelaide wolfed down her food and then went to have the med bot check her out. She was having slight pains when breathing. She was sitting on the med table, when Dante walked in.

"Have you heard anything more from Axis?" she asked him.

"There's now a price on my head," he said sourly.

"Crap. That'll make things more difficult. You'll need to stay hidden."

"I'm not hiding like a little girl, no insult intended."

"Well, I am. You've no right to talk, with the decisions you've been making lately. You're staying hidden, because I don't feel like getting in the line of fire again. Look where I ended up." Dante shut his mouth looking sullen, and Adelaide continued, "Where can we find Axis?"

"He's usually on Zartuth."

"So, he's mad about the profits he lost, when you disposed of the drug?"

"Also, the hardship of controlling the slaves," he grimaced.

An idea was formulating and she grinned.

"I have another idea. You're going to contact him and say you want to make up for your blunder."

"No way in hell! He'll kill me," Dante protested.

"No, he won't. You're very apologetic and will do anything he wants."

"Why?"

"Because we're going to stop him. I'm sure the authorities would love to have him in custody."

"How will that help me?" he demanded.

"Because he won't be around to pay the price on your head anymore," Adelaide said smiling.

Once Dante agreed to contact him, Axis responded in record time, surprising Adelaide. Dante arranged a meeting on Zartuth with her standing behind him, threatening bodily harm. There was no way Dante would have gone through with it otherwise. She insisted the meeting would be at Narwhal Tavern. It would be idiotic to let Axis choose the location. Afterwards, Adelaide walked to her room and collapsed. The last few days had taken their toll on her, and sleep came swiftly.

*   *   *

Adelaide jerked awake. In her nightmares, she'd kept watching Dante get shot over and over. There hadn't been anything she could do. The face of his killer was fuzzy and had morphed into someone unfamiliar. She swung her legs over the bed and leaned forwards, breathing deeply.

"ALICE, how much farther till Zartuth?"

"Approximately two hours."

Well, no point in going back to sleep, then.

"ALICE, pull up everything you have on Axis and send it to my monitor." Adelaide stood up and paced around her small room until she heard beeping. Scooting to her bed, she swung the monitor around and perched on the edge of the bed.

"This is it?"

"Yes."

"Well, damn."

There wasn't enough information to cover a full page. He had originated from a planet bordering the edge of their solar system. Axis had dropped off the radar until this past year, popping up as the leader of a new faction on Zartuth. Then, there were plenty of incidents of piracy, smuggling, murder and other deviant acts. It seemed like several different governments had been trying to capture him for awhile. Now, she just had to figure out her plan to ensure Axis didn't escape. Adelaide's mind wandered to the whispers of war. Her curiosity was now piqued about the Cradesions, and she remembered the conversation she'd overheard on Gaeaf. Since they were heading to Zartuth, maybe a quick detour was in order.

"ALICE, change direction to Biyaha."

"Arrival will be in three hours."

"Good." There was plenty of time to check out the location and still make it to Zartuth before the meeting.

To kill some time, Adelaide paid a visit to the gym. Exerting some energy would hopefully tire her out enough for a quick snooze. Adelaide decided to do a little Wado kai. Going through her katas, she soon had sweat pouring down her body. The familiar moves relaxed her, hopefully enough to crash. Adelaide was bent over breathing heavily, when the door slid open and Dante stormed in.

"Where the hell are we going?" he demanded.

She slowly lifted her head, wiping the sweat from her eyes.

"I'm doing a little investigating," she replied.

"Why? You made me arrange this meeting. We can't miss it." His voice had slowly risen an octave as he spoke, and he paced in front of her.

"Calm down. I've been hearing mumblings about a fleet amassing. We have time."

"I'd better not be late," he warned her, before stomping out.

Adelaide shook her head. The meeting was scheduled for 1700 hours Zartuth time. She wanted it right at dusk, so if escape was necessary, the wildlife would hopefully slow down the pursuit. There was plenty of time to satisfy her curiosity and make it back in time for their rendezvous.

Chapter 14

"Captain, we will be arriving at the specified location in ten minutes," ALICE announced.

Adelaide slowly rose from her bed and grabbed a black jumpsuit. Hopping around, trying to pull her one leg through and then the other, she stumbled against the bed and stubbed her toe. Grimacing in pain, she quickly zipped up and hurried through the corridor to the bridge.

"ALICE, display." The screen flashed, and then she could see the vast expanse of space in front of them.

"The destination is set for the Outer Rim, near the planet Biyaha."

"Have you picked up anything on the sensors yet?" Adelaide asked.

"No, I am monitoring the area."

"Continue on course, but slow to one-quarter impulse. I don't want to be detected."

Adelaide felt the ship slow, and she continued staring at the screen. Biyaha slowly rotated, and the multiple water sources on the planet's surface became evident. That she knew of, Biyaha wasn't inhabited by any lifeforms. With the planet's surface around 90% water, only a few creatures had managed to survive, and they were microscopic.

"Captain, I'm detecting multiple ships. They are Cradesion warships."

"Crap!" Adelaide muttered, tapping her fingers on the armrest. "Are we close enough to calculate their numbers?"

"Not yet."

"Proceed with caution. We want to stay out of their sensor range." Adelaide was thankful that, with the computer and weapons upgrades the ZOO had received, she had ensured their sensor range was increased. She only hoped that the new sensors would be better than what the Cradesions had, which would make them worth the exorbitant amount she had paid for them.

"Yes, Captain." Moments later, ALICE announced, "There are 100 ships."

Adelaide swore and ordered, "Get us out of here. I'll send a message to the members of the Accords and our military. They need to be warned."

The ship slowly reversed and changed direction for Zartuth. Adelaide pulled up communications and wrote a brief message. Someone needed to be sent on a reconnaissance mission to determine what threat the Cradesions posed. The trip to Zartuth would only take an hour, so Adelaide didn't have much time to finish planning. She needed to put aside the worry of an impending war and concentrate on saving Dante's ass.

As Zartuth came within range, Dante walked onto the bridge.

"Find what you were looking for?" he asked.

"Yes, but it's not good." Adelaide didn't elaborate, and Dante didn't question her any further. He paced behind her chair until she was tempted to yell, but instead she said, "Once we reach Zartuth, I'm going planet side to do some reconnaissance before the big meeting. I want you here on the ship until the last possible moment. No point in giving Axis any more chances at doing you bodily harm."

"Fine. You'll keep me informed?"

"Of course. You just be ready for the performance of your life."

"Who do you think is the best gambler out there," he stated.

She looked at him in astonishment and said, "Not lately. That's why you're in this mess." Adelaide looked back at the controls but didn't miss the finger Dante flipped her. She slowly pulled into the space station and stopped inches from the bay doors.

"Gil, I'm heading to the surface. Keep an eye on Dante and ensure he's on time."

Dante growled at her, "I don't need a fucking babysitter."

"Sure thing, boss."

Adelaide ignored Dante's arguments, as she scanned her chip and then headed to the cargo bay.

"ALICE, ensure we are ready for a quick departure if everything goes to shit."

"Yes, Captain."

Adelaide stepped into the crowd and debated her first move. She needed to gather more intel on their quarry to ensure optimal chances of survival. But, she also couldn't shake the doom that was filling her body. Maybe someone on Zartuth knew about the fleet amassing. She shouldered through a group of Gaeaf females. It was difficult to tell the difference between males and females. The only visual difference was the size and colour of their horns; the females' horns were thinner and blue, while the males' horns were as thick as her arm and green. All the females carried massive swords across their backs as well as side arms. Adelaide found it interesting that so many species still used swords when they were technologically advanced. She'd never seen the appeal of getting up close and personal with her enemy. Give her a blaster any day. On Gaeaf, everyone had been fighting and hunting since they were young. She wasn't sure what their children looked like, as they weren't seen in public.

"Etu pai ytpomh ya vjuey qu?" a Tu'Val yelled at a shopkeeper. A crowd had gathered, and she slowed her pace.

The shopkeeper yelled back, "I'm not cheating you. This is high quality. If you aren't willing to pay, leave," he snarled and grabbed the sword from the Tu'Val's hand. Many of the spectators began betting on the outcome, most in favour of the shopkeeper. The female Gaeaf standing beside Adelaide explained the reputation of the stall owner to her companion. He was massive, and most customers weren't willing to tackle him after the last body had been recovered from his shop.

Adelaide continued on, pushing through the throng, until she reached a stall where she recognized the patrons. A Tu'Val, a human and a Gaeaf were lounging in the back of the stall, enjoying tall mugs of green swirling liquid. *It sounds like the beginning of a joke.* Adelaide snorted as she walked towards them. She knew Arnold from the military and had met the two others through him.

"How's it going?" she asked, grabbing a chair.

"Waiting for some action," Shandu said. The Tu'Val slouched, fingering his sword.

Adelaide shook her head and asked, "Haven't you had enough?"

"Of course not. We need it to survive." The males laughed as she sighed.

"I need some information on Axis. Have you heard of him?"

Three pairs of eyes swivelled towards her.

"Are you nuts?" Arnold asked, scratching his bald head. For a human, he was large, just over six-foot-four.

"You know the answer to that. So, why are you asking?"

"Djud vtacq," Shandu said, sliding his sword into the sheath.

"That's for sure," Arnold muttered.

"No, I'm not crazy. This is just necessary."

"What's going on?" asked Cancho, the Gaeaf male who was scratching his long beard, before taking a swig from the large mug in front of him.

"Dante," was all she said, and the others nodded. "So, what do you know?"

"He showed up here and wiped out the competition in a couple of days," Arnold said.

"All of them?" she asked in surprise.

"Yes. He then set up his operation on the planet, towards the edge of the city," Arnold replied.

"I heard he's nuts," Adelaide commented looking around.

"More than you?" Arnold joked.

"Haha," Adelaide quipped and smacked his arm.

"He'd have to be, if the rumours are to be believed," Shandu said.

"Does he have any weaknesses?" she asked.

"Not that I've heard," Arnold said, as the other two shook their heads in agreement. Adelaide looked down at the mug the shop owner had just plopped in front of her and smiled.

"Thanks," she said and took a long swallow. "I'd better get going. Don't want to be late."

"Be careful, Adelaide. We don't want to find your body," Arnold cautioned.

"Aww, you guys care about me."

"Not really. We just don't want to deal with the mess," Shandu replied. They all laughed as she downed her drink and then headed back to the shuttle.

Time to check out Narwhal Tavern, Adelaide thought.

RAYKAR SPECIES

PLANET: ZACARAN

OVERVIEW:
- Steal and scavenge all their technology. They lived by one rule: "Why build what can be taken from another?"
- Attacked earth in skirmishes over many years. Lost last battle in space surrounding Earth2
- Warrior species, brutal. Mercenaries for hire.

PHYSICAL DESCRIPTION:
Broad shoulders, lean muscles, sinewy arms, strong. Dark green scales. Small black eyes. Small snout (more rounded). Teeth more similar to humans but still pointy. Small spikes down center of head. Large feet with four toes.

WEAPONS:
2 Blasters strapped and crisscrossing across chest

PERSONALITY:
Vicious, temperamental, strong, cruel

If things went her way, the meeting would be quick and painless. She checked her wrist comm. There were still thirty minutes until Gil would arrive with Dante in tow. She had time for a drink or two. Pushing the large heavy door open, Adelaide gazed around the tavern. Dante's description of Axis had been vague at best. No one she could see was even close to it. There were just the usual weird, creepy and unusual customers. Her shoulders began to relax as she sidled up to the bar.

"Can I grab a garpel?" Adelaide asked the bartender. He nodded in her direction, grabbing a short glass. She could see a few smudges on it and grimaced. The alcohol would hopefully kill off anything on the glass. The bartender slid her garpel across the bar, and she picked it up, taking a drink. The liquid warmed her throat on its way down, pooling in her stomach. Smiling, Adelaide turned around and leaned back against the bar.

The dim lights hid the many illegal transactions that occurred in the bar. Laughter rang out on the other side of the room, as two Tu'Val pounded each other's back and swung their swords. Customers scrambled back, not wanting to connect with the deadly blades. Taking another sip, she stared at the door, willing it to open. *Looky, looky.* A man with a sparse head of black hair matching Axis's description strutted into the tavern. Two large Raykar stalked in behind him, their hands hovering over the large laser blasters that were strapped across their broad shoulders. *What the hell were the*

Raykar doing here? she thought, resisting the urge to jump up and slaughter them. They looked just like someone might think a typical alien looked. Their dark green skin rippled like scales, as their sinewy arms swung with their body movement. Their lean muscles were no competition for the Tu'Val, but the Raykar were definitely strong. Their small black eyes surveyed the bar, and their snouts sniffed the air. She couldn't tell if they were tall or if they only looked it because Axis was so short.

Axis himself looked to be barely over five and a half feet, and he was scrawny. She couldn't believe he commanded so many. In the military, it was dangerous to underestimate an opponent because of their looks, but really, him? Adelaide was reminded of a rodent, as she stared at the little black mustache growing under his long pointy nose. When he chortled, his thin lips stretched what little flesh there was over his cheek bones, pronouncing them even more. What made him more interesting, though, were the two antennae protruding from his head, extending 6 inches above his tufts of hair.

The three men pushed their way to a back table, yelling out their drink orders. A server hurried by Adelaide, muttering under her breath. She grabbed the drinks off the bar, slamming them on her tray before stomping to Axis's table. Adelaide watched as one of the goons laughed at the server, slapping her ass. Before Adelaide could move, the server wound up and slapped the Raykar male across the face, swearing at him.

Adelaide couldn't hold in her laughter and turned back to the bar, her shoulders shaking. The door swung open again, letting in another layer of dirt that swirled around and landed on the floor. Gil and Dante stepped in, and she waved them over.

"That him?" Adelaide asked, gesturing to the ass in the corner.

Dante grimaced and nodded.

"Yeah."

"This is how it's going to work. You'll be contrite and ask Axis what you can do to make amends. Agree to anything."

"Are you nuts? I'm not going to agree to anything. What if it's murder?" he demanded.

"You're the second one to call me nuts today," she mused. "And I don't care. We need to get you out of here alive, and hopefully, he'll rescind the contract on your head." Heads were turning their direction. "Crap, let's get over there."

She all but dragged Dante to the table, with Gil following behind them.

"Well, look who showed up." Adelaide tried not to smirk as Axis's high, squeaky voice yelled out to them.

"Hi, Axis," Dante said.

"What do you want?"

Dante fidgeted and looked down. Adelaide elbowed him and whispered an encouraging order in his ear. Axis glanced her direction as Dante grimaced.

"I'm sorry, Axis," he apologized, affecting a contrite-looking expression.

"For what?"

"Losing your drugs. What can I do?"

Axis stretched his thin lips into a slimy grin.

"Well, isn't this interesting," he mused.
Dread was climbing up Adelaide's spine. *Great*,
she thought. "I do have a job where your skills
would come in handy," Axis continued, stroking
his scraggly beard and staring at Dante.

"Well, what is it?" Dante demanded,
straightening up.

"So, anxious. I like it," Axis replied, and his
voice dropped. "On Opica, there is an alien
artifact that is supposedly a deadly weapon. I
want it."

Dante looked at him in surprise and asked,
"Isn't it already being used?"

"No. The locals think it's special and have it
locked away," he snorted. "What idiots. To have
something with that much power and not use it."

Dante looked in Adelaide's direction, before
answering, "Fine. What about the price on my
head? I can't do this if I'm looking over my
shoulder."

"You'll have a reprieve until either I get the
weapon in my hands or you fail. And by the way,
Bravock will be accompanying you."

"The hell he is," Adelaide burst out with a
frown.

"Who are you?" Axis demanded leaning
forwards.

"No one," Dante said, stepping in front of
her. "Do you have any intel?"

"Yes. Bravock will bring it. He'll also be reporting back with your progress or lack thereof."

"Fine," Dante agreed. "We'll leave in a couple of hours. Tell him to meet us on the station." Dante turned and walked away. Adelaide muttered as they left, barely noticing the nod Axis gave to the other patrons, who then backed away, letting her party go unmolested.

"This isn't good, Dante."

"You said anything."

"Not that. His stupid goon watching us. I'll have to change my plans. Have you heard of Opica?" she asked.

"Vaguely. It's an average-sized planet. From what I've heard, the natives refused space travel, because it might offend the monkeys they worship, who can't fly. Sometimes, they'll trade with passing ships, but they aren't overly friendly."

"Worship how?" Adelaide pressed.

"They leave them tributes. I'm not sure how accurate this is, but sometimes that includes people."

"Great." She swore a few choice words. "We'll be travelling with a spy in human-eating monkey territory. It's getting better and better. How far away is it?"

"I think a couple of days."

"Even using a gate?"

"Yeah."

"So, two days there, a few to snatch up this thing, and another two back. Damn it, Dante, I have shipments!" she complained.

"What am I supposed to do?"

"You'll owe me the lost profits. I'll have to find someone to take over the shipments." Adelaide strode ahead, trying to control her anger. Giving in wasn't an option.

The whole time she hadn't heard a peep from Gil. He walked up beside her and whispered, "We could leave him to his own devices."

She sighed, "No. I would love to but, Axis would kill him. Ensure everything is locked up, so Bravock can't enter any important rooms."

"Yes, Captain," Gil agreed.

They were able to reach the shuttle without any attacks, which was a relief.

* * *

"ALICE, we're having company soon. I don't want access to any part of the restricted areas by anyone other than Gil and myself. You know what to do as the deterrent?"

"Yes, Captain. What about Dante?"

"I don't want him snooping around either." Adelaide reached the bridge and headed for the monitor. "ALICE, send me any information on the planet Opica."

Before looking at the information, Adelaide needed to find someone to take her shipments for the next week. There were a couple of cargo outfits she was friendly with, and hopefully, they'd be willing. When all the arrangements were completed, she spent the rest of her time reading. The place didn't sound too bad. No way would she live there, though. Hopefully, the spy had some maps, as she had no desire to tramp around another jungle.

When it was time, she met the men in the cargo bay.

"We're going to be in and out, you hear." They both nodded and followed her out. Only a few people were milling around, and a lone Zartuth male was leaning against a stall, looking out of place. Adelaide made a beeline towards him.

"Bravock?" she asked.

"Yes."

She was surprised Axis had sent a Zartuth to try to keep them in line. They weren't known for their strength or agility. The better for them, Adelaide hoped.

"You have what we need?" she asked.

"Yes." He held up a memory chip.

"Let's go. No point in wasting time."

When they reached the ship, she took the memory chip and said, "Gil, show Bravock to his quarters."

"Sure."

She watched until Bravock turned the corner, before she headed to the bridge. She had a really bad feeling about this. They were probably expendable. Not sure how Bravock expected to fly away from Opica after the mission. Maybe he was getting picked up.

"Let's take off," Adelaide commanded. I'm imputing our new destination."

Once they cleared the station and headed towards Opica, Adelaide pulled out the memory chip from her pocket, turning it back and forth and inspecting it for anything unusual.

"ALICE, I have a memory chip from our guest that needs to be analyzed. Be careful, they may have put a trace or a virus on it."

"I will inform you when the analysis is done."

Adelaide inserted the memory chip. Sitting in her chair, she watched as they flew by various stars and planets, thinking about what their next move would be. Hopefully, they had received some helpful information from Axis. It was bliss for a couple of hours, with no one disturbing her. Then, the computer blipped, and simultaneously, she heard a roar. She jumped up with a grin, leaving the bridge and arriving in the corridor by the engine room. Adelaide found Bravock sprawled on the floor, howling in pain and holding his hand. She started laughing.

"Need any help Bravock?" she offered gleefully.

"What the hell!" he hollered. Gil walked out at that moment giving her a questioning look as well.

"Maybe you shouldn't try to access something you shouldn't. If you need anything, you can use the med bay."

"I don't need it," he snarled, slowly standing up and stomping away.

"Make sure you keep out of my things, or you'll be confined to your quarters," she called after him. Bravock muttered something in Zartuthian and disappeared around the corner. When he was gone, Adelaide and Gil burst out laughing. She bent over, holding her stomach as tears rolled down her cheeks.

"What did you do?" Gil asked.

"I didn't do anything. ALICE has instructions to zap anyone other than you or I who tries to access the ship's computer or any of the storage panels."

"Good one. He's going to be trouble."

"I know. Keep your eyes peeled."

"Will do," Gil replied, heading back to the engine room, and Adelaide went to work out. She didn't know what they would be encountering on Opica, so she needed to be prepared.

Chapter 15

Over the next two days, Adelaide rarely saw Dante or Bravock. They both stayed in their quarters, only coming out for meals. ALICE tracked their movements, sending her updates throughout the day. Not that she expected Dante to do anything to harm the ship, since they were helping him, but he might steal something. She decided it was time for a powwow with everyone. She'd studied the intel from Axis, which was surprisingly detailed. He must have been planning this heist for a while.

They met in the galley. The three of them sat facing Bravock, hopefully as a united front.

"Okay. I checked over the information Bravock brought from Axis. Gil, you'll need to stay with the ship, and we'll retrieve the idol."

"I'm not staying back again, Captain. You need me," Gil argued, shaking his head as Bravock watched them with interest.

"How about Dante stays behind," Gil suggested.

"Sure," Dante agreed.

"No. It's your fault we're here. Fine, Gil, we'll all go," Adelaide relented. "ALICE, show us the maps of Opica." The screen came alive, and a map popped up.

"It looks like we'll have to travel about one day to reach the location, if this is accurate," Adelaide informed them. "I'm not sure the locals will want us trekking through the jungle. The native monkeys are revered, and having us tramp through their habitat could disturb them."

"Screw the monkeys. Kill them if they get in the way," Bravock said.

"That's a good way to get the locals to attack us. We're not killing them," Adelaide disagreed. "I don't think Opica has many visitors, so we'll be questioned as to why we're leaving the ship."

"Why don't we have the ZOO drop us off away from civilization?" Gil asked.

"Bravock, do you know if they'd have sensors?" Adelaide asked.

"I don't think so. They're pretty ass-backwards."

Adelaide glared in Bravock's direction; she didn't like his attitude.

"I wasn't sure either. From what information I could gather, they stay away from most technology."

"What technology do they have?" Gil asked.

"They've accepted a limited amount. Their weapons are still from the stone age, just spears and other handmade weapons," Adelaide said.

"See, they'll be no trouble compared to our blasters," Bravock mocked.

"A spear to the gut will kill you just as much as a blaster," Adelaide snarled. "Enough about killing everyone. It will be a lot quicker if we can avoid a fight."

"I say, let's take a chance and land farther away," Gil said.

"Do you guys agree?" Adelaide inquired. Both Dante and Bravock nodded their heads. "Alright. I'll have the ship find the location that's farthest from civilization and closest to the jungle entry point. Right now, the weather is similar to our fall, so pack for a cold night. Not sure if a fire is going to be possible."

They discussed their options for a bit, then both Dante and Bravock left.

"I wasn't staying back again, Captain," Gil said apologetically. "Not after the last couple of excursions."

"I know, but I wanted you here monitoring our progress from the ZOO in case a quick retrieval was necessary. I'll program the ship to ensure no one can board it. With the upgrades, rescuing us should still be possible."

"You know, one of my shots could go wide," Gil said cautiously, glancing over at Bravock's retreating form. Adelaide smiled.

"It may come to that," she said grimly, then grabbed some food and headed to her cabin for some shuteye.

*   *   *

Adelaide had just finished categorizing the essentials. Most of the food and medical supplies were going with her and Gil. If it were possible to leave Bravock somewhere, she wouldn't hesitate. But, he was in constant contact with Axis, and the end exchange was essential. The military would be at the rendezvous. Maybe the relic would still draw him out, even if she killed his guy, but it would probably mean revenge. She could probably work with that.

While waiting for the others, Adelaide confirmed that ALICE had the necessary instructions to ensure their safety. She was worried about having no one on board, but they'd deal.

"Where is everyone?" Bravock questioned, as he swaggered in.

Adelaide handed him his rations and commented, "You speak English very well, do you have a translator chip?" she inquired, as her own translator chip had already informed her that he was speaking the language on his own.

"I do alright," he replied, not answering her question, as the other two came through the door.

"Here are the supplies. I split them among all of us, in case we're separated," Adelaide explained. "The maps have been sent to your comms. Once we land, arriving at the jungle quickly is important. From what I read, the monkeys inhabiting the jungle might give us trouble, and no, we aren't killing them unless necessary. Keep your eyes and ears open." Everyone nodded and added the supplies to their packs, throwing them over their shoulders.

"We are beginning our descent to the selected location," ALICE said. They all grabbed a handhold as the ship descended. There was a slight lurch as it landed, then the doors slid opened.

Adelaide cautiously stepped into the hip-tall green grass, which covered the ground for as far as the eye could see. A sharp smell, which she couldn't place, reached her nose, making her sneeze. She shaded her eyes from the bright sun, staring into the distance and just making out their destination.

"Okay, boys, let's get a move on. With this grass, we won't be able to hide our movements. ALICE, keep monitoring us."

"Yes, Captain. I will wait for the signal."

They all stepped away from the ZOO and watched it slowly rise then shoot away.

"Where is it going?" Bravock demanded.

"Out of sight," Adelaide said, marching away.

"How are we getting out of here?" Bravock demanded and tried to reach for her arm.

"Don't you worry about it. Your priority is to ensure that we get the idol and survive," Adelaide said, stomping away. The others silently followed. Even with the sun, she still shivered through her jacket. Glancing back, Adelaide saw the fallen grass laying flat behind them and cursed. It was like a big flashing sign saying, "Intruders, come and get us." From what she'd discovered, this location was far enough away from any settlement. *Not that the huge flattened area from the ZOO wasn't a dead giveaway.*

They marched for a couple of hours, before stopping for a rest. The landscape was deceiving;

they looked no closer to their destination then they'd been when they started. Sounds surrounded them, and she was constantly swivelling her head to look for the sources. Adelaide wouldn't be surprised if her neck developed a crick. Rustling and chirping sounded to their left, and they searched the trees, hands resting on their weapons. When nothing jumped out, they slowly relaxed. A power bar was quickly devoured by each of them, and the three humans drank some of their precious water. She was a little envious of Bravock. The Zartuth species didn't rely on water; they didn't need it to survive. Their bodies used other specific nutrients to stay healthy, which were found in many of their foods. When off world, they had to eat a special blend of supplements. Once everyone finished eating, they continued to tramp through the heat. There was no way Adelaide wanted to camp out in the open. She wasn't sure the jungle would be any better, but it did provide some protection. As they trekked, Adelaide thought back to the last time Dante had asked for help. She'd still been in the military, and he'd conned her into meeting on Earth2.

* * *

It was dark and eerie as the wind whipped through the leaves. A whistling sound reached Adelaide's ears, and she pulled her leather jacket tighter. Ahead, Dante waited in the shadows of the trees, shuffling his boots. A small furry red rodent-sized animal chirped, as it ran by her towards its home, making her jump. She recognized her brother's tall, slim figure in his standard jeans and t-shirt that showed his ripped muscles and tanned skin. The breeze picked up, blowing her long red hair around her face. Adelaide muttered irritably, as she swiped it out of her eyes.

"What took you long?" Dante demanded with a frown, as he stepped out of the shadows.

"I had to finish something. What do you need?"

"70,000 credits."

Adelaide gasped and demanded, "Holy crap, Dante! What do you need so much for?"

"Things."

"I need to know what, before I hand over that much. Are you in trouble?"

"I owe it to Tamber."

"Who is that, a loan shark?"

"I had a losing streak, so yeah, he loaned me some credits."

"You need to stop this, Dante."

"I'm a grown man. I don't need your advice."

"But you need my credits?" she stated frowning.

"If I can't get it from you, I'll have to ask Mom and Dad."

"Don't you dare. They don't have that much."

"It looks like we're at an impasse," he said, crossing his arms, with a small smile playing on his lips.

"I don't know how quickly I can get that much," she snarled, pacing with her hands clenched at her sides.

"I can wait a few days."

"Fine. I'll get it, but that's it," she threatened.

"We'll see."

"I'll contact you when I have it," she said, before stomping off.

It was after that incident that Dante began conning their father to start smuggling. The feelings of betrayal and loss were still close to the surface from the memory.

"How much further?" Gil's voice startled Adelaide out of her musing.

"Not much longer," she answered, not even glancing at her comm. The sun was already setting, and she picked up the pace. The sounds seemed to have multiplied, covering the men's stomping. *How could they make so much noise?* she questioned, continuing on silently. They had travelled for four hours when the treeline finally came within spitting distance, and she sighed in relief. Plodding through tall grass and trying to leave as little impact as possible was difficult. Her legs weren't used to this anymore. Military exercises had conditioned her body differently than the training she did now. Maybe she needed additional exercises.

"That sure wasn't much longer," Dante said sarcastically, dropping his pack.

"Oh, shut up," she said. "Gil, do you want to venture into the jungle to see if there is any wood to burn? Don't go in very far." She glanced into the darkening sky with a frown. Opica only had a twelve-hour day rotation. It really sucked for travelling.

"No problem," Gil agreed.

"Hopefully, we can have a little fire. I haven't seen any signs of the indigenous people." She looked questioningly at the others, and they shook their heads. The trees towered over them. With dusk falling, shadows could be seen everywhere, and she couldn't decide if something was alive out there. At least no glowing red eyes were staring back at them. She shivered and hugged her body, watching Gil step into the trees and disappear.

"Let's clear a small area at the edge of the treeline. We don't want to leave visible tracks for someone to find and follow. There could be dangerous creatures or plants lurking on the ground, so be careful." Adelaide had a flashback to the killer plant on Raau and shuddered. Branches snapped nearby, and she hoped it was Gil. Calling out would be a mistake, so she waited for either a scream or Gil to emerge. Dropping her pack, Adelaide inspected the ground with the toe of her boot, pushing anything she found out of the way. Thank goodness, nothing squealed or bit her boot.

Adelaide looked around their little safe haven. The tall grass ended abruptly at the treeline as if someone had come along with a weed cutter, making a straight edge down the length of the jungle. The ground they stood on was covered by dirt, rocks and different types of foliage that she didn't recognize. Adelaide was surprised that dead branches didn't litter the ground. *Was there someone close by that collected them?* She looked around, peering into the coming darkness. Just then, Gil walked out of the trees, and she saw Dante jump.

She grinned and asked, "How did it look?"

"I didn't spot anything unusual, but it was getting too dark to see clearly."

"Okay, that might be a good sign."

They all squatted to the ground, surrounding the meagre wood pile Gil had made. Adelaide threw in a fire block from her pack, which would help sustain it through the night. She aimed her blaster at the bottom of the pile and fired. A glow started to spread, and soon, a small blue-red flame burned, engulfing the offering. They all rubbed their hands together, smiling as the warmth penetrated their little circle.

"We'll need to keep this low," she cautioned. "At least we have the grass and the trees surrounding us. I'll take first watch, then Dante, Bravock, and Gil, you're last."

Dante grumbled a little but made no comments as he opened his pack. The thermal blanket came out first, then the food, which he unwrapped and began munching on.

"This isn't very appealing," Dante complained of his rations.

"It has all the nutrients your body needs to survive, so eat it," Adelaide said and took a swig of her water. She'd never noticed how much Dante whined, or was that just a recent development? He'd always been the cool kid, the tough guy who took care of anything that came up. "I'm going to use the facilities. Be right back."

Adelaide stood up, threw her wrapper in the fire and grabbed some wipes. Stepping into the trees just out of sight from the boys, she stared at the ground hoping nothing would grab her bare ass. Quickly whipping down her pants and squatting, it was only a minute later that she practically ran back to the welcoming warmth. The fire was great, even if two of her companions were questionable. Adelaide didn't want to lump Dante in with Bravock, but he hadn't been much help up to this point. The guys were talking quietly about tomorrow and what could be expected.

"We aren't killing any natives unless absolutely necessary," Adelaide reiterated. Bravock's large eyes stared at her, unblinking, making her want to look away. "Understood?" she demanded, glaring in his direction.

"Fine," he muttered, looking away.

"We'll try getting in and out with the least possible damage. Tomorrow will be an early start."

Everyone shifted on the hard ground, trying to find a comfortable position. Adelaide moved slightly away from the fire, and her eyes slowly adjusted. She could feel the heat warming her back, as she fingered her blaster and monitored the surrounding area. Her gaze would wander back every so often to Dante, and she watched his snoring form. Before showing up at the ZOO, Adelaide's interactions with Dante had been minimal. She recalled an encounter earlier in her military career, when she was home on Earth2 and Dante had frequented it more often. They had met at Narwhal Tavern to discuss a military deserter. Dante had been able to provide information on the possible location of the deserter. Adelaide had drunk quite a bit with Dante, and they both stumbled back to her place and crashed. The next morning, he had left, before she rose with a wicked headache. *He wasn't all bad,* she thought, as she drifted off to sleep.

Chapter 16

"Adelaide, rise and shine," Gil said, shaking her shoulder.

She groaned, as her back protested the harsh treatment. Rubbing the grit from her eyes, Adelaide stood, arching her back until she felt it crack. The place hadn't changed since she'd fallen asleep. A lovely jungle stood in front of them and waving grass behind them. The sun was just rising, and there was a nip in the air. *Thank goodness for the blankets.*

"Any issues during the night?" she asked.

"Nothing," Dante said.

"There was some screeching and a lot of rustling," Gil replied.

"You didn't see anything?"

"No."

"Hopefully, that's good news. Let's erase as much of our presence as we can."

They made quick work of disassembling the camp, then Adelaide pulled up the map on her holodisplay.

"If we follow the map, barring any horrible incidents, we should reach our destination by midafternoon." She should have known not to jinx them.

They walked single file into the jungle with Adelaide leading the way and Gil guarding their rear. She pushed aside a large leaf and ducked around a cluster of green hanging vines. All around, there was movement and noise, making her imagination run wild. She was gun-shy, since her last visit to a jungle. Something buzzed around her ear, and she swatted it, watching as the thing spiralled to the ground and landed on a pile of leaves, under which creamy white objects could be seen vaguely peaking through them.

"What the hell." She came to an abrupt halt. The men almost ran into her and demanded an explanation. "Look down, and tell me that's not what I think it is." They all crowded around and searched beneath the roots and foliage covering the ground.

"Are those bones, as in from people?" Dante whispered, frantically searching around.

They spotted more bones littering the ground, and Adelaide groaned, praying, "Please, nothing horrible. Please, nothing horrible. Hurry, guys, I want to get as much distance from here as possible."

"Maybe, it's a burial ground, and the animals just dug them up," Gil suggested.

"Man, I hope so," Adelaide said. "But, knowing my luck, that isn't the case."

They picked up the pace slightly, but it was still slow going, navigating through the dense brush. The sun barely filtered past the treetops and moving helped hold off the chill. As they moved through the jungle, Dante and Bravock discussed the benefits of Zartuth and where the best places to visit were.

"ALICE, are you monitoring our location?" Adelaide asked over her wrist comm.

"Yes," the voice came through the comm.

"Have there been any problems?"

"No detections."

"How many lifeforms are in our immediate vicinity?"

"Millions."

Adelaide frowned, as a swarm of insects flew towards them.

"Take out all the small ones. How many are two feet or larger?"

"What radius?"

"Two kilometres."

"There are fifty."

"Oh, good. On the one hand, we don't have as many large creatures to eat us. But on the other, we'll be consumed by creepy crawlies," Adelaide said sarcastically, shivering in the chill air. There were a few snorts, and she swivelled around with a glare.

"Sis, are you scared of a few bugs?" Danted teased.

"Damn right, don't you remember the ones from Zartuth? We're not on Earth anymore with the tiny bugs we had there. Gil, have you seen anything behind us tracking our movements?"

"No."

She turned around and continued onwards for about an hour, before changing directions to stay on course.

"I need to stop," Bravock said.

"Why?" Adelaide asked suspiciously.

"My leg is cramping up."

"We've only been walking for a couple of hours. We can't keep stopping, or we'll never make it."

"I'm stopping," Bravock said, stomping over to a log, and collapsed staring at them in defiance. Adelaide glanced over at Gil and motioned slightly with her head. She wasn't sure why Bravock would make a move this quick. She didn't think he could survive here on his own.

"You have five minutes," Adelaide said, "or we're leaving without you."

"No, you won't, and who made you queen?" he said with a sneer.

"Try me. It's my ship, my supplies and my rules," she snarled, pulling out her water canteen and taking a quick gulp before stomping a few feet away.

"You think we're going to make it out of here?" Dante whispered, as he stepped up beside her.

Adelaide looked over at him with a grimace and replied, "I think so. I'd be more confident if that idiot wasn't here."

"Looks can be deceiving," he warned. "But you'll keep him in line," he said with a grin. She smiled slightly and turned around to see Bravock standing up.

"Let's get this over with," he said.

"We're heading south." Adelaide pointed in the correct direction.

"So, why haven't we seen any signs of the indigenous people?" Dante asked, swinging his blaster around as he moved through the trees.

"Watch what you're doing," Gil yelled, ducking out of the line of fire.

"I know what I'm doing," Dante argued. Adelaide shook her head.

"Not sure. It's not like we're really deep into the jungle yet. Keep your eyes and ears open. We'll probably run into something soon," Adelaide replied.

They trudged at a good clip. She found an overgrown path, which was heading in their current direction. This could be the path the guards used. Everyone had been swatting at the flying pests, and Adelaide was sure welts were growing everywhere on her body. She was already beginning to scratch. Hopefully, these creatures didn't inject poison like some that she'd heard of.

"This sure sucks," she moaned.

"Hold up," Gil whispered. They all came to an abrupt halt.

"What is it?" Bravock asked, pulling out his blaster.

"I heard something. How close are we to the target?"

Adelaide glanced down at her compass and map.

"About forty minutes."

"It could be the natives," Dante said.

"Let's go, but be careful. Do you hear that?" she responded.

"What is it?" Dante asked. They all looked up, trying to locate the source of the screeching.

The branches shook, causing falling debris, and they all covered their heads, scooting further ahead and out of range. "Crap, what is that?" Dante demanded, as his shoulder was struck by a falling branch.

"Don't know, don't care. Let's get the hell out of here," Adelaide said, dodging the falling branches and hanging pitfalls. They hurried as quickly as possible. The noises suddenly stopped, and she feared the worst.

"Maybe, that's why there aren't more guards. An early warning system is already in place," Gil said.

"Or, they just keep getting eaten," Bravock said with a nasty grin.

"That, too," Adelaide agreed. "It looks like there's a clearing ahead."

They all crouched and scuttled forwards, peering ahead. Adelaide spotted a large clearing, and at its centre, there appeared to be a stone temple. It rose as tall as the surrounding trees. Moss and vines covered most of the two-tiered structure. The same tall grass they'd already encountered spread across the clearing, just a smidge shorter. Two guards stood blocking the entrance; they looked approximately six and a half feet tall, but what caught her attention were the four arms they each had. Two hands held blasters, and the third held a wicked looking sword, leaving one hand free. Their hair was tied back, falling to the ground in long ponytails. What looked like armor made of skin covered their massive chests and hung partway to their knees. Adelaide shuddered, hoping that it was animal skin. Each of the guards kept watch with a single eye. Something Adelaide had only read about in stories had become a reality. Two cyclops stood in front of her. There was a first time for everything.

"Holy cow!" Gil said, leaning forwards. "Don't know if I want to fight them. We need to get past them somehow."

"Any ideas?" she asked.

"We have blasters. Shoot them from here," Bravock said, lifting his arm and aiming.

"No!" She rammed her fist down onto his arm.

Bravock snarled, "You'll regret that."

"We just need a distraction. Even if one leaves, maybe we can overpower the other."

They volleyed suggestions back and forth, until a plan was agreed upon. Dante stayed behind, and the other three ran along the treeline until they were almost abreast with the guards. They continued a little farther, then stopped and hunched behind some trees.

"ALICE, we found our target, and we're going in," Adelaide informed the ship.

There was some static and then the voice came faintly through the comm answering, "Yes, Captain."

"When the guards leave, we'll make a break for it," Adelaide instructed.

"And if they don't?" Bravock asked.

"They will," Gil said, watching for the signal. It wasn't long before there was a small fire burning across the clearing. Adelaide held her breath and crossed her fingers. The guards shouted, as one of them pointed towards the jungle and took off at a run. *Boy, was he fast*, Adelaide thought.

"Let's go," she whispered and scooted across the clearing with the guys behind her. As they drew closer, Adelaide could see the short light hair covering the guard's body. But the male also seemed to be growing taller, which wasn't good, in her opinion.

The tall grass was both a blessing and a curse at that moment. They all silently dropped to the ground as the guard shifted views, still not looking in their direction yet. Adelaide glanced back and saw Dante catch up with them. She reached the side of the temple and waved the others over. Peering around the side, she watched the smoke rise from the trees, along with multiple flames shooting up into the air.

"How big did you make the fire?" she hissed.

"Not very," Dante answered. "It's keeping them busy." She rolled her eyes and stared at the guard, waiting for a minute before gesturing the others around the corner. Thank goodness, the men were quiet on their feet this time. As Gil ran by, he took the butt of his blaster and rapped the guard on the back of the head, catching him as he fell. They all hurried into the temple, struggling to carry the fallen guard between them. Adelaide pulled out a rope and ripped up her spare shirt.

"Put him here," she whispered, pointing to a dark corner.

"Man, is he heavy," Bravock grunted, as they heaved the body.

Adelaide turned the one-eyed man onto his side, quickly tying his hands together and joining them with his legs. Next, she shoved the gag into his mouth and tied it behind his head.

"Good job," Bravock said sounding impressed.

"Thanks. Let's get this over with and fast. His buddy will be back." She stood up, glancing around her. The stone surrounding them was covered in hieroglyphics. She walked over to the nearest wall and traced the writing. "It's not something I recognize. You guys?"

"No," they answered.

"It appears to be very old," Gil said, stepping up next to her. The ceiling was approximately nine feet high, giving them plenty of room as they investigated.

"Bravock, you stay back and guard the entrance," Adelaide ordered. "Hopefully, we won't be long. Boys, let's go." Adelaide pulled out her blaster and slowly advanced down the tunnel. Lamps were scattered along the walls, casting a faint glow and lighting their way. Carefully placing her feet, Adelaide watched for any traps; there were always traps. Her favourite shows to watch, when she had the time, were the old treasure-hunting movies. Someone always died from a booby trap at the beginning — *not her.*

"Remember to walk in my footsteps," she called over her shoulder. Dust rose from the sandy floor, causing her to sneeze, and the air was stale, which made breathing unpleasant. As they advanced, the tunnel narrowed until she was able to reach out and touch both sides. Good thing she wasn't claustrophobic, but Dante was. His breathing had risen until it sounded like he was panting. "You doing alright back there, Dante?" she asked.

"I'm fine," he almost snarled. "This isn't good," he muttered. Adelaide agreed but didn't respond. Coming to a fork, they halted, debating on which direction to take.

"I'm feeling a breeze down this tunnel," Dante said.

"Maybe it heads to an opening," Gil answered.

"So, we go the other way," Adelaide said and turned towards the darkness. A shudder ran up her spine as she stared into the abyss. There was no telling what was down there. "If this is a temple why aren't there more worshipers?" she asked.

"This could be an old temple. They could just use it for keeping treasures safe," Gil said.

"There might be something to this relic," Adelaide replied thoughtfully. "I sure as hell don't want Axis to get his claws into it."

Dante pulled a flashlight out of his pocket and handed it to Adelaide with a grin.

"Lead the way, fearless leader," he urged. She grabbed it out of his hand and grimaced. A few steps in, she jerked to a halt with her foot still raised.

"Stop, damn it," she yelled, holding up her hand. "There's a wire."

They all bent down, gazing at the trap.

"Should we set it off?" Dante asked.

"No, you dumbass," Gil said smacking him. "We don't know if it'll close off this tunnel."

"They have to have a reset," Dante argued, rubbing his head glaring in Gil's direction.

"Yeah. But we don't have time to find it," Adelaide said, stepping carefully over the tripwire. It was tense for couple of moments, until they reached the end of the tunnel and faced a large wooden door covered in intricate carvings. Adelaide quickly touched the handle and waited. When nothing fell on them, she held her breath and pushed. It didn't budge. "Damn it. Give me a hand."

All three of them pushed against the door with their full bodyweights, and it slowly groaned open a crack. A putrid smell wafted their way.

"Oh my god!" Dante said, holding his nose. "What could that be?"

"Probably a body," Gil said, peering through the crack and trying to see into the darkness. Adelaide tried not to gag as she continued pushing the door open, thinking she didn't want to know. Eventually, the door slid open enough that they could squeeze through it into a large cavern. The ceiling reached towards the sky, and in the centre, was a veritable horror show.

"Holy crap!" Adelaide said, staring at the altar. Dried blood was encrusted down the sides of the waist-high black stone slab. A rotting corpse lay on the top of it. She stepped a little closer and saw a huge, gaping hole where his heart presumably used to reside. Glancing up, she spotted a door on the other side of the room, and Dante headed towards it. As he placed his foot down in front of the door, there was a grinding sound, and the floor sunk beneath his foot.

Adelaide whipped her head around to stare at him and demanded, "What the hell, Dante?" His eyes widened in fear, and he swiveled his head around frantically, looking for the impending danger.

"Drop to the floor!" Gil yelled the instant a small crevice opened in the wall, darts shooting out in every direction. Adelaide dropped and watched from the floor as the missiles shot across the room where their bodies used to be.

"Is everyone alright?" she called out.

Dante groaned in pain but answered, "I'm good. Just banged my knee when I dropped. Is it over?"

"Let's wait a few more minutes."

When nothing else blew up or came out, they slowly stood.

"That was lucky. Thanks, Gil," Adelaide said.

Gil nodded and slowly walked towards the door, staring at his feet. Jiggling the knob, he frowned and announced, "It's locked."

"Shoot it. We don't have any more time," she commanded.

Gil pulled out his blaster, aimed and shot. It made short work of the lock, and he was able to swing the door open. In the back of the small chamber stood a bunch of shelves. There were real books on them, and shoved between the ancient tomes, there was an idol.

"I think I've found what we're looking for" Gil called out. Adelaide stepped up beside him and looked around the room in wonder.

"Books," she said in awe. I haven't seen any for years. Digital is all that's available now." Picking one of them up reverently, she flipped through the pages. "This language looks similar to the hieroglyphics at the entrance. But these pictures are self-explanatory." Sacrifices were depicted in great deal detail within the volume, making her gag. She slammed the book closed with a look of disgust. Beside the vile things stood a stone figurine shaped like a freaky monkey. Nothing seemed special or out of the ordinary about it. "Dante, get in here," she called. Gil moved aside so Dante could reach Adelaide.

"Time for your job. Do you see anything?" she asked pointing to the shelf.

"Move out of the way." Dante inspected the shelves before touching the monkey. "Here goes nothing." He slowly lifted it slightly off the shelf, then waited, nothing. "Grab me a bag." Adelaide pulled a small brown satchel out of her pack and held it open. Dante dropped the monkey in with a grin and twist of his hands.

"Done. Let's get out of here," he said. They got three-quarters of the way to the door, when the room suddenly began to shake.

"Run for it!" Adelaide yelled, hugging the satchel close to her body and squirming through the slim opening. A loud grinding noise filled the chamber, and they escaped just as the door slammed shut.

"Man, that was close," Dante said, bending over and panting.

Adelaide took a deep breath, wiped the dirt from her face and trudged towards freedom. They crept down the tunnel, ensuring the first trap was still set, and cautiously stepped over it again. She pulled out her blaster as they drew nearer to the front entrance and slowed her pace.

"Why are we slowing down?" Dante whispered.

"Because I don't trust Bravock, and I don't hear anything."

As they turned the corner, she spotted the prone figure of the guard. *Was that blood by the body?* She knew it had been a possibility, but she'd hoped it wouldn't happen. Cursing a blue streak, she stalked over to the body.

"Where is he?" she hissed, peering around the chamber but finding no traces of Bravock.

"He wouldn't have just left," Dante said, with a question in his voice.

"No, not if this thing is what Axis claims. I hope the natives didn't come back. Maybe he had to deal with the other guard. Let's go look. I'm not waiting around for him," Adelaide declared. Gil went ahead and looked outside the temple. When no alarms were raised, he waved them forwards.

"I don't see any signs of either Bravock or the other guard. The fire is out."

"This isn't good," Adelaide muttered. "ALICE, can you track Bravock? ALICE? Shit, something's happened. Let's get out of here. We'll head back to the landing area."

They were running at full tilt towards the trees, when a spear landed in front of them, quivering in the ground at their feet. Coming to an abrupt halt, Adelaide glanced around in fear. Twenty warriors stepped out of the trees dragging a tied-up, motionless Bravock behind them.

"ALICE, where are you?" Adelaide demanded in a whisper. *Still nothing.*

"We can shoot our way out," Dante screeched in her ear. "You're a crack shot." She couldn't believe Dante would compliment her only in the face of death.

"There are too many," she replied. "Did you not see how accurate that throw was? I don't want to be skewered. Maybe we can talk our way out of this."

"Probably not, since the idiot killed their friend," Gil stated.

"Thanks, you're a ray of sunshine." Adelaide grimaced, watching as they were surrounded.

Chapter 17

Adelaide was being dragged through the jungle by the ropes tied around her wrists. Her two companions stumbled in front of her, while Bravock was being carried over the shoulder of one of the larger males. Their captors yelled out commands every now and then, but their language wasn't computing with her translator, and she still hadn't been able to contact the ship. There must be a jammer somewhere, which was surprising since no other technology was visible.

"We mean you no harm," she said to the warrior beside her. He glanced over but didn't respond. "Ru zuem pei me jetz," she tried in the Raau tongue. Neither language elicited a response, and she gave up with a grimace. The ropes were tight and rubbed her skin raw. Hopefully, they didn't have far to travel, as the sun was already dropping below the treetops. She stumbled over a root and was yanked up by her captor, pulling on her shoulder painfully. Adelaide choked back a yelp and grimaced at the man.

A clearing came into view, and Adelaide gasped. There were modern houses clustered around a large fire. A few huts made out of wood and what appeared to be mud stood out like sore thumbs. A male Opican stepped out of one of the huts and signaled the warriors forwards. The one beside her began talking and gesturing wildly, before pulling the idol out the bag. A unified scream rose from the tribesmen surrounding them, followed by hissing and what looked like stones being thrown their way. One hit Adelaide on the cheek, and she bit back a yell, feeling along her cheek with her fingers. A few drops of blood dripped down, landing in the dirt. You didn't need to be a genius to figure out what the crowd wanted.

Dante glanced in her direction and said, "We need to escape."

"I figured that much," she snarled, trying not to blame him. *Who was she kidding? Of course, it was his fault, again. When would she learn to leave him alone?* Adelaide wondered. *He was like a fungus that kept coming back.* "Do you understand what they're saying?" she asked.

"No," Dante responded. Their guards yelled something and lifted their fists threateningly.

Adelaide watched as the new man carefully wrapped the idol and carried it into the hut. She wondered if he was the leader — *or maybe a shaman?* Reading about different cultures, she'd noticed many had a shaman or someone similar who guided the tribe. The male had a large headpiece built from feathers and what appeared to be a skull. Hopefully, it hadn't come from a

person. The man's eye seemed to stare right
through her, giving her the willies. One hand held
an intricately carved staff, while his other three
hands were clenched tightly into fists. She
glanced down at her hands and grimaced; his
were twice the size.

They were herded to the other hut, behind
the welcoming fire, and pushed through the hide
hanging across the entrance. Adelaide barely
stayed upright, as she stumbled across into the
small, empty room. Bravock wasn't so lucky; she
watched as he was dropped onto the dirt, but he
didn't move.

"Do you think he's dead?" Gil asked, staring
down at the body.

"Not sure." She bent down and poked his
shoulder. "Bravock," she whispered. The only
response was a groan. Adelaide looked over his
brown body and noticed the many cuts and
bruises already forming. They were going to be
nasty in the morning. Dante moved to the flap
and peeked outside.

"Two guards," he said. "I can't believe they
left us unbound."

"Because we'd have to escape through the
village," Adelaide said, frowning down at the
immobile Bravock.

"Should we leave him here?" Gil asked. "It's
going to be hard to escape dragging his ass." You
could tell there was no love lost there. Adelaide
sighed.

"We can't," she answered regretfully. "We
need to try our escape tonight. Maybe he'll be
conscious by then." Feet stomped by outside the

hut, accompanied by a lot of loud discussion. The hide flap opened, and two males walked in, one carrying a large platter. *Thank goodness, she was starving.* He dropped it the tray on the ground, and they both left.

"Really! What is it with me and bugs?" she demanded, staring down at the offering. At least they seemed to be dead, mostly. She stared in horror at the insects laying in front of her. Adelaide poked one with her finger, and Gil snorted.

"Be my guest," she offered. Gil knelt down and quickly grabbed one, plopping it in his mouth. Adelaide grimaced and gagged.

"How can you do that?"

"Easy. I need to keep up my strength."

"This looks like fruit." She reached for a gelatinous orange mass and shoved it into her mouth, before she could change her mind. There was no real flavour to it, and it slid down her throat.

"Well?" Dante demanded.

"Better than those."

Gil attempted to wake Bravock, but no luck. Adelaide bravely tried one of the bugs and was sure the legs were still kicking on their way down.

"Am I ever thirsty," Dante said, looking around. There was a pile of blankets and nothing else.

"We'll wait till full dark and then try our escape. You guys sleep for a bit. I'll keep watch," Adelaide said, staring at the entrance. "The longer we wait, the weaker we'll be, and the greater our chances of torture or death."

"What! You think they'll torture us?" Dante yelled.

"Shut up! What do you expect them to do with us?" Gil snarled, glaring at Dante. "If you weren't such a dumbass, and Adelaide didn't have a good heart, we wouldn't be in this mess. At least, two of us wouldn't be," he said, gesturing to himself and Adelaide.

Adelaide coughed, trying to cover up her laughter, as Dante opened and closed his mouth like a fish. He then stomped over to the pile of blankets, grabbed one and dropped to the floor. She shook her head.

"Thanks, Gil," she whispered.

"No problem. I don't think I would have helped his ass." Gil gave her a nod, before finding a spot on the floor, and closed his eyes.

* * *

It was awhile before Bravock began moving and groaning.

"Hey, you alive?" Adelaide asked him in a whisper.

"I guess. Where are we?"

"In the locals' village. We're going to escape tonight."

"Good. Did you get it?" he asked.

"Yes. But they took it when we were captured."

"We aren't leaving without it," Bravock stated, shifting on the ground until he was leaning on his elbow.

244

"Yes, we are. I'm sure as hell not looking for it. You can stick around if you want."

Bravock snarled, "Why didn't your almighty ship rescue us?"

"Because I can't make contact. There's something jamming the signal."

"Then, how are we going to be rescued?"

"I'm hoping, if we reach our pickup location, the ship will find us."

"What about weapons?"

"They took them." Adelaide glanced to the door flap. "It looks like it's time." She quietly rose and stepped to the entrance, pushing the hide aside.

Two guards were silhouetted by a large bonfire further into the village. They each held both a spear and a blaster. She gave a start, as they weren't supposed to have any modern weapons. Not that it changed anything, since they still had to escape. She was a little envious — *having multiple arms would be handy in combat, pun intended*. These beings must expect an attack at anytime with the amount of firepower they were carrying. She wouldn't have thought there'd be anything valuable enough here to attack them for. Laughter and music drifted towards them, and she could see figures dancing — was it a celebration? Probably, they'd decided on their fate. Letting the hide drop, Adelaide walked up to Gil and Dante, shaking their shoulders to wake them.

"Rise and shine," she whispered. Gil jumped quickly to his feet, blaster at the ready, while Dante groaned, rolled over and mumbled under his breath. "Damn it," Adelaide swore and lightly kicked him.

"What?" Dante said, grimacing in her direction and rubbing his side.

"Get your lazy ass up. We need to get out of here."

Dante struggled to his feet and glanced at Bravock.

"You're still alive," he commented. Bravock just glared in his direction, as Dante snorted. "What's the plan?" he asked.

"There are two guards outside. I don't see anyone else close. Gil and I will take them out," Adelaide replied confidently. Dante nodded and ripped off a few strips from the blanket he'd been using, before helping Bravock stand and move beside the entrance. Adelaide and Gil moved as one, quietly slipping out the door flap. Luckily, the dirt absorbed the sound of their steps. In one swift movement, both guards were down and dragged into the hut. They put the guards back to back, tying their hands together and gagging them.

"Gil and I will take the spears. Let's go," she said.

"Why you guys?" Dante demanded.

"Because you're helping Bravock, and he's injured." She peeked out the entrance and then waved them through. "Let's make a break for the trees to the left. Gil, go first. I'll bring up the rear," Adelaide whispered.

Gil glanced around before booting it across the open stretch. He could sure move for a guy his age. Dante and Bravock waited for the signal then made their way slowly to Gil. Thank goodness, the bonfire gave off enough light for them to see. Adelaide held her breath until they were safe. *Time to go,* she thought. She crouched and crab-walked towards freedom. Hopefully, they had time to put distance between them and their captors. A couple of spears weren't going to cut it. Luckily, even if communications weren't working, her compass was.

"Everyone good?" she asked.

"Yeah," Dante confirmed.

"We need to head straight," she said, pointing the way.

"It's going to be impossible to see where we're going," Bravock commented.

"We can't have a light, because they'll spot it. The glow from our comm screens will have to be enough. It'll slow us down, but hopefully, it won't matter," Adelaide responded. Holding her arm out slightly, she used the faint light of her comm screen to carefully place her feet. Movement could be heard all around them, and Adelaide tried not to freak out with every noise. The screeching started after they had been walking for about ten minutes. Gil and Adelaide held out their spears, searching for the source.

"I am going to kill those things," she snarled.

"Shit!" Dante swore, pointing above them. They all looked up, staring at the multitude of red eyes glaring back.

"Do we keep going?" Gil asked.

"We don't have much choice. Maybe veer to the right a little," Adelaide said. She was tempted to cover her ears, as the screeching reached a new high. It wasn't long before they heard shouts from the village and saw lights bobbing through the trees behind them.

"I don't think we're getting far," Bravock said, panting as he tried keeping up.

"Don't give up," Adelaide said over the noise. It was like those stupid animals were directing their captors. Soon, about ten Opicans converged on their location. Adelaide almost felt insulted. Did they think so little of her skills and those of her companions? Bravock was recaptured quickly, but the other three put up a good fight. *The trees surrounding them were a godsend,* Adelaide thought, facing another warrior in front of her. She parried the first two swipes of his weapon, successfully ducking closer to his body under the third arm, which was swinging her way, and thrusting up with her spear, hopefully into some vital organ. Her breathing was laboured, as the body fell to the ground and was replaced by two others. It felt like an hour, but it was probably closer to five minutes, before all four of them were shoved to the ground. Adelaide swore under her breath as she was yanked upwards and her arms were twisted behind her. Disgruntled, she agreed that maybe their captors hadn't needed more warriors to subdue them after all. *It was all those arms,* she thought, jealous of the extra appendages.

There was plenty of yelling from the locals and screeching from above. The branches shook from the force of the unknown beings in the trees, and Adelaide shivered, imagining the worst.

"ALICE!" she frantically whispered.

"Wyib iz!" the male said, before cuffing her on the side of the head. Pain exploded in her head, and she stumbled, trying to stay upright. *Damn, did that hurt.*

This time, their captors left all four of them tied up, locked in one of the houses. Adelaide was so tired that sleep came almost immediately.

Chapter 18

A door slammed open, startling Adelaide awake, and she groaned. Her body ached everywhere. Opening and closing her dry mouth, she lifted her gritty eyelids and blinked into the darkness. Two muscled, four-armed males stood outlined in the doorway, and she glared defiantly in their direction. After some discussion between the two, they grabbed Bravock and hauled him out.

"Hey, where are you taking him?" Adelaide demanded. Their response was to slam the door, and she heard the click of the lock.

"What now?" Dante asked, looking defeated.

"I'm not sure. But escape will happen one way or another. If we could discover what's jamming our signal, I could contact the ship. I don't understand why my stupid translator chip hasn't figured out this language yet. They've talked enough around us."

Gil shrugged his shoulders, replying, "Maybe, since it's a completely different language, it takes longer."

"It could also be because it's an older model," Adelaide admitted. "I really need to upgrade it when we return. This shouldn't be an undiscovered language. There have been traders on this planet."

"These people seem quite isolated. Their dialect could be distinctive," he replied. She nodded her head and wished again that one of the others had a translator chip. Since Gil was an engineer, he hadn't required one to work on the ZOO, and of course, Dante believed they were not necessary. He'd learned the one common tongue, and that was it.

In the ensuing silence, Adelaide imagined what was happening behind the closed door, and then the screaming began.

"What the hell is that?" Dante surged to his feet.

"Is that Bravock?" Adelaide asked in horror.

The door swung open, and a guard motioned them forwards with a blaster. It was painful for Adelaide to stand with her arms tied behind her this way. She ended up rolling onto her side and pushing herself up with her elbow. They were led to the centre of the village, towards the loud chanting and yelling. Adelaide felt her body fill with dread, as she peered through the mass of writhing bodies.

Bravock lay naked on the ground, with ropes tied to all four of his appendages. Each rope was held by one of the villagers, and they were slowly pulling him apart. Even at that distance, she could see the fear in his large eyes. No one could stay tough in that situation. It looked like Bravock was trying to hold in his screams, but once in awhile, one would escape.

"What the hell are you doing?" Adelaide screamed. The looks on the faces of the spectators sickened her. It was like they were watching one of their favourite shows. She, Gil and Dante strained against their ropes, trying to reach Bravock. She wasn't sure what they could do, but it had to stop. They all froze in place, when these creatures from out of a nightmare shuffled out of the jungle. She could never look at a cute little monkey the same way. Two of these monstrosities came closer with a loping gait. They were about four feet tall and mostly hairless, with patches of coarse hair all over their bodies. Their molten red skin looked like scabs between the patches of hair, and a long tail dragged on the ground behind each of them. The creatures let out an awful screech, and she could see that each of them had a mouthful of sharp, pointy teeth. The villagers cleared a path for the monkeys leading straight to Bravock.

"I don't like this," Gil said.

Adelaide wasn't sure which was worse, the monkeys' screeches or Bravock's screaming. It was like a train wreck, though; she couldn't look away. With one more mighty yank, there was a horrible wet noise that she didn't want to identify, and Bravock's body pulled apart. The two creatures fell upon his limbs, and Adelaide gagged, turning away. There was cheering from those around her. Out of the corner of her eye, she watched the body parts being gathered up.

Aside from the ones already being devoured, they were carried to a large waiting pot.

"Oh my god. Are they going to cook him?" she asked in horror.

"I think I'm going to be sick," Dante said, bending over and heaving. Adelaide felt the same way but held it in by sheer force of will. She wasn't going to give these monsters the satisfaction. Yes, they had stolen from the Opicans, but the plan had been to return the idol once Axis was captured. They had to escape, and quickly. Although she could turn her head away from the monstrous sight, the munching and slurping sounds couldn't be ignored. It was over quickly, and the carnage left behind by the monkeys was devastating. The bystanders parted like the sea for them to pass through. Adelaide could see the blood coating the monkeys' fur and dripping down their grinning faces. And, yes, she was sure the stupid things were smiling.

"Korl fi," said one of the Opicans. *Thank god*, Adelaide thought. Her translator was finally starting to work.

"I'm not going anywhere with you," she snarled, digging in her feet. The guards stared at her in surprise and then began yelling a mile a minute. Her brain couldn't keep up, and she shook her head moaning. "Not so fast."

"How can you speak our language?" they demanded. She still didn't know all the correct words.

"It's hard to explain," she said simply.

"You will be punished for your crimes," the male growled. "No one steals the Monkey God."

He yanked on her rope, and it felt like her shoulders were pulled out of their sockets.

"We were going to return it."

"No infidel can touch the idol. You have defiled it, and now, we must complete a cleansing ritual."

"What is he saying?" Dante asked.

"I'll tell you later," she said dismissively. "I want to speak with your leader," she addressed the Opicans. Maybe, she could get them to understand the situation.

"We will see if the Holy One is available. Preparations have already begun for the cleansing ceremony."

They reached their prison, and Adelaide renewed her struggling.

"I'm not going in there," she argued.

"You can take your friend's place," he threatened.

"He wasn't my friend." Her struggles lessened, and they were all pushed across the threshold. "What about these?" she demanded, showing him her bound hands.

"We will see," he said, and the door slammed shut.

"What's going on?" Gil asked.

"We're being punished for defiling their Monkey God."

"Like Bravock?" Dante cried out.

"They never said." She slid down the wall to the floor. "Can you believe those creatures?"

"We're lucky one of those things didn't drop down on us in the jungle," Dante said, leaning against the wall. Adelaide's stomach growled, and her mouth felt like sandpaper. The prison food had left much to be desired, and if it continued like this, she'd waste away to nothing. *It was forced dieting*, she snorted to herself. It wasn't long before they had company.

"Here." The male threw a platter down on the floor.

"Do you have anything to drink?" Adelaide begged. He muttered something, blinked his eye, then left. They all stared at the plate and wondered what it could be. The male returned with a jug. "This isn't Bravock?" Adelaide asked, giving voice to what they were all thinking.

He snorted at her and growled, "The meat of our enemy is only for our warriors. Not for the likes of you."

"Can we be untied?" she asked, showing her back to the guard and wiggling her arms.

"Over there." He waved them to the corner.

"Over here, guys," she said. Dante and Gil shifted beside her as the male towered over them, holding out a knife. Praying she wouldn't be stabbed in the back, Adelaide held her breath. The instant her wrists were released, she pulled them around in front of her, rubbing where it ached. Rolling her shoulders, she watched the guard back out of the room, leaving them alone. "It's not Bravock," she assured her companions. Dante sighed with relief and scooted over, staring at the options. Adelaide slowly forced down her portion and tried to formulate a plan. It looked like their options were running out. She was afraid this might be the one time they couldn't escape. There were plenty of times during the war when she had been in dicey situations but nothing this bad.

When they finished eating, she had the boys turn around, so she could do her business in the bucket. It was very demeaning, but Adelaide couldn't hold it any longer. *Who'd have thought she'd miss the lovely gel showers?* Even those were sounding good to her now. The stench was increasing, and their running and tramping through the jungle hadn't helped their cause. She pulled her crusted shirt away from her body with a grimace. There were no blankets this time, so Adelaide huddled in the corner shivering. She dozed fitfully, trying to recover some of her stamina. Their future looked pretty grim.

* * *

"Come on, Dante." Adelaide giggled, swinging her stubby legs under the swing.

"I'm coming. Hold your horses."

"I don't have any horses." Laughter burst from her lips, as Dante stepped behind her and gave a mighty push.

"Higher, Dante, higher!" she yelled, feeling the air blow across her face. The sun shined happily down on them.

"Get ready!" he warned her.

She was almost level with the bar by then and felt a little fear trickle down her back.

"You'll catch me, right?" she asked.

"Always, shrimp. Always."

* * *

Adelaide jerked awake, disoriented. *Why was she dreaming of that time?* It was one of her happier memories with Dante. There were so few of them after she was a teen. The little nap hadn't helped, and she felt worse than before. Dante was snoring in the other corner, but Gil was pacing in the middle of the room.

"What's wrong?" she asked.

Gil looked over and replied, "I'm antsy, and I need to move. I think the next time we are graced with their presence, we should make a break for it. I'm too old and gristly to be eaten."

"Agreed," she replied. Gil frowned and growled at her. "Haha, I meant that we should run. Not that you're old and gristly."

"Have your laugh, but if they get hungry, they'll pick you first. Looks like you've put on a few pounds." He grinned when Adelaide looked down to inspect her body. He waited a minute, before erupting with laughter. She glanced up and grinned.

"You'd better watch it, or I'll restrict your rations," she teased. Dante quickly sat up at the sound, looking around.

"What's the commotion?" he demanded.

"Nothing," she said. "We're deciding on a course of action." Slowly standing, she stretched a little and was grateful that the aches and pains had receded somewhat. Her back was killing her, but the floor could be blamed for that. Then, the door swung open, and before any of them could react, four males crowded into the room carrying swords and blasters.

"You all stand here," one of them demanded, pointing where his eye gazed.

Adelaide looked over at Gil, but he shook his head. They probably couldn't take all of them without some casualties on their side. She stepped up to the guard, with the boys behind her. A collar was snapped around her neck before she could say "boo."

"What the hell!" she reached up, grabbing hold and pulling. It didn't move but just squeezed her throat. A chain was then attached to the collar, and they yanked her away. Gil was next. At that point, he started putting up a fight, but they made quick work of it, and soon, all three of them had *lovely* new jewelry. A chain was then strung between them, joining them all together. She lifted the heavy chain with disgust. No privacy at all. The assholes still hadn't said anything. "I asked, what the hell are these?"

"As a slave, you must be controlled."

"We're slaves," she repeated. Both boys responded with colorful words. Adelaide agreed with them, as the chain was yanked and all three of them were dragged out into the light. She blinked from the glare and shaded her eyes. It was amazing, the difference in sunlight and temperature between the building and the outside world. Out here, she felt like ripping her clothes off, as sweat dripped down her back.

They were being led to the huts, when there was a loud explosion, and flames shot up towards the treetops behind them. Everyone dropped to the ground, and pandemonium broke out. There was screaming and crying coming from all directions. Through it all, Adelaide heard a welcome sound.

"Captain, are you alright?" She felt like crying.

"ALICE. Thank you. Where are you?" she answered the ship's computer.

"You need to head north about ten miles to a small clearing."

"Got it." Adelaide grinned at Dante and Gil lying beside her. "Move it. We're being rescued." They all looked to the two remaining guards, who were slowly standing. As one, the three of them stood and wrapped the chains around the guards' necks, grabbing their weapons as the bodies fell. "We need to travel north to a clearing — quick."

No one noticed their escape amidst the commotion. Adelaide led them to the edge of the village, and then continued north along the buildings, keeping out of sight. She couldn't distinguish if the yells were from the destruction or if they had been discovered. Hopefully, their captors would give up on them. Adelaide felt a tug on her neck and glanced back. She saw Dante stumbling, and she came to a stop panting.

"We need to keep going," she stated, and they both nodded.

It was a mad dash through the jungle with no signs of pursuit. They began coughing, as smoke slowly moved between the trees. Adelaide hoped the fire could be brought under control. She didn't want to be responsible for the destruction of the jungle. Eventually, the trees started to thin. *We're almost there*, she thought in relief. Adelaide gave the thumbs up, so Gil and

Dante could see. The ZOO was a sight for sore eyes. The doors slid open, and everyone cheered, as they entered the cool cargo bay and collapsed on the floor.

"ALICE, get us out of here. Head to Zartuth," she commanded.

"Yes, Captain. Glad to have you back." Adelaide grinned and listened to wheezing Gil beside her. Her smile slid off her face, and she looked in his direction.

"You guys alright?"

"I will be, once this is off," Dante said with disgust, rattling the chains. Gil nodded his head and kept silent. Adelaide slowly crawled to her knees.

"Do you have something in your collection that would take these off?" she asked Gil.

"I think so. Let's go have a look."

They all tottered down to Gil's private stash in the engine room and waited while he shuffled things around, muttering to himself. Grinning, he soon pulled out a nasty looking tool with a spinning blade on the end of it.

"Here it is."

"No way, man," Dante said shaking his head. "There's got to be something else." He backed up as far as the chain allowed.

"Don't be a baby, Dante. We're doing it," Gil said waving, his deadly tool around in the air. Adelaide looked at him doubtfully but nodded her head in agreement.

"First, let's go grab some food, so we're not so shaky," she suggested warily, watching Gil lower his arms.

"Fine," Dante said. "I'll go last."

They almost ran to the galley. Adelaide ordered a 12-ounce steak, mashed potatoes and vegetables and smothered everything in gravy. Her stomach may protest the large meal, but she didn't care at that point. *The smell was amazing.* As she shovelled the food into her mouth, a foul stench slowly filled the room. Shifting her head to glance at her comrades, she inadvertently pulled on the chain, making her grimace. It ticked her off both at Dante and their captors. So, then, Adelaide ended up glaring in his direction. The food was demolished in record time, and Gil sat back, patting his stomach with a grin.

"That hit the spot. Let's get this off."

The trek back to engineering was quick, and Gil grabbed his tool. *He seemed a little too excited holding that thing,* Adelaide thought.

"Step right up." Gil motioned for her.

"Are you sure?" she asked hesitantly.

"Don't you trust me?" he asked with a frown.

"Of course."

"Then hurry up. I want a shower."

"Fine," Adelaide consented. She offered Gil her back, so she wouldn't have to watch. Gil fired up the rotary saw, and she could hear the buzzing as he neared her neck and began cutting. The vibration could be felt throughout her body, and she tried not to flinch. The collar started heating up, causing her to yelp, "That's getting hot."

"I'm almost through. Hang on just a minute." There was a snap, and the collar fell away. Adelaide grabbed her neck, sighing in relief.

"Thanks, Gil. Do you want me to do yours?"

"No. I'll do Dante's first and then mine."

"Alright. I'm heading to my cabin. How about, in a couple of hours, we meet on the bridge to debrief?"

"Sure," they both answered.

Adelaide hurried to her room and striped out of her clothes, throwing them in the garbage incinerator. *No way was she keeping them.* Even though the shower was small, she couldn't be happier. It took two gel showers to wipe away the smell, and her body was now squeaky clean. She grabbed some underwear, pulling it on.

"ALICE, wake me in two hours," she ordered.

"Yes, Captain."

Adelaide's eyes were closed before her head met with the pillow.

Chapter 19

Adelaide strode through the corridor, feeling much calmer. Her eyes were a little sore and tired, but she felt a hundred percent better. Stepping onto the bridge, Adelaide raised her arms, spinning around, so happy to be home. If ALICE had a body, Adelaide would kiss her. It wasn't long before Gil and Dante joined her.

"You guys look ten times better, and I don't have to hold my nose," she said and laughed at their expressions.

"I wouldn't talk," Dante replied, collapsing in a chair.

"Alright, let's get some answers. ALICE, what happened after we left?"

"I went into the upper atmosphere and monitored your progress. I received your final communication, before you entered the temple. In twenty-two minutes and three seconds, your signals disappeared. I could no longer detect your location."

"That must be when they brought out the jammer," Adelaide interjected.

"Yes. I waited for twenty minutes, but when nothing changed, I travelled to your last known coordinates. Once there, I had to ensure no one could detect me, so flying low wasn't an option."

"Were you able to see anything?" Gil asked.

"The sensors didn't pick up any body signatures. I did detect smoke residue. There were no other clues as to your whereabouts."

"So, how did you find us, then?" Dante asked.

"I completed a grid search in a 20-mile radius from the temple," ALICE replied.

"If there was a jammer, what were you searching for?" Dante demanded.

"A void. With the jammer, there would be nothing there," the ALICE said. Adelaide nodded her head in agreement. "There were some dead spots in the jungle that took awhile to eliminate, before I moved on. I eventually pinpointed the possible village. There was one location that had a large dead spot. I calculated the odds that the jammer was there. After it was destroyed, your signatures appeared on my sensors. It was then possible to contact you."

"Thank you," Adelaide said profusely. "I'm so glad you were installed before all this crap began."

"I second that," Gil said nodding.

"What do we do about Axis? There's no more Bravock," Dante interjected.

"We should be able to enter the description of the idol into the computer, and ALICE can create a duplicate. He's never seen it," Adelaide replied.

"Yes, Captain," ALICE confirmed.

"Then what?" Dante asked.

"What do you think? We'll arrange a meeting, and we're not taking no for an answer."

"I don't think it'll work."

"Enough. That's the plan."

"Fine," Dante said, storming out in a huff. Adelaide rubbed her face and sighed.

"I don't know how we're so different."

"Are you going to inform one of your contacts in the military about the exchange?" Gil asked.

"Yeah. I also want to find out if anything has happened with the Cradesions."

"That is a concern."

"Do you know anything about them?" she asked Gil.

"Not a lot. When Earth finally got to travel outer space, the wars were over. I did hear talk from a few different species that the Cradesions were vicious. Their only concern was conquering any planet that was discovered by their scouts."

"I've seen pictures of them. How could they destroy so many? I know size doesn't matter as much… Hey, I said that with a straight face," she said laughing. Gil grinned.

"They wear exoskeleton suits that are larger than their bodies."

"None of the survivors talk about that," she said with surprise.

"Because anyone who encountered them was slaughtered. All the stories were second-hand."

"Then how do you know about it?"

"When I was on Gaeaf, I met a Mali ljudje. His planet was decimated, only a few of them survived," Gil answered. Adelaide's eyes widened.

"I've never heard of these Mali ljudje," she said, slowly trying to pronounce the unfamiliar words.

"Because they aren't around anymore. People more than likely whisper their names in the dark because of superstition. They don't want to invoke their tragedy down upon themselves. The Mali race inhabited a peaceful planet filled with artisans. I've heard their artwork is renowned, and of course, it is now priceless."

"Why were they attacked?" Adelaide pressed.

"Because the Cradesions wanted the planet's resources."

"Don't they usually wipe out the inhabitants and then colonize?"

"Not always. Depends on the planet. No one knows if the Cradesions are searching for a suitable home, or if they just take the resources," Gil answered. She shuddered.

"I really don't want to meet them," Adelaide replied. Gil nodded, before leaving the bridge, heading to the engine room. "ALICE, did you run into any other problems while waiting for us?"

"No."

"So, there weren't any other ships? I'm wondering if Axis came there for Bravock."

"I was alone," ALICE confirmed.

"Good. I need to contact General Williams from the Earth base."

"Yes, Captain." A few minutes later, ALICE said, "There is no response from the general."

"I'll send a message, then I'll contact Axis."

Adelaide sat in her chair, contemplating how many details to provide. If she explained everything about Dante, the general might be obligated to arrest Dante. She sure wasn't going to tell him about their adventures together. Skirting the truth would be prudent. Once the message was sent, she headed to the ship's 3D printer, inputting all the details she could recall. The computer began building her a fake idol. Ten minutes later, she picked up the monkey with a grin. *Not too bad,* she thought. Axis wouldn't be able to tell. *Time to get this show on the road.*

* * *

"Where the hell is Bravock?" Axis demanded the instant the call connected.

"Dead," she said impassively, staring at his furious face.

"I will hunt you down!" he threatened.

"To hell with you! Do you know what we had to go through to get this?" she demanded, shaking the fake idol.

"Hey, hey. Be careful with that," Axis said, worry creasing his brow.

"We were captured, Bravock was beaten and pulled apart, while he was still alive. And then you know what?" Adelaide responded angrily, almost yelling by this point. "They ate him." Axis looked sick and angry, while he paced in front of the screen.

"We need to meet immediately," he stated.

"Fine by me. I don't want this cursed thing."

"We can meet on Zartuth…"

"I don't think so. How about Segundo?"

"The Accords' base. Are you nuts?"

"I want somewhere neutral. How about Earth2?" Axis growled and pulled his hand through his hair.

"How the hell is it *neutral*? It's your home."

"Yes, but it's still primitive and doesn't have many civilians or allies around yet."

"Two days from now. I'll send you the coordinates," Axis said relenting.

"I'll be waiting." Adelaide signed off and grinned as the screen went blank. "That went pretty well, ALICE."

"Yes, Captain."

"Change directions and head home," she commanded. Adelaide couldn't wait to step foot on Earth2. After Axis was dealt with, and she said *sayonara* to Dante, her life would hopefully settle. General Williams still hadn't responded to her message, and she was a little worried about the Cradesions. By tomorrow, if there was still nothing from the general, she'd try again.

Instead of heading to bed, Adelaide went to the gym and began working out. She pushed her body to the point of exhaustion. Laying on the ground panting, she stared up at the ceiling, strategizing the coming days.

"Captain, a secure call is coming in from the general," ALICE informed her.

"Great, put it through." She hobbled quickly to the panel turning it on. "Hello, General Williams. Did you see the intel I sent?"

"Yes. When is the meeting?"

"In two days. I'll send you the coordinates, when I receive them. Make sure your guys aren't spotted, so they don't spook him," she cautioned.

"I know that, Captain."

"Sorry, sir. I just don't want him getting away. Is there anymore news about the Cradesions?" He sighed heavily and a frown appeared on his face.

"We sent out scouts, and they've disappeared."

"What! When?"

"A couple of days ago. The scouts were in constant contact, and then, nothing."

"Crap. How close did they venture? I didn't have any problems."

"Maybe, they've expanded. We're sending another scout, and they can use a probe. Hopefully, the thing can collect some useful data," the general said.

"I hope it's nothing, but I don't think so," Adelaide replied. The general nodded in agreement, before signing off.

It was time for another shower, and then Adelaide would pass out until she woke up.

* * *

An insistent beeping, woke Adelaide from a very pleasant dream involving Taurian. She grumbled trying to peel her eyelids open.

"ALICE, what is it?"

"We're at the gate," the computer announced.

"Fine. I'll be there in a minute." She stumbled around her room, searching for something appropriate to wear, then made her way to the bridge.

"Adelaide!" Dante yelled running after her.

"What? I'm needed right now."

"Have you contacted Axis yet?" he demanded, following behind her.

"Yes. We're meeting him on Earth2."

"Why in the hell didn't you tell me?" he demanded. They had reached the bridge, and Adelaide collapsed in her chair, waving her hand in his face. In truth, she hadn't told Dante because she had forgotten. Adelaide wasn't used to discussing her decisions with anyone.

"ALICE, put them through," Adelaide snapped.

"Hello, Captain. What can we do for you?" asked the jump gate's guardian.

"I'm heading to Earth2."

"Please send the credits, and we'll be happy to open the gate." Adelaide scanned her personal chip, as Dante paced behind her. "Thank you," they said.

"ALICE, continue to the coordinates," Adelaide commanded.

"Yes, Captain." Adelaide turned to Dante.

"I was going to inform you. I just haven't had the chance. One of my contacts will be there to arrest his ass, and then we can go our separate ways," she assured him.

"Fine by me," Dante said leaving.

Adelaide closed her eyes, leaning her head back. *Why was family so difficult?* She still craved the closeness they used to have. After this was over, Adelaide knew in her bones that Dante wouldn't be back unless he needed something. With another day to wait, all there was to do was plan and stay active.

Chapter 20

The ZOO arrived at Earth2, and Adelaide couldn't contain her excitement at being home. After ensuring the precious cargo was tucked safely in Adelaide's bag, the three of them strode out of the ship.

"Let's go to the Hollow Peasant and have a drink before the excitement."

"Sounds good. I could use a cold one," Gil said.

"I have a few things to do. I'll see you later," Dante said, starting to walk away.

"I don't think so," Adelaide said. Her hand snaked out, snatching his arm. He looked down in surprise. "You're not ruining this. If you're out and about, Axis will find you, and our bargaining power is gone."

"I've survived just fine until now without you. I think I can handle this." Dante jerked his arm with a frown.

"You'd better listen to her, laddie. Coming with us is the only option. You don't want us to have to cart you off," Gil threatened, his hand making its way to his blaster. "A drink will calm us all down and kill some time." Dante's lip curled, as he looked at both of them.

"Fine. Don't get your panties in a knot," he acquiesced sullenly.

*   *   *

Laughter and music reached Adelaide's ears before they even opened the door to the Hollow Peasant. Dante had sulked the whole way there and entered first, heading straight for an empty table. She waved to a few regulars and sat down beside him.

"Hopefully, this will be over soon," she sighed, tapping her fingers on the table.

Dante just grumbled, as he waved over the server.

"I'll have what's on tap," he said.

"Do you want your usual?" the server asked, smiling at Adelaide.

"Sure."

"Make that two," Gil said.

Once the server left, Gil asked, "Everything ready?"

"Yes. The general's troops will be dispersed throughout the area," Adelaide confirmed.

"I'm sure Axis will have his own men, who'll spot the idiotic military men first," Dante snarled. Adelaide ignored his tone.

"I asked the general a similar question, and they're trying out these new high-tech gadgets. Supposedly, they won't be detected," she reassured him.

Drinks came and were consumed, all the while Adelaide kept an eye on the door. She was surprised that none of Axis's goons came in. Only regulars littered the space.

Glancing at the time Adelaide said, "Time to go," and stood up. Dante shot back his drink with a grimace. Adelaide held back a snicker, knowing about the swill kept on tap. Dante should have known better, even if he hadn't been through these parts in awhile. Someone might wonder how she knew this, if they hadn't been on speaking terms, but she still kept tabs on him. Adelaide had used some of her sources to check up on Dante, whispering about him in her ear.

They stepped outside as dusk fell. The last rays of sunlight peeked over the bar roof. Adelaide stepped onto the worn path and into the light. The temperature was slowly dipping, and a breeze blew through the trees. She slung her bag over her shoulder, and zipped her jacket closed. *Time to finish this*, she thought, taking a deep breath. She loved springtime, when the scent of clean air and flowers came alive. It was a ten-minute walk through the trees from the bar to their rendezvous point.

"We're almost there," Adelaide whispered, slowing her steps. Leaves crunching were the only sounds as they continued. There was no sign of General Williams or Axis.

As they neared the clearing, she could see Axis's little figure through the sparsely covered tree branches, surrounded by four Raykar males. Each held nasty looking weapons. They stood a few metres from the edge of the trees, requiring

Adelaide and the boys to walk out into the open. *Yeah,* she thought with a frown, *of course, he'd have his goons with him.* The little weasel, the bane of her existence, was even shorter than his body guards. His beady little eyes shone between the shoulders of the two males. She had difficulty holding back her laughter at the ridiculousness of the situation and snorted instead. Gil looked at her quizzically, but she just shook her heard. Adelaide had a momentary impulse to just pull out her blaster and shoot Axis. *What could go wrong,* she sighed, *other than it was murder, and she still had a conscience?*

"Hello, Axis," she called out, waving at him instead. A frowned marred his face, making her smile widen.

"Do you have it?" he demanded. Adelaide looked around, searching for the extra bodies she knew were close by. "What are you looking for?"

"More of your goons," she hedged.

"You don't need to worry about that. Where is it?" he demanded, holding out his hand. Adelaide shook her head, her eyes shifting from side to side.

"Oh, Axis, I would never trust you." She laughed, reaching for her bag.

"So, Dante, you're going to let your little sister talk for you?" Axis taunted. "You haven't said anything. Did you help with the retrieval or just sit in the safety of the ship?" Dante snarled in reply, taking a step forwards, but Adelaide whipped out an arm to block him.

"Ignore him, Dante. He's an ass," she whispered, pulling out the idol. "Here it is. What does it do?"

"Something you don't need to know." Axis nodded at one of his goons, who lumbered over, grabbing it out of her hands.

"So, we're good?" Dante demanded.

"He speaks," Axis sneered. "Yes. Hope to see you again."

"Not bloody likely," Dante responded.

"Everyone, hold it!" a voice yelled. Chaos ensued, as Axis was surrounded by his Raykar thugs and shuffled back towards the waiting cover.

"Don't let him escape," someone yelled.

"Scatter!" Adelaide said, and they split and ran for cover, as the clearing filled with blaster fire.

"Damn you, Dante. You'll regret this!" Axis's voice could be heard saying over the noise.

"Come and get me, you bastard!" Dante taunted back.

"Don't worry, I will. With this beauty in my hands, the sky's the limit."

Dante began laughing and replied, "You're in for a shocker. It's a fake."

"Shut up, Dante," Adelaide hissed.

"You're a lying asshole."

"You should have seen Bravock's face, when they ripped his body apart," Dante goaded him. There was a roar of fury, and the idol sailed into the clearing, shattering on the ground.

"Give it up, Axis, you're surrounded," the general yelled.

"If I'm going down, a lot of you are going down with me," Axis snarled back at him.

Adelaide returned fire, as part of the tree beside her exploded. The fading light was making it difficult for her to target her foes. She muttered under her breath, peering towards the enemy. She didn't want anyone to get hit by friendly fire. Dante was just a faint outline to her left and Gil to her right. Both of them were concentrating on the scene unfolding in front of them. Ten minutes of exchanging firepower felt more like an hour. A movement out of the corner of her left eye caught her attention. Before Adelaide could shout out a warning, Axis stepped out, firing at Dante. She watched in horror, as her brother screamed briefly, before dropping to the ground.

"You bastard!" Adelaide yelled, directing her blaster fire towards Axis. He never had a chance; the shot exploded his brains all over the trees. She was up and running towards Dante before Axis's body fell to the ground. "No! No!" she screamed, sinking to her knees and holding Dante's body close. There was a large hole seared right through his chest. *Imagine that*, Adelaide thought. *There's not a lot of blood.* In the distance, the blasts stopped, but she didn't look up from the last member of her family. Tears flowed down her cheeks as she cradled Dante, rocking back and forth. A hand gently touched her shoulder, and she looked up.

"I'm so sorry," Gil said, with sorrow on his face.

Adelaide nodded, gazing around her. She could see the general coming their way.

"It's over?" she asked quietly.

"Yes. They're all dead," the general confirmed. He looked down at what was left of Axis. More men arrived at the scene, and General Williams gently moved Adelaide aside, so Dante could be carried to the middle of the clearing for retrieval. Adelaide felt numb as she followed. *There was no one left. She may have been willing to part ways with Dante, but to never see him again! Her protector and friend growing up.* A sob broke free, and she gasped, clenching her hands and staring straight ahead. The men placed light signals around the clearing to direct the transport in the dark. Wind swirled, and she heard the engine, before seeing the transport glide over the treetops. It settled gently on the ground. *Good pilot*, Adelaide thought absently. The doors opened, and General Williams yelled, "Everyone on."

She hurried forwards, so Dante didn't get too far away, and Gil followed at a distance. Once all the bodies and survivors were aboard, the transport lifted off. Travelling to the medical centre was a blur. The transport had first stopped to release the soldiers, before continuing on. A few were still aboard in order to help with the bodies. Adelaide hadn't immediately noticed that the bodies of Axis and his goons were in the transport, too. No way was she helping with their removal; she would much rather dump their bodies somewhere or leave them behind in the woods. Adelaide's eyes hadn't left her brother's body. Her hand unconsciously touched his shoulder, periodically. She felt the transport engines slow and braced herself. Loosing Dante was imminent, and she wasn't ready. The doors opened, and a medical team stood in front of them. *What are they needed for,* she thought? *There was nothing they could do. No! They can't have him,* Adelaide's mind screamed, as she gripped Dante's cold hand. *Why was he so cold?*

"Adelaide," Gil said quietly. She looked up in surprise. He was still here. "They need to take him." She shook her head in denial, but slowly, she released his hand. The other bodies were already gone, and the remaining medical team stood patiently outside the transport. She nodded, and the men stepped forwards, lifted Dante up and carried him away. Adelaide broke down, and Gil gathered her close.

Chapter 21

Sitting in a stark white room, Adelaide glanced at the time on the wall again. It felt like hours, but the clock showed only twenty minutes had passed. The medical staff were in the next room preparing Dante for the incinerator. She had refused to leave and was going to be there for the end.

"Thanks, Gil," Adelaide said, turning to her stolid companion.

"No problem, Adelaide. I'm here for however long you need me," Gil replied. She nodded and took a big gulp, staring at the video screen. Something was playing, but it was all a blur.

"Are you the next of kin for…" the woman who stepped into the room trailed off and looked down at her board, "…Dante?"

"Yes." Adelaide jumped up.

"You can come with me," the woman beckoned Adelaide.

"Thanks, Gil. I'll be alright by myself."

"Are you sure?" he asked, standing with her.

"I need to be alone. I'll contact you later." Adelaide gave him a brief hug and watched Gil walk away before she followed the woman.

This was too much, Adelaide thought, staring through the glass at her brother's body. It was her last glimpse of Dante, as his body rolled along to his fiery grave. The sobs started, and she stuffed her fist against her mouth trying to stem the flow. It felt like she was going to break in two. *She was all alone.*

*   *   *

Adelaide stared down at the swirling drink in front of her, her body numb. After watching Dante burn, she'd stumbled home and collapsed on her bed for almost twenty-four hours. Now, her butt was resting in one of the uncomfortable seats in the Hollow Peasant with no plans of moving. Her life was spiralling out of control. It would be a miracle if her business survived, with the number of cancellations she'd had to make in the last while. She was beyond caring at this point. Tipping the glass back, she emptied the glass down her throat and then slammed it on the bar.

"Another one."

"I'm buying," a voice said, as its gorgeous owner dropped into the seat beside her.

"I don't need you to pay," she said in a quiet voice.

"It's in remembrance of your brother," Taurian said gently.

"Fine. What are you here for?"

"I figured this was where you'd be. I'm sorry about Dante."

"Thanks," Adelaide replied softly. She looked up at him with tears in her eyes. Taurian gently wiped an escaped drop off her cheek before dropping his hand. "What about the whole 'we're getting married' issue?" she asked, swiping at a stray hair, conscious of how terrible she looked.

"It's on hold until your mourning time has passed," Taurian replied. She snorted, and a little smile played across her lips as she gazed down at her glass. The music and laughter surrounding them seemed miles away and couldn't penetrate her bubble. The same question kept popping up in her mind. *Why did her brother have to be such an idiot?* Then, she'd have to berate herself for speaking ill of the dead.

"What did you do with that fancy jewel?" Adelaide asked, as another full glass was placed in front of her.

"Your brother didn't know what its true worth was. The Darvish value it above all else. To them, it's priceless."

"So? Why do you care about them?"

"I don't. But it'll save my people."

"How." She looked over at him, curious despite herself.

"I traded it to them for weapons. Thousands of advanced weaponries."

Anger filled her and she snarled, "You're going to start a war?" *Just when I was starting to like him,* thought in disappointment. *Damn it, where did that thought come from?*

"No. War with the Cradesions is coming, and we're simply preparing," he stated. She looked at him in surprise. "You're not the only ones with scouts," Taurian said laughing.

"What have you discovered?" she demanded.

"Just that they have a force amassing and will be coming for us all. Soon."

"You're going to fight with us?"

"We will be defending our home. You need to come with me. You'll be safer on Raau."

"Didn't you say the wedding's on hold?" Her body stiffened, waiting for an attack.

"Yes, but this is about your safety," Taurian persisted.

"Don't worry about me. I'll be fine. I'm not running away if the Accords need me. Thanks for the drink." Adelaide nodded her head and slid off the stool. "See you around," Adelaide said, as she practically ran out of the bar. The first thing she had to do was inform her contacts in the military. If Raau was gearing up for war, it wasn't a good sign. The Tu'Val were a cocky race and normally held the belief that no other race was above them.

Adelaide was panting and a little nauseous by the time she reached her home and pulled up the comm.

"Makar, we need to talk," she said breathlessly.

"Hello to you, too," Makar said with a grin, taking in her dishevelled state. "What were you doing?"

"Not that you idiot," she said, trying not to smile. "Have you heard about the fleet amassing?" she asked him. Makar's eyes darted back and forth.

He whispered, "You know I can't answer that. But there has been talk. They're keeping it hush-hush."

"The Tu'Val are preparing for war," she stated. Surprise crossed his face.

"Oh, crap. Have you told anyone?" he asked.

"Earlier, I informed the military of some ships that I spotted on the Outer Rim. I need you to pass this along."

"Sure, but why not you? You've already communicated with them."

"It'll be better coming from you."

"Do you know who they are?"

"The Tu'Val believe the Cradesions are back. Just keep me in the loop," she said, signing off before Makar could respond. *For not wanting to fight any longer, she sure kept sticking her nose in it*, she thought with a frown.

"Hey, Captain," Gil's grinning face popped onto her screen. She smiled in return. "I'm checking in," he continued. "Are there any jobs?"

"Sure. Quite a few."

"Pick one, and I'll meet you at the ship shortly."

"Sounds good," she agreed.

Adelaide took a deep breath and headed to her room. A shower was needed, to wash away the stench of her grief and her race to get back home earlier.

* * *

"Glad to see you," Gil said, giving Adelaide a quick hug. She soaked in the warmth for a moment then stepped back.

"Thanks. Glad to be back. What do we have?"

"Gaeaf needs an emergency shipment."

"Sounds right up our alley," Gil said. Adelaide grinned, stepping into the ship and patting the hull along the way.

Once the ZOO was on course, Gil joined Adelaide on the bridge. He gave her a onceover as he stood beside her.

"I'm fine, Gil," she said grimacing. "It'll take a while, but eventually, the pain will recede. I've wallowed enough. I need some action. Taurian paid me a visit at the Hollow Peasant." She paused, glancing up at Gil before continuing, "He had an interesting story to tell. Raau is preparing for war. You know that large gem Dante stole for Taurian? They used it to buy weaponry."

"Who are they fighting?" Gil demanded.

"Remember that fleet we saw amassing near Biyaha? The Tu'Val think it's the Cradesions." Gil let out a few choice words and began pacing.

"Our military knows, right?"

"I called Makar. He didn't deny anything. I hope Earth's military is preparing," Adelaide said and stood up. "I'm going to take a quick nap before we arrive."

"Sure. I'll wake you up."

Adelaide gave Gil a little smile and walked out. The smile slipped away the instant she was alone in the corridor. Her body slouched, and she shuffled slowly to her room. The exhaustion was catching up with her. *Who would have thought that three days without sleep could affect someone this way?* she thought, with a grimace. Her door slid open, and the bed called out to her, promising a peaceful rest. Adelaide's body moved in the right direction automatically and collapsed on the mattress, her eyes closing in a dreamless sleep.

* * *

Adelaide's heart felt lighter, as she wandered through the marketplace towards Kranth's stall. The sounds and laughter reminded her of better times. She was almost to her destination, when suddenly, there was shouting and a stampede of bodies. Adelaide tried to elbow and push her way through the throng, but eventually, she gave up and allowed her body to follow the flow of the crowd. There was a sudden halt, and they all gazed up at the large screen that hung from the ceiling. Horror filled Adelaide as she stared at the video, a reporter stepping into view on the screen.

"I am standing on the edge of the once peaceful city of Kahoon," he said. The camera zoomed in behind him, showing the devastation. No building remained standing as far as the eye could see. A picture taken from above was displayed on the screen, and the crowd gasped as one. Multiple craters lay throughout the city, each one at least fifty feet across. *What the hell happened?* She remembered previous visits to the planet Janpar, and its beautiful city of Kahoon. *Now, it was destroyed.*

Dread prickled up Adelaide's spine, and her stomach churned. She knew the cause. The sight of the massive fleet flashed in her brain. She hadn't heard from Makar since providing him with the intel. Kahoon was light years away from the fleet's last known quadrants. Something tickled the back of her mind but quickly disappeared. *What was she forgetting?* she wondered. *Could there be more than one fleet? No, that wasn't it.*

People were beginning to mutter and shift, trying to shove their way through the crowd.

"Captain," ALICE came over her wrist comm.

"Yes," she whispered.

"Incoming call from General Williams."

"Damn it," she muttered to herself. "Give me a minute, I have to find somewhere private." She turned around and began pushing with her body and her elbows, eventually sliding out of the crowd with a pop, and she stumbled, falling to one knee. Swearing, she quickly stood and hurried to a quiet corner. "Put him through," she said, looking at her wrist comm. "Sorry, General. I had to move somewhere more private."

"We are recalling all our troops. The military needs your services."

"Is it the Cradesions?" she asked.

He looked at her in surprise and admitted, "Yes. They have begun bombing cities."

"They were responsible for Kahoon," she stated.

"You are quite informed," he said. "Good. You are expected at Earth's base of operations in two days' time." Before she could respond, his face disappeared. Pandemonium had broken out on the station, and she had difficulty reaching her ship at a decent speed.

Upon arriving back at the ZOO, she shut the door behind her and yelled, "ALICE, get us to Earth's military base immediately!"

"Yes, Captain."

"Gil, I need you on the bridge once we clear the station," she commanded him over the comm. She collapsed in her chair with a groan, scanning her chip and praying for a quick departure. Even though they were lucky enough to be one of the first few trying to escape the station, it still took half an hour to reach the gate.

"What's going on?" Gil asked, walking through the door. Adelaide glanced at him and motioned for him to sit.

"I'm being recalled. Did you see Kahoon?"

"Yes," he said quietly, nodding his head.

"It was the Cradesions," she stated. Gil swore under his breath, pacing in front of her. "I hope you'll serve with me on my ship," Adelaide continued. "I need someone in engineering who I can trust." Gil's eyes dimmed, and he rubbed his head.

"I don't know if I can handle that again," he said quietly.

"Please," she begged, despite knowing that asking Gil to follow her into battle was selfish. He sat for a few minutes, thinking, before slowly nodding.

"I will. Can't leave you to yourself. You might get yourself killed. I'll be down in the engine room." He stood up, patted her shoulder and left.

As they passed through the gate, heading home, it finally clicked. *Do the Cradesions have the new gate technology? That's what she'd forgotten!* If they did, the Accords might not stand a chance.

THE END

OTHER BOOKS BY
YVONNE YOURKOWSKI

KAILA PORTER SERIES 1

MURDER
FROM BEYOND
THE GRAVE

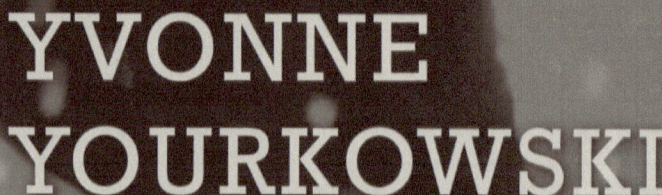

YVONNE
YOURKOWSKI

Officer Kaila Porter gasps for breath as she stares at the corpse of her mentor. It has been years since the town, or herself, has seen a dead body. Struggling to move past the devastation, with no clear motive for the vicious attack, Kaila doesn't see the stalker dodging her every step. When the only suspect shows up dead, Kaila is plunged into the midst of the criminal world. Suspecting a leak in the department, Kaila strives to connect the two victims, one, a beloved woman of the community, and the other, a newcomer. Kaila finds courage within herself to defy the conspirators who attempt to kidnap her and sabotage the investigation. The town is in an uproar, demanding protection. Time is running out. She must stop the deadly string of murders, before she's next.

KAILA PORTER SERIES **2**

SWEETEST REVENGE

YVONNE
YOURKOWSKI

The only way to stop the voices is to appease them with more blood, and he's more than capable of obliging.

Detective Kaila Porter can't explain the motive of a brutal stabbing of a young woman, and it's keeping her awake at night. Time is of the essence--bodies start piling up and the murders become increasingly vicious. The worst is believed; a serial killer is on the loose, gaining confidence with every kill.

As the investigation progresses, evidence begins implicating the victims' parents. Is it possible? Kaila can't fathom what would possess parents to kill their own children. There must be a crucial clue they're missing. In desperation Kaila follows their last lead: money. The trail leads to a suspect with the age old motive...Revenge.

KAILA PORTER SERIES 3

INCINERATED

YVONNE
YOURKOWSKI

Fire cleanses and regenerates life. But when arson is used to stop a blackmailer, the pressure mounts. More than one person will be burned.

Detective Kaila Porter leaves the scene with blackened nightmares etched into her mind. When investigating the victim brings up more questions than answers, Kaila knows it's time to turn up the heat. Not even an explosion can thwart her determination to reach the truth.

As the body count climbs, Kaila needs to stop the killer before she's facing the wrong side of the flames.

LOOK FOR
BOOK 3 OF
KAILA'S STORY
FALL 2018!

THANK YOU
FOR READING!
I WOULD APPRECIATE
IT SO MUCH IF YOU LEFT
A REVIEW ON AMAZON.

www.ingramcontent.com/pod-product-compliance
Lightning Source LLC
Chambersburg PA
CBHW031109030726
47496CB00002BA/451